THE AGENT'S WIFE
A Novel

Carol Morley

BookLocker
Trenton, Georgia

This book is a work of fiction. Names, characters, and incidents either are the product of the author's imagination or are used fictitiously. Any resemblance to actual persons, living or dead, events, or locales is entirely coincidental.

Copyright © 2023 by Carol Morley

All rights reserved, including the right to reproduce this book or portions thereof in any form whatsoever.

The Library of Congress has cataloged this edition as follows:
Name: Morley, Carol Anne, author
Title: The Agent's Wife: a novel
Description: First Edition
Library of Congress Control Number: 2023906532

ISBN Paperback: 979-8-9880836-0-3
ISBN eBook: 979-8-88531-491-6

Facebook: MorleyCarol
www.morleycarol.com

ALSO BY CAROL MORLEY

Beyond Public Image

To my loving husband and amazing three sons.

Yet hasty marriage seldom proveth well.
~William Shakespeare
1592, Richard of Gloucester, Henry VI Part three,
Act 4, Sc.1, 1.18

The Agent's Wife

1

DIMINISHED

Dru would never understand her need for therapy. As far as he knew, his wife was taking a sculpturing class at Georgetown University on Tuesday afternoons. It wasn't as if he would be curious, not enough to ask to see her art projects. These days, his mind was self-contained in the going and coming of snipers, arsonists, and terrorists. As long as there were clean socks and underwear in the bottom draw, he was content.

    Doctor Katz greeted Élise O'Neil with his hand extended and directed her into his office. She sat on the plush leather sofa feeling like Alice in Wonderland in the strangeness of her surroundings. "There's no reason to be nervous," he said, placing a glass of water and a box of tissue next to her. He watched as she tucked her long, dark hair neatly behind each ear as if to better organize her thoughts. He couldn't help but notice his new patient appeared less photo-shopped than the host of glammed-up women he counseled each day. Instead of fake eyelashes, plumped-up lips, and salon manufactured tans, she let her natural, girlish good-looks speak for themselves. How refreshing! It was a message he attempted to preach at home to his two teenage daughters. *But then I digress,* he thought.

"Shall we begin?" he ventured, getting down to the business at hand.

It was like watching her life flash across the big screen as Élise began to explain how, in seven years of marriage, her life had gone from negotiating million-dollar investment deals to squabbling with the butcher over the price of pork chops.

"So, you feel diminished?" he summarized.

"Yes, diminished. It's as though I'm living someone else's life. Certainly not mine. This is not the life I imagined. It's like I have everything, but I have nothing."

The doctor recognized her in the face of a hundred other women who sat in the same seat, divulging the identical story of an unrewarding marriage in which they were lost. It seemed the higher they registered on the economic chain, the more desolate their situation. With perfectly manicured nails and sculpted bodies, they slumped in despair, sniffling into fistfuls of tissue, while choking on their own words. Unlike the others, however, he couldn't help but notice, Élise O'Neil had yet to shed a single tear.

Doctor Katz, a tall dark-haired man, was beautifully accessorized from his custom-tailored tie to his alligator leather shoes. His long fingers looked as though they had never known a callous. He scribbled a single word on his tablet now and again without looking down or losing eye contact. "So, you say your husband has no idea you're here?" he asked without judgment. "Why is that?"

Élise confessed, since the birth of her third son, there were a number of things she was keeping from her husband. "First and foremost, I'm planning to leave him," she stated, as though it were hardly worth mentioning.

"That is a major decision!" he replied, his previously expressionless face displaying concern. "When did these thoughts of leaving your marriage begin?"

"Oh, Doctor Katz," she sighed. "When have I not thought about leaving? It's the *how* and *when* that fills my every waking hour. This past year, I've had plenty of empty hours to carefully think it through."

"I see," he said, with a furrowed brow. "Earlier, you referred to your recent pregnancy as your pregnancy from hell," he probed with an empathetic tone.

"Yes," she uttered softly, head down, as if she thought an apology necessary.

"Pregnancy for many women can be a difficult time," Dr. Katz added gently, mindful of the havoc hormones often play in a woman's body and mind. Even so, his sixth sense told him, in this instance, he was dealing with more than a common case of postpartum blues.

Élise wasn't in the habit of sharing details of her dismal married life. It wouldn't be easy, but nevertheless, she would have to put her trust in someone. Dr. Katz was, perhaps, her only hope.

"This might take longer than you care to hear," she smiled, turning to the notebook she had brought along.

"Take your time," he said, returning the smile. "That's what I'm here for."

With a deep breath, she settled into the oversized sofa, and in a confident voice began to tell her story, listening, as though she too were hearing it for the first time.

2

THE CLAN

"I never should have gone home with him that first Christmas," she sputtered aloud, like the accused pleading innocence to a malcontent jury. "If I had just taken a stand from the start," she admonished herself when dropping her oversized Jockeys-for-Her down the laundry chute. "In hindsight, I knew better," she added, deliberating her own guilty verdict.

Dru's persuasive powers triumphed every time. "And, who's to blame?" The accusatory finger pointed to herself. Snubbing the lacy night dresses spilling forth from the top three bureau drawers, Élise fished for the grey-blue checked flannels and a pair of Dru's thermal hiking socks.

"I can't believe I let you talk me into this," she confessed when Dru insisted she join him that first Christmas at the O'Neil's. "Honestly," she argued, "I'll be perfectly fine by the fireplace with my cappuccino latte machine and a freezer full of low-cal mac & cheese. There's work to catch up on, books to read, and plenty of movies to watch. It's not like I've never celebrated Christmas alone before." In truth, she felt meeting his family was entirely premature. "What's the rush?" she insisted.

"You can't spend Christmas alone and, besides, my parents are expecting you," his timbered voice finalized their holiday plans. So, it was on that December 25th, despite her better judgment, when Élise found herself on I-95 en route to Greenwich, Connecticut, scrunched in the front seat of Dru's BMW.

"Why would you let him talk you into this?" she repeated silently as the vehicle motored nearer an undesired destination to meet people she was disinclined to meet.

It's not as if her family, the Saint-Cyrs, were counting on her this holiday season. Last she heard, her parents had rented an apartment in the south of France, and weren't expected home until May. They had long ago disconnected from tradition, as well as from Élise. She had an older brother, but hadn't heard from him in over a year. No one was going to be misty-eyed over her absence.

The weatherman had delivered on his forecast. It was indeed a white Christmas. Élise shivered in her fox lined coat, more from the dread of meeting Dru's family than from the sight of frost gathering on the windshield, or the mounting snowdrifts. Driving through sleet never failed to frighten her with someone else at the wheel. By the time they pulled curbside at 49 Aspen Road, she was relieved to have arrived, even if it meant making nice with the O'Neils. Hoofing through the snow banks, her high heeled leather boot sunk deep into a pothole, hurling her forward onto all fours.

"Oh, hell!" she gasped, just as the front door unhitched.

"Mom, Dad," said Dru. "Let me introduce the woman of my dreams."

The senior O'Neil raced to the rescue, offering his arm, and hoisting his flustered guest to an upright position. Mrs. O'Neil stood in the doorway, hands doused in powdered sugar and with a smile as wide as the door she swung open. She greeted her youngest son with a hearty, motherly hug. Her cropped, yellowed hair gave off the unmistakable scent of onion as she planted a kiss on both of Élise's cheeks.

"So glad you could join us Alice," chimed Rose O'Neil, wiping her dusty hands on the front of her ruffled apron.

"It's Élise, mom. With an E," Dru said. The correction went unheeded.

Dru's father, Patrick, barely reached his son's chin though he appeared to be a large man. His military buzz haircut, reminiscent of boot camp days, framed the temples of his boyish grin. In his own mind, he was still very much a soldier.

All the O'Neil men were expected to enlist in the Marine Corp. "It's a calling," Dru had explained. "Like a Mormon boy who knows he's going to Australia or New Zealand to serve a coming-of-age church mission."

"A pleasure to meet you, sir," Élise replied as she stretched a gloved hand toward Mr. O'Neil, while stifling an urge to salute or tender a Semper Fi.

Amidst babies squealing and toddlers chasing through the kitchen, Rose O'Neil baked, boiled, seared, and brined a lavish lamb dinner. Of course, there were no recipes; simply a dash of this, a lick of that, and a smattering of the other.

The women of the house invited Élise to join them in setting the dining room table, a task they took very seriously. Sooner or later, she would have to learn their names but, for now, they would collectively be thought of as the O'Neil women.

Seventeen-year-old Katy, red-haired with thick glasses, placed a stack of pale pink linen napkins on the table. Dru had disappeared. Élise found herself tackling the impossible, folding square table napkins into the shape of rosettes.

"Like this," instructed Katy, wrapping, flipping, and twirling.

I'm not sure if I'm more humiliated or enraged, she thought, hoping she hadn't spoken aloud. If she had, the women were too absorbed in laying silverware, dusting Waterford, and toweling Lenox to pay heed. There was little conversation, no laughter, and few smiles.

Clearly, I am an unsuitable match for this family. If homemaking were a prerequisite to joining the clan, her fate was sealed. At this point, that didn't seem a bad thing.

The back hall was suddenly filled with the sound of man-like horse-play as Dru and his twin brothers, Dennis and David, hobbled through the door, and dismantled frost from encrusted boots, gloves, and hats. In record time, they had scraped ice from windshields, and shoveled snow from the walkways, all under Mr. O'Neil's command. Amidst the raucous sounds, Élise could hear Dru's infectious laughter. Obviously, he was having a good time.

"Let's eat!" bellowed Mrs. O'Neil, which was apparently her way of formally announcing the dinner hour.

Amidst the shifting and scuffling of chairs, Élise faced the fourteen O'Neils seated around the banquet-sized table. Mr. and Mrs. O'Neil sat at the head of the table looking very much like proprietors of the inn. The young mothers adjusted their babies in high chairs, and began to cut vegetables and meat into childlike, edible portions.

Oh God, this is all too Norman Rockwell for me, thought Élise, wishing she were anywhere but here.

Dru unfurled a rosette napkin onto his lap and reached for the truffles. "You've got to try these," he said, dishing several nuggets onto her dish, and offering her a clumsy it'll-be-ok smooch.

That was his idea of a peace offering, she supposed, as she tapped out a forewarning on the face of her watch that said, 'Immediately after dinner, we're history.'

He nodded a 'Yes dear.'

The absence of alcoholic beverages did not go unnoticed by Élise. Though a polite wine sipper, her anxiety yearned for a tall glass of Merlot to ease the surging muscle spasm tugging at the back of her neck. "Diet coke with ice please," she replied as Mr. O'Neil filled her goblet to its brim.

By four o'clock, the last lick of cherry compote was cleaned from every plate. Regrettably, her plan of stealing away immediately after dinner, was catastrophically spurned by the O'Neil women, who insisted she join them for their customary after-dinner tea. Without warning she found herself pressed into a line up, wedged between Katy and Rose, advancing to the corner study.

Dru waved to her from across the room as he watched the oak doors slide shut on the assembly of ladies. She could hear Patrick O'Neil call out from the kitchen, "Let's go men. Man your stations."

Without question, my worst nightmare, Élise's mind screamed in helpless protest.

The O'Neil women kicked off their shoes, and nestled into lumpy sofa chairs shrouded in red and green Scottish plaids. "It's a family tradition that the men do the dishes and care for the children for the hour after Christmas dinner," David's wife explained, her diction that of a woman who had spent years in elocution lessons.

"I'll be dammed!" Élise blurted, with a quick apologetic glance toward Rose O'Neil, who pretended not to hear. Not only was alcohol not a part of the O'Neil household but Élise was certain, profanity was harshly frowned upon.

Katy confirmed the notion with a piercing glance, erasing all doubt.

Just then, Patrick O'Neil entered the room rolling a highly polished silver urn of freshly brewed tea resting on a marble serving cart. With the grace of a duchess, he poured a round of tea, melting two lumps of sugar into his wife's heirloom china cup and then handed it to her as if it were the holy grail and she, Mary, Queen of Scots.

Without a word, the soldier turned butler exited the room, closing the door gently behind him. All eyes were directed toward their honored guest as Mrs. O'Neil raised her cup, and officially began the questioning. "So, Alice, is it your intent to marry my son?"

3

TOMFOOLERY

"Hell no, Ma'am!" Élise screamed, as the car door slammed shut. "I have no intention of marrying your son. Not now, not ever. That's *exactly* what I told your mother."

"Oh Christ! She was that brutal?" Dru asked, as soon as their car hurled from the curb. How do you answer a question like that with only a two-hour drive back to the city?

"I'm sorry," he said, assuming a politically neutral stance. Élise swallowed her words, fully aware that a verbal attack on a man's mother was as self-sabotaging as thrusting a steel rod through one's own chest.

Élise huffed, unclenching her gloves from the door handle and unleashing her hair from its perfectly formed chignon. Clearly, there were more icicles to melt inside the car than outside. She settled back, padlocked to her seat, for the long, wintery drive home.

"Not everyone celebrates holidays in the traditional way," she spouted, after thirty minutes of silence in which she had been orchestrating how their breakup would play out.

"You're right, sweetheart," Dru muttered in the manner of a man who'd been married half his life. With his focus on the treacherous road conditions, he kept his eyes glued to the road ahead.

In hindsight, Élise knew, this was the day she should have parted ways, forever, from Agent Dru O'Neil. Ending their relationship, then and there, would have saved them both undue anguish in the years to come.

The fact was, after this abysmal day, she realized that, she and Dru were much too different to ever be a suitable match. His values were that of a man raised in an ultra-traditional family home, while hers revolved around a family best described as unconventional. Worse still, his career choice, that of solving crime, made her terribly uneasy. Though she knew nothing about the works of a federal agent, her instincts told her, it was something she might want to steer clear of.

It could never work, she thought, nuzzling her nose into her fur-lined collar, as she peered out the fogged-up car window at the mounting snow. Once they were pulled up safely in front of her Manhattan apartment building, she would tell him it would be best they not see each other anymore.

"I think we should take a break from each other," she said calmly. "Maybe see other people."

"Absolutely not!" he roared, offended, more than shocked.

From that moment, Dru O'Neil became relentless to prove he was the only man for her. He would dig deep, with whatever charm he could muster, to win her over and become the perfect, most attentive, caring, loving man any woman could ask for. She got to experience, firsthand, that when Agent O'Neil set his mind to something, he usually won. Whatever it might take, he had his sights set on marrying Élise Saint-Cyr.

Élise had always been methodical, analytical, and painstakingly sensible in all her decision-making endeavors. Haste had never been her style. She imagined she was smarter than that. But when a beau rings your doorbell at two in the morning, hand-delivering six dozen long stemmed red roses, and a bottle of chilled Chardonnay, one is easily enchanted. Wasn't it such tomfoolery that lured the doomed Princess Diana into marrying the ill-suited Prince of Wales?

It was with such complete disregard of commonsense, logic, or reason, that she fell in love, and the search for the perfect man screeched to an end. It was that simple.

4

BUNNY SLIPPERS

She couldn't be the only woman to regret poor decisions made long ago, thought Élise O'Neil, as she surveyed the thirty pounds of baby weight propped in her lap. This, the third trimester of a third pregnancy, held all the debilitating symptoms of pending motherhood.

It was hard to imagine that seven years ago, to the day, Élise had walked away from a six-figure income as one of Manhattan's most visible investment brokers. The twenty-seven-year-old financial wizard had no reservations on the morning she strutted into the CEO'S office, resignation in hand, to trade in her pinstriped suit and corner office. The additional announcement of her upcoming marriage to government agent Dru O'Neil nearly floored Mr. Bogurt, the stoic, sophisticated figurehead of Stearns, Bogurt & Dunn

Investments. No one suspected Élise Saint-Cyr had the time or inclination to dabble in love.

"You've thought this through?" he asked in a scornful, fatherly tone.

The future became sealed with the simple, "Yes, sir."

The ever elegant, silver-haired Mr. Bogurt, not often caught unaware, cleared his throat before awkwardly stammering through the appropriate best wishes. He had hedged his bets on this ingénue financier who had been hired sight unseen and freshly graduated summa cum laude from Harvard. She had not disappointed, delivering far beyond expectations. Feeling older than his sixty-four years, the senior executive had no choice but to gallantly escort his most favored employee to the back stairwell with her belongings as one would an ex-con.

When Henri Saint-Cyr, father of the bride-to-be, answered the call later that day from his daughter, he laughed heartily thinking her news a practical joke.

"No, Dad. I'm serious," she explained. "I resigned from the firm, and am getting married."

"Why have I never heard of Dru O'Neil?" he asked in a voice shriller than he liked. Visits from his daughter to the family homestead in Cape Cod were usually brief, and best described as obligatory. Physically, she was present but her mind was otherwise occupied by margin calls, short sales, and commodity market trades. The cell phone, which never left her side, beeped and chimed incessantly, not unlike the cry of an ornery child. Henri understood his daughter's serious side in ways his wife was incapable.

"I'll never understand that girl!" Jacqueline Saint-Cyr protested with each toxic ring of the phone. "Rude and disrespectful," she insisted, holding her head as if it were about to topple from her shoulders.

"Sorry," Élise would mouth, while apologetically scampering from the room to take another call.

"Honestly, why does she bother to visit?" whined her mother.

This impromptu marriage announcement was yet but another grievance the mother of the bride felt obliged to suffer. It was no secret that the mother-daughter relationship between Jacqueline and her only daughter was exclusively biological. It was always her father, Henri, forever the peacemaker, who was able to gently step into the fray and mediate a positive spin between the two.

Merely six weeks after notifying their respective families of the pending nuptials, Dru and his future bride walked into the lobby of the historic old manor, the Oceanside Inn on Main Street, in the quaint village of Seawood on the New England coast. Relatives from either side of the family bustled about in varying stages of readiness for the evening candlelight ceremony. Bloody Mary refills flowed generously from the open bar, manned primarily by avuncular attired men, while women rushed about in miscellaneous stages of dress and undress. Fingernail polish and hairspray permeated the air. Unrecognized among the bustling collection of strangers, the soon to be newlyweds muscled their way to the reception desk like any other new arrivals.

"The woman in hair curlers with the bunny slippers…One of your relatives?" Dru asked, stifling an accusatory grin.

"I have no idea," replied Élise, maneuvering toward the bridal suite on the upper landing. The guest list and elaborate wedding fuss was entirely their parents' doing. Quietly eloping was never an option. Best to hire the orchestra, and throw the damn bouquet.

The closely knit O'Neils filled the entire left side of the small, cobble-stoned chapel. Broadly smiling, hugging, hi-fiving one another, they appeared more a team at the fifty-yard line than a family about to celebrate a holy union in a place of worship.

Across the aisle sat the mother of the bride, Jacqueline Saint-Cyr, dressed from head to toe in ice blue lace, sobbing uncontrollably. An unknowing observer would think her soulfully bonded to the sophisticated woman now reciting *I do* at the altar. Henri smiled bravely, veiling mixed emotions. It was a moment of concession solely owned by fathers who have ever escorted a daughter down the aisle. Símone, Élise's older brother, arrived late for the ceremony, and quietly took a seat in a secluded corner.

A two-week honeymoon in Monaco, far from bosses, family, and daily hassles was precisely the right choice. Tanned and rested, the young couple returned to D.C., eager to settle into their newly purchased red brick Georgetown home as man and wife.

"Cinderella, those dishes washed yet?" Dru would tease, his nose nestled in the nape of her neck as she scoured the last of the evening pots and pans. His nightly tub of buttered popcorn spinning in the microwave, filled the room with its tantalizing aroma. "It's movie time," he'd announce, while untying her apron strings, and stripping the dishtowel from her soapy wet hands. With two wine goblets wedged between the overflowing bucket of sizzling warm popcorn, he'd grab his wife's hand, and head to the study. She couldn't help but glow, recalling every aspect of those euphoric post-honeymoon days.

5

SETTLING DOWN

Dru was well aware of the unspoken sacrifice his wife had made in forsaking a high-powered Wall Street career. *Would I have walked away from my career for love?* he asked himself. *Not a chance!*

"Fund raising might work," Élise thought as she continued to scan the financial pages of the morning paper.

Raising money had always come second nature to the one-time financier. Within months, the name Élise O'Neil topped the list of nearly every major charity event planner in town. Unrelentingly, her cell phone rang night and day. With practice, she managed to text with the right hand, sort laundry into piles of white, light, and darks with the left, while compiling mental notes for the next grand event.

"You see," said Dru, "it's not only me who finds you irresistible, my dear."

But, as much as he loved his wife, his mind was already across town working out the logistics of his next case. "Gotta go," he sputtered, adjusting his gun holster. With a quick kiss to her forehead, he headed to the door. "Another late one tonight babe," he said, the word *sorry* filtering through the screen door as it squeaked itself shut.

"Okay, I love you, too!" she mouthed.

The years were racing forward at the pace of a pedigreed greyhound at the finish line. First came the birth of their son Oliver, and then Will. Dru's workload had evolved so that the long, sleepless nights, and endless demands of crying babies, fell solely upon Élise. Apologetic and remorseful as he was, he could offer little to the parenting scene.

"You knew about my work when you married me," Agent O'Neil was quick to remind his wife in his defense.

That was not entirely true.

She hadn't understood the world she was stepping into by marrying an ATF agent; surveillance, stake-outs, gun raids, bomb squads, mug shots, firearms, explosives, and lengthy undercover assignments. She hadn't asked enough questions, or listened closely enough.

The weary mother of two young sons could barely recall her former dynamic self. How trivial her past successes had become once laid aside. Regardless, the fact remained, a third child was about to be born.

"Seven years of utter bliss," winced Élise sarcastically, her reflection seemingly mocking her in the hallway mirror. She tugged at the seams of her ill-fitting jersey maternity top, the fabric barely stretching across her oversized breasts and weighted belly. Dr. Leon assured her the pregnancy was normal, but how could outgrowing Baby-Bump X-Large possibly be normal?

From its corner nook, the upright antique clock struck the hour in muted monotonous tones, prompting her to drop the floral needlework piece into the wicker basket. Mercifully, another evening had come to an end. Dru seldom, if ever, made it home before midnight. Élise found this role of accommodating housewife and mother increasingly unbearable. In truth, she had supposed married life to be less of a soliloquy.

6

PRINCE HAL

Oliver and Will were asleep, soundly burrowed beneath pillowed feather comforters. Élise smiled in the darkened silence to the quiet sounds of their trusting breath. It was the purring of puppies when they snore; sounds that restored one's sense of purpose and of self.

Slipping from the boys' room, she trudged down the hallway before tumbling into her side of the empty, king size bed. Shivering at the chill of the sheets through the layers of bedclothes, she flipped on the preset radio resting on the nightstand. The late-night drone of *Coast to Coast* helped ease the eerie darkness of the room. Ironically, the silky voice of the radio talk show host comforted her with his real and imagined myths of ghostly demons and pending national disasters. Visions of space alien abductions permeated her mind as she drifted into an unsound sleep.

Suddenly, Élise sprang upright in bed at the piercing sound of a barking dog, made all the more alarming since the O'Neils did not own a dog! "What the...?" Jumping to her feet while still half asleep, she waddled down the unlit hallway, clinging to the wall, and clutching her pillow to her chest.

"Quiet, Hal!" a man's gruff voice rang out in a hushed holler. "Get over here, boy," said the voice at the foot of the stairs as the front door hurled itself shut behind him. The lights turned on in the downstairs study as three burly men deposited heavy wooden crates onto the thickly carpeted floor.

Dru met her at the foot of the stairs. "Sorry, hon. We have the bomb dog with us and he gets mouthy in the aftermath of a gun raid," he said apologetically, brushing a kiss on her cheek, and rushing off to join the others.

It was 4:20 a.m.

"You scared me to death," Élise said, left standing alone on the staircase, her heart pounding like a jack hammer.

Two of the agents were unloading boxes in Dru's study. The third was in the corner, emptying a manila folder stuffed with mug shots. The now silent barking dog moved cautiously as Élise entered the doorway, a restless growl throttling in his throat. His bottom teeth were aligned and Élise could see saliva seeping from both sides of his mouth. She cowered past him, avoiding eye contact. The certified explosives detection canine brushed her leg with his practiced nose before settling down.

"Get over here, Hal!" said Agent Paul Martin, quick to recognize unadulterated fear on the face of his terrified hostess.

"Thanks, Paul," she said gratefully, inching her way to the corner desk.

"Hey, gorgeous," he said, gallantly kissing her hand, and guiding her to the over-stuffed leather chair. Seated amid the assembly of broad-shouldered men, her swollen, pregnant body felt grossly conspicuous though no one except Paul and the bomb dog paid her any notice.

The two younger men and her husband focused exclusively on dismantling the contents of the cartons. One by one, the rifles were laid side by side on the tarp surface. "Holy Jesus, if we didn't hit the mother lode," said Dru, holding a sawed off shot gun into the light like a kid on Christmas morning who had just unwrapped his first BB gun. With rubber gloves, the trio examined each piece of the cargo with the satisfaction of felons fingering embezzled currency. Élise felt more like the devoted wife of a mobster after a heist than an innocent spouse awakened from a dead sleep by the fervor of an ATF firearms bust.

"Now that's one scary dude," Paul said, surveying a photo of a man with gaping hollows where teeth ought to be.

Élise leaned over, gazing at the image of the young man whose life was reduced to a series of numbers running along the border of the print. *4593.* She read the numbers, staring at the photo as one stares at a fatal wreckage. This whole business frightened her but she was indirectly a part of it whether she liked it or not. Crime was a constant, which too often invaded the threshold of her home. She wondered how its ugliness would eventually affect her children as they became more and more aware. Oliver carried a mock badge in his rear pocket, pining for the day when he would become an agent. As if by osmosis, he had already adopted his father's strange way of probing every situation with painstaking scrutiny, to the point of alarming his preschool teachers.

Paul winced, tossing the photo back to the top of the pile. Élise couldn't help but stare into the blackness of the suspect's eyes in search of a trace of self-worth, a hint of self-respect. At any moment, she expected a grief-stricken woman to storm into the room, and drop to her knees, begging for compassion for her son. His innocence she would defend with her last breath. In the darkness of the city, multitudes of inconsolable mothers lay awake, praying for the young men whose photos now sprawled atop her husband's littered desk. Élise shuddered at the thought, grateful that both her young sons lay safely asleep in their beds.

Prince Hal, the yellow Labrador Retriever, pawed his way around the room, and saddled himself adjacent to the weapons. His canine eyes oozed disapproval as they remained guardedly fixated upon Élise's stiffened bare feet.

"He's likes you," Paul said teasingly. "You just don't want to be overly anxious, or move abruptly, or he'll take you down like a sumo wrestler." Bomb dogs were primarily interested in inanimate objects. That's what guaranteed their next meal. Hal was trained to uncover explosives, not to exchange particulars with an agent's wife.

"I'll remember that," she promised, cautiously retracting her legs from the dog's reach. ATF's finest breed continued to eye her ankles as though they were a rib roast. His eyes darted back and forth, from the illegal stash of guns to her bare feet, as though connecting dots. Élise shrunk deeper into the safety of the cowhide leather chair in an unobtrusive attempt to exude trust, and lessen Hal's groundless misgivings.

Paul studied the photo of a Caucasian male searching for certifiable markings. Agent Martin was the only friendly face in the room. Élise and the children had long adopted him as a family friend. *How was it he's still single? Makes no sense.*

He and Dru began working together more than eight years ago. They were both transferred to the D.C. Alcohol, Tobacco, Firearms, and Explosives (ATF) central office from New York City. At thirty-five, Paul's boyish good looks and dark skin typecast him as the textbook undercover agent for the bureau's top juvenile linked cases; cases involving eighteen-to-twenty-one-year-old gang members. As a black man, he had lived a privileged life. The son of an influential corporate attorney, he earned a law degree from the University of Virginia.

First to poke fun at himself, he laughed heartily, sharing details of an assignment as a part-time server at a burger joint in Baltimore. "Only in the movies do agents get the undercover jobs with the penthouse, the Porsche, and the girl! Me, I get a baseball cap, and an apron," he would joke.

Dru and the two kneeling agents were inspecting and inputting make, model, and serial numbers of the rifles and handguns into their database without speaking to each other, except through eye contact, nods, and gestures. It was clear to Élise that these bounty hunters would be non-responsive to anything she might add to their non-conversation. As for Prince Hal, his heaving breath appeared to rise and ebb in response to each repositioning of her limbs. She was the intruder in his domain.

"Can I put a pot of coffee on for you guys?" she offered, purposely confronting the more offensive of the two men who kneeled on all fours. As he rose, revealing his towering height, the unshaven, muscular man begrudgingly nodded as if he had just consented to ingesting calamine lotion in order to rid himself of a pesky rash.

"No problem," she grunted back, easing her way past the growling Prince Hal to the open door. "I'll get right on it," she said, heading for the kitchen, and leaving the men and their dog to do what they loved best. Wallowing in crime.

This was not the first time Dru and his buddy agents set up shop at the house in the middle of the night, though it never failed to alarm her. The sight of sawed-off shotguns, hand guns, and ammunition violated her sense of being, and left her feeling defiled. Weapons were physical reminders of the dangers of her husband's work. Knowing a .40 caliber handgun was resting beneath the bed stand, or watching Dru slip into his holster and bulletproof vest before leaving the house, would never seem ordinary. She never lost sight of the bulge beneath her husband's jacket, knowing he was armed, whether attending the Saturday matinee of *Bambi*, or high mass at Washington National Cathedral. *How could that be normal?*

She envied other women whose husbands pulled into the driveway nightly at 6:00 p.m. to take part in a routine dinner hour, where family debated insignificant events. If only she had married any one of the men who had all but stalked her the years at the brokerage firm. There was the banker, the attorney, and the dentist. Frankly, even that short, shoe salesman from the Bronx seemed intriguing as she now plodded her way to the kitchen. What's the worst he would have brought home in the middle of the night? Maybe mismatched Manolo Blahniks.

The pantry door slammed shut behind her, empathizing its displeasure at her plight. It was, after all, an ungodly hour. The coffee trickled into the pot, slowly filling the kitchen with an aroma that induced conversation. Élise heard herself replying to the bubbling inquiries of the steamy brown brew. "If your husband, who you hadn't seen in two days, turned up unannounced in the middle of the night with a troop of G-men and a truckload of weaponry, how would you feel?" The pot snapped back with a loud, bristling gurgle, its red light blinking on and off.

Paul Martin was ATF's rare exception. Despite the odds, he had succeeded in maintaining a healthy persona. It seemed the ATF academy in Georgia turned out armies of gingerbread men, oven baked at 400 degrees for exactly six months of arduous training, crisped to specifications. Except, now they interrogated rather than inquired, expected rather than requested, petitioned rather than coaxed, and served rather than cared. Their cookie cutout bodies, armed and credentialed, buff and sinewy, reentered the real world speaking a new language; the language of weaponry, car bombings, explosives and snipers. They formed a people of and unto themselves. *G-men should have their own country,* she thought.

Through the hallway she caught a glimpse of her husband who had spent the better part of the last forty-eight hours holed up in an unheated surveillance van while munching on beef jerky and pretzel sticks, and washed down with Pepsi and Sprite. His work was grueling and dangerous but he wouldn't have it any other way. The reality was that his wife and children could never come first. And, now there would be a new child. Pouring cream into grandmother Saint-Cyr's cut-glass pitcher, and sugar into its matching bowl, Élise surmised the coffeemaker with a grain of skepticism.

"Can I trust you?" she asked. The pot remained silent. Élise took that for a yes. "My marriage, it's in trouble." There, she'd finally said it. The pot didn't look surprised. "I guess you already knew, huh?" The two quietly shared a moment like two friends openly confronted by a mutual problem. Gathering four coffee mugs from the armoire, she filled each cup with a steady hand. "Can we talk about this again later?" she whispered, while propping the tray on the shelf of her extended belly. The half-empty pot vibrated as it watched her walk away.

7

BELLE

Élise sat on the edge of the bed as Dru folded and refolded the contoured, checkered shirt and stone-washed denim jeans before precisely positioning them into the leather satchel. Meticulous about his clothing, he would sooner leave the house without trousers than sport a crease or wrinkle. He planned a quick change at the office before heading to Ramrod's, a gay country western bar in the city.

"Why you?" she asked.

He and two other agents had drawn the short straw. That's how he explained the uncharacteristic late night undercover assignment to his questioning wife. Should she suggest scuffing up the shiny western foot gear? *No, let it go.* His stride across the room flexing the black, cowhide cowboy boots brought to mind a flamingo dancer she once knew. All attention pointing to the toes.

"You forgot a tag," she chided, pointing to the price sticker on the monogrammed belt buckle. She watched as he pulled a black cowboy hat from a deep box feathered with yellow straw, and bent closely into the mirror, tilting the stiffened brim this way, then that. *Vanity, thy name is...*

"So, if I should go into labor tonight, will you be available to take my call?" Their due date had passed four days ago.

"I'll be a phone call away, love," he gestured, holding his cell phone over his head without looking up. She was slightly reassured.

"The important thing is you make it to the rodeo," she said with a tinge of sarcasm while heading to the door.

There was a time he would have indulged her with a forced grin. Indifference cuts directly to the bone. You know you've crossed the line when the injured party abandons indignation and wrath, opting silent rage. Dru interacted as if their differences were no longer his concern. His every exchange begged a disconnect. Élise found herself guessing, supposing, speculating, and presuming. *What did he mean by that? Had he just scowled? It's my hair, he hates my hair.*

Face to face with the clownish reflection in the hallway mirrored wall, she glared defiantly at the belly full of baby. The Mediterranean mules on her feet underlined the caricature of an inflatable, weighted punching bag. She put her hand to the wall, hoping to dispel the ghastly image. In an amusement park funny house, the distorted figure might have triggered rollicking laughter. But, not here, not now.

The Agent's Wife

Lately their togetherness unleashed an inner cattiness that even she couldn't tolerate. It was something akin to an adolescent batting baseballs toward the neighbor's bay window, hoping to warrant a response. If only he would yell, or stomp his feet, curse, or punch the wall. Ironically, for Agent O'Neil, it was just another sunny day doing what he loved. Fighting crime was his antidote to all life's concerns.

Dru had been gone six hours when the first labor pains began. *Gas pains, maybe?* As the late-night television host bowed to raucous applause, Élise gasped at the gushing, torrential stream of water erupting between her thighs, and splashing onto the floor. "Oh, Je-e-e-sus!" she roared, shoving a nearby sofa pillow between her legs, and scrambling for the phone. Doubling over, she rocked her convulsing body to quench the excruciating pain. Anticipating Dru's annoyance was equally as grating as the unrelenting contractions now firing spasms through every cell in her bloated body.

Why was she not surprised when Dru's phone forwarded to voice mail? *Bastard!* "Dru, it's me. I'm in labor. Please call me right away," she inhaled and exhaled into the mouthpiece.

The next call was to Belle, the O'Neil's nanny and housekeeper. Having Belle for a neighbor was like harboring Mother Teresa two doors away. At a moment's notice, despite the hour, the day, or the weather, the saintly woman made herself available, always making you feel she'd been waiting for your call. Tonight was no exception.

"Belle, I'm in labor. Dru should be on his way home soon, but... Belle, Belle... Are you there?" The unlocked front door burst open before Élise had time to pocket the phone.

"Stay calm, sweetie," Belle chimed with the air of a seasoned midwife as she traipsed across the mahogany wood floor. Born and bred in the deep south, the squatty, sixty-year-old neighbor assured the young mother that she was fully capable, if need be, of boiling water, gathering linens, and delivering this child.

"I thought Dru would have called back by now." Élise apologized, embarrassed more than troubled by his delay. "Oh my God, here comes another one!" she wailed, as the older woman headed for the hallway closet.

"Well, sunshine, if there's one thing I've learned," sputtered the practiced woman while lifting the yellow page directory from the closet shelf, "Never wait for a man to do what you can do yourself."

Thumbing through the yellow pages, Belle sounded out the letters, "t-a.x..."

"No! No, Belle! There's no need for a taxi. Dru will be back to us any minute," Élise panted as the labor pains raged convincingly enough to arouse a dogged, "Damn him!"

"Hello," Belle sang into the phone with a flowery, Georgia drawl as though she were calling a salon for a hair appointment. "We need a taxi as soon as possible. I have a pregnant woman in labor who needs transportation to Georgetown University Hospital." The long pause on the other end of the line indicated what had to be every cabbie's worst nightmare. "Yes, could you please hurry?"

No response from Dru.

Élise shook her head, mortified at the thought of having to turn the poor cab driver away. "It won't be necessary," she'd explain to the man. The next wrenching pain, however, forced her to nose-dive into the corner, withdrawing all prior rebuttals. An escalated series of spasms sent her clutching her stomach, and pounding the marble table, demanding, "Where is that frigging cab!"

Belle escorted her young friend to the taxi, swaddling her in an eiderdown comforter. "Don't you worry about a thing, Princess, except delivering that healthy, precious baby." She placed the overnight bag on the back seat, and gave the laboring mother a heartfelt embrace. "I'll take care of the boys. They'll sleep like little lambs through the night. It'll all be fine."

The cab driver slouched over the wheel, snapping a wad of chewing gum, and shifting gears while tapping his foot impatiently to the gas pedal. "Hey lady. She is running," he informed Belle gruffly in broken English, boldly pointing to the numbers flashing on the metered screen.

"Now you listen to me, young man," scolded Belle, sternly wagging her forefinger inches from his elongated, crooked nose. "I expect you to drive this woman to the hospital. You do not leave her side until she is laying in a bed with a doctor by her side. Tell me you understand!"

Sitting upright, the man nodded as she crumpled a fifty-dollar bill into his fist. Belle stared wide-eyed into his thickened, black brow, keeping a grasp on the door handle until he gave her a hard, fast confirmation. "Yes, ma'am. I go straight there," he promised. "I take mother to doctor. We go now."

Satisfied, she shut the taxi door, and stood in the empty street making the sign of the cross, blessing the tail-lights as they turned the corner, and disappeared from the tree lined street.

8

OLIVER AND WILL

Six-year-old Oliver sprawled across the upper bunk bed, his blond tangle of curls much too pretty for a boy. At least that's what others said whenever Belle accompanied the youngsters to the nearby park.

Below, in the bottom bunk, slept Will. Tall for a four-year-old, he nearly fit into Oliver's clothes. A cluster of freckles spattered across his nose and cheeks, the cause of much unwanted attention. "So adorable," the neighborhood women would gush as the boy shifted his baseball cap to shield his face.

The brothers were unified in vetoing any discussion involving that of a baby sister. "We've decided we'll call him Luke...Luke Skywalker," they chimed one day at lunch. Belle had glanced up from spreading peanut butter and jelly evenly on two slices of bread to see their mother cringing in the corner.

"Well, I know how Oliver got his name," the housekeeper had said to Élise with a chuckle. "But, how about Will?"

Belle knew how the tradition of selecting theatrical names had begun on Dru and Élise's first date; fifth row center, opening night of the musical production of *Oliver*. Dru had leaned over, and whispered in her ear, "What do you say we name our first-born son Oliver?" She had laughed politely at his presumption that there would be a second date since she knew nothing of this man who had just been introduced to her the prior Monday.

"Will, as you might guess," said Élise with a twinkle in her eye, "is named after the great William Shakespeare, the Bard of Avon." Bowing low in dramatic form, she began reciting a favorite quote; "*Deny thy father, and refuse thy name*, Act II, Scene II." Belle applauded heartily, recalling Dru boasting that his wife could quote nearly every line from *Romeo and Juliet*.

"Good thing your dad didn't have tickets to *The Adventures of Huckleberry Finn* or your names might be Huck and Tom," Belle teased, handing her giggling charges a tall glass of milk.

What a sweet, young couple, the O'Neils. They had taken Belle into their fold soon after moving into the house on Jefferson Row. When asked if she could help with household chores, the sprightly woman nearly skipped all the way home. They had no idea how desperately she needed joy back in her life. Caring for a husband of forty years, now bedridden, had taken its toll. Cliff Stevenson, a victim of Hodgkin's Disease, was a mere shadow of the brilliant civil service engineer he had once been. Since the loss of their only son many years ago, he had severed friendships, sold his prized violin, and slept past noon each day.

Quickly, Belle had proved herself indispensable to the O'Neil household, running errands, cooking meals, and washing windows. Handsome Agent O'Neil's politeness reminded her of the gentlemanly, southern manners she was accustomed to back home. "Belle, here, let me get that for you," he would offer, carting the vacuum up the stairway. She suspected military training had done some good, but she'd bet her socks that, behind that deep-seated courtesy, hailed an unyielding mother.

Despite age differences, she and young Mrs. O'Neil immediately connected, as sometimes happens. "Please, call me Élise," insisted the brown-eyed bride. Names didn't much matter since Belle was going to call you darlin', honeybunch, or some such name of endearment anyway. Initially, the newly married Mrs. O'Neil spent forever on the phone or running off to yet another of *them* glitzy D.C. charity events.

According to Mr. O'Neil, his wife was the most gorgeous financial wizard on the planet. He was a federal agent, like the ones you see chasing across your T.V. screen; alert, armed, and ready to rescue.

"I like that boy," Cliff Stevenson had told his wife after his new neighbor paid him an introductory visit.

The approval plumb near knocked Belle off her feet. "Well, ain't that the berries! I thought Cliff didn't like anyone." For so many reasons, the arrangement with the O'Neils made the brooding silence between the elderly man and his wife so much more bearable.

In time, the O'Neil babies began to arrive and Belle's mothering skills superseded silver polishing, waxing of floors, and rearranging closets. The children adored her, clinging to her chest as though their ship was sinking, and she their lifeboat. What a gift this family was to a lonely old woman.

Lately, however, during the last of this third O'Neil pregnancy, things had taken a turn. Belle worried about the uncharacteristic troubled look her young friend sported nowadays. A furrowed line seemed to deepen across her forehead even while singing Sesame Street lyrics with her giddy sons.

Charity work had long been set aside and the expectant mother seldom found reason to leave the house. Physically, to Belle's eye, her young friend still had the unblemished look of a homecoming queen but to see her moping about with hair tied back in an unruly knot, wearing Dru's old sweats, near to broke the older woman's heart. It wasn't her place to lecture the dear girl. If truth be known, that baby couldn't get here soon enough. Mr. O'Neil, bless his heart, was working night and day, which appeared to be a subject of contention between the two.

Belle knew not to get involved.

"My husband got his two boys," Élise spouted, as the two ladies sorted through baby clothes. "Now, I get my girl," she declared holding a soft pink bunting up to the light. "We'll name her Cosette," she said with certainty, half expecting opposition since the child's gender was yet unconfirmed.

"Cosette, as in *Les Misérables*?" asked Belle, knowing she was right.

"Oui," answered Élise, slipping into her mother's annoying habit of weaving French into every conversation. "It's time we balance the genetic score." The blond hair and green eyes of Oliver and Will screamed of Scotland, as Jacqueline Saint-Cyr all too often reminded her daughter.

Like a sentry, Belle settled into the corner rocker chair of the boys' starlit room. Soft as a lullaby, the breath of the two youngsters calmed the night. It would be morning before any baby news. *Dear Lord, let it be a girl,* thought Belle as she felt herself begin to dose. Pulling the warm blanket up under her chin, she prayed that dear boy Dru would make it to the hospital in time for the delivery. At times like this, a woman needs her man.

9

DELIVERY

"It's a boy!" gushed Dr. Leon, dangling the wailing baby boy by its ankles.

An unexpected, "Oh no-o-o-o-o-o!" flooded the delivery room. The sob-filled lament from the new mother hung midair like a mean-spirited Sunday sermon. The doctor and attending nurses continued to clamp, suture, swipe, and swaddle, exchanging silent puzzled glances.

The infant cried hungrily as the nurse lathered his downy black hair with suds, and gently scrubbed afterbirth from his loins. His howls of protest permeated the room while Élise clenched her eyes shut, fighting the urge to join him in a feral scream of her own. Instead, she fostered a weary smile at the post-delivery nurse who hovered about, layering warm, soothing blankets atop her.

"He's a beauty," the nurse squealed, placing the squirming newborn in his mother's arms, his skin sweetened with powder and lotions. Stretching spastically with an exhausted man-sized yawn, the child recoiled into the familiar fetal position while fingering his mother's breast with a ravenous gumming tug. He began suckling like an old soul who had nursed more than once. It appeared the child did not sense any disappointment in his being a boy.

A seasoned nurse scurried into the room late in the day to remove the dinner tray of soggy lettuce, untouched chicken, yellowed mashed potatoes, and quivering green gelatin. "You really should eat something, sweetheart," she added, raising her brow.

For the hundredth time, Élise listened to her cell phone repeat itself in Dru's baritone voice. "I'm not available right now. Please leave a number."

Searching for any reason to forgive, she sputtered, "That must be one hell of a case he's working. But, aren't they all?"

When Belle answered her phone, Oliver and Will could be heard shrieking at the news of a baby brother in what sounded like tribal yelps known only to young boys.

"You doin' okay, peaches?' asked her faithful friend.

"I'm fine," lied the new mother. "No word from Dru?" she asked cautiously.

"Not yet, honeybunch. Now, don't you worry 'bout a thing. You just get yourself some rest."

The day passed slowly as the unnamed baby boy slept soundly in his bedside bassinette. By late afternoon, the maternity ward bustled noisily with doting husbands, boastful grandparents, and overly-friendly volunteers mingling freely amidst hospital staff. Unhurried, directionless people swarmed about, resembling a dreamlike cast of Kafkaesque-like actors from a fictional world. At any moment, she would awaken forty pounds overweight, anticipating her first labor pain, Dru by her side, holding her hand, telling her everything was going to be okay.

Finally, after an endless day of drowsy exasperation, she found herself applauding the loudspeaker as it boomed out its final farewell. "Visiting hours are now over."

"Thank the good lord," she sighed in relief as flocks of guests exited through the swinging double doors. Lights flickered and dimmed. Muffled sounds of televisions filtered down the emptied hallways, diminishing to a silenced hush. Her sleeping newborn breathed softly, contently cradled amidst downy blue blankets, with no inkling what turmoil he had been born into. Élise kissed his tiny forehead goodnight, and quietly shuffled across the room to huddle beneath the sterile, overly-starched, white hospital sheets. It wasn't the first time she'd felt so alone and abandoned.

At 12:17 a.m. her cell phone lit up the room. Élise, still wide-eyed, watched it vibrate its way across the night stand, its face flashing the familiar words SECURITY SCREEN.

"It's me, babe," Dru spoke deliberately. "I'm in the lobby and the nurse at the desk is trying to tell me I can't come up there. Hold on and let me straighten this out." With that, the line went dead.

Three floors below, her irate husband was confronting the night crew, voice raised, flashing his badge like a madman, attempting to make clear why he is not subject to their damn rules.

Once again, the cell phone light flashed.

"These yahoos say you distinctly requested no visitors till tomorrow. Goddamn it! I'm not a visitor. I'm your husband!"

"I understand," she said as calmly as possible. "But I think it best you come back tomorrow." She could hear him cussing as she ended the call.

A night nurse appeared in the darkened doorway, and described the events going on in the lobby below. "Seems Mr. O'Neil is causing quite a ruckus. Security has warned him to calm down or he will be removed."

"I'm sorry," is all Élise could think to say.

The phone blinked. "These clowns will answer for this," were his final words before the disconnect.

"I love you, too," she blurted in answer to the dial tone and then realized Dru had never asked about her or his newborn child. How could he be so heartless?

10

HANNAH

Grandparents are usually the first to know so Rose O'Neil was stunned to discover her newest grandson had arrived two days earlier. "What do you mean he was born Thursday morning? It's Saturday!" the riled grandmother demanded of her son.

"Sorry…" he said apologetically, dismissing any mention of the tumultuous details surrounding the blessed event.

Delay in notifying Élise's parents proved irrelevant since they were en route from Paris to Naples on the 11th of April. "That's wonderful," glowed Henri to his daughter, over international phone lines. "We'll be home first of May, and can't wait to see you and the new little one. Have you called your brother?" inquired the ever-peace-making father.

"Is he still living in Chicago?" Élise hesitated to ask. The last phone call made to her brother Símone was four years ago to announce Will's birth. "I'll be sure to call him," she promised reluctantly.

Printed announcements were in the mail and life was returning to normal three weeks after the birth of the O'Neil's third son; normal, that is, relative to a household dedicated to the whims of a wailing newborn. Élise's puffed eyes reflected her youngest child's inability to distinguish night from day.

Dru left early before she or the boys were up. Nothing much had changed in his world. After offering a series of progressively unconvincing alibis for missing the birth of his son, he acted as if it had never happened. He assumed his wife would forgive and forget like all the times before. What he didn't realize was that she had neither forgiven, not forgotten.

Oliver's carpool mom arrived at 8:00 a.m. to drive him to school and the preschool minivan honked its horn for Will at 8:15. Élise had an early luncheon planned with her best friend, Hannah, downtown at Café Orléans. It had been months since she'd been out socially and it would be Jean-Jacques' first outing. Nearly tripping over the baby seat and scattered toys lying about the room, she hustled past the clutter and up the stairs to fix her hair, and slip into a flowery spring dress.

"He's gorgeous," gushed Hannah, greeting her friend with open arms. "Let's go inside, and get a look at this seven-pound ten-ounce wonder." Élise led the way through the backside of the narrow, elegant café overlooking the cobbled streets of Georgetown.

"How I've missed this place and you!" chimed Élise, delighted to reconnect with her friend. It had been so long since she had dined out that she wondered if she'd remember how to act.

The young waiter, André, distributed menus in his affected French accent. "Mrs. O'Neil, we haven't seen you for ages. Now I see why," he said acknowledging the sleeping infant. "Congratulations! Looks like a boy." There was no mistaking Jean-Jacques for a girl with his bronzed skin, shock of dark hair, and fists tightened to his chest. Élise was reminded she would soon have to strip the nursery of its feminine frills.

"André, I know exactly what I want. Potato and leek soup, and Quiche au Crabe," she ordered from memory.

"I'll have the same," Hannah quickly agreed.

Before a word had been exchanged, Hannah sensed all was not right beneath the glowing smile of her long-time friend. A true friend recognizes the signs when something is amiss. Cosmetic companies don't manufacture a concealer to erase such telltale markers.

"So, how are things going with the addition of this new little guy?" she asked, delving into the basket of sweet warm bread, her eyes glued to the baby carrier. Chuck and Hannah had a childless marriage. Not for lack of trying. They had devoted years to exploring every groundbreaking fertility method to conceive a child. Over the years, it had caused its problems in their marriage. With her husband recently turned forty-five and she two years his senior, it seemed they were resolved to growing old together gracefully, each with their own private regrets. "Sometimes, you simply give up on your dreams," she'd once told Élise.

Jean-Jacques squirmed uncomfortably in his seat as if considering whether to create a disturbance. With a soothing touch, Hannah stroked his tiny wrinkled brow just enough to lull him back to sleep. "But, now, it's too late for me," she confessed, while caressing the child's billowy cheeks. "I sometimes wish I had left my marriage long ago."

"Those are pretty grave words, my friend," replied a startled Élise, her soup spoon clumsily slipping from her hand, splattering soup on the pristine white tablecloth.

"It's no secret that an agent's home life is far from family-friendly," continued Hannah. "We only have to look at the women in our small circle. I can't name one agent's wife who is truly happy. Can you?"

None came to mind.

"For most of us, happiness is measured by the balance due on our monthly Visa statement. We shop our way through the emptiness." Hannah was right. Doesn't matter if it's a new tube of mascara, or the latest self-help book, ordered on-line. Anything to make us feel whole.

"I never had the luxuries you do, dear," Dru's mother, all too often, pointed out, in a tone that implied her ungrateful daughter-in-law had brought nothing to the party. But, then, Rose O'Neil was purposely kept unaware of grandfather Saint-Cyr's trust funds which afforded Élise and Dru the gorgeous Georgetown home in their exclusive neighborhood.

Hannah's situation was similar, having brought substantial family monies to her union. And, the fact that her husband, Chuck Connelly, held a prestigious management position, insured them a more than modest life style. It would seem, neither women should have a care in the world. Yet, glancing across the table, she could see without being told, that was not the case.

"You, okay?" she asked.

"Not really," Élise whispered. "Actually, I've considered going to therapy," she added softly, as though gossiping about someone other than herself.

"I have a wonderful therapist," Hannah offered with unaltered poise, simultaneously sorting through her Kate Spade handbag for her psychiatrist's business card. "Half the women we know are patients of Doctor Katz," she shared almost boastfully, as if it were a service made available to a privileged few.

The baby stirred in his carriage seat. His mother lifted the blanket to surround his ears as if to shield him from what she had to say. "It's probably a simple case of post-partum blues," she shrugged, as if to dismiss its severity or attach blame to her child.

Hannah's arched brow supposed otherwise. "Honey, you've been sad for a while," she responded knowingly. "I don't need to tell you this life of an agent's wife tries one's soul. Every time the phone rings you wonder if your husband is going to be sent on yet another long assignment, and for how many months. Hell, the annoying part is Chuck used to volunteer if it involved travel. I've got pictures from the African safari to prove it. Suntanned, all smiles. A zebra and a majestic lion over his shoulder in the near distance. He was gone two months. Meanwhile, I was home recovering from an appendectomy. I remember it vividly."

André interrupted apologetically with a dessert tray. "Ladies, you must try the Mousse au Chocolat, non?"

"That would be lovely," Hannah spoke for both.

Reaching across the table for her friend's hand, she continued to state her case. "Truth is, our husbands are part of a brotherhood of which we are not. We can either accept it or leave it." She stated the hypothesis as though the theory had been tested in controlled and measured laboratories worldwide.

The clamor of the afternoon rush had dwindled to a murmur as André arrived with a tray of complimentary digestifs. "Eaux de Vie for two of my favorite guests," he cooed. "You must, however, promise a repeat luncheon very soon, oui?"

"Absolutely," Hannah assured him, while leisurely signing off on her credit card with a more than generous tip, and bidding him a fond goodbye.

Maneuvering through the parking lot to their adjoining separate cars, the friends parted ways as girlfriends do; hugging and blowing kisses till they were out of sight. Miraculously, angel baby Jean-Jacques had slept through two hours of entrées, desserts, and exhaustive male-bashing girl talk. With courteous muffled whimpers, he began to articulate his growing hunger as the silver Mercedes traveled down 31st street heading for home.

11

DRU

Most of what Élise knew of her husband's work was what little she overheard on his early morning or late-night phone conversations. He had a hard and fast rule not to discuss business at home. But, on occasion, snippets of information trailed after him as he paced room to room on his cell phone. The topic commonly centered around street crime but, when the venue turned to explosives, his voice grew weighty with rage.

"Shit! A twelve-year-old can mix a little potassium nitrate purchased from the pharmacist, scrape enough charcoal from any charred board, and discover he has gun powder. But now these damn kids hook up on the Internet and they've graduated from exploding toilet paper tubes to serious lead pipe bombings. It's like a Timothy McVeigh self-help course for teens. Next thing you know, they're blowing up federal buildings. It's fucking demented!"

"I'll be in court testifying all morning," he informed his partner Paul. "Don't look for me in the office until mid-afternoon." So, that explained the white starched shirt and silk tie draped on the bed post. Élise rolled over, eyes shut tight as if asleep. It was 5 a.m.

"Turns out our guy eating out of the dumpster made a drop in the woods near a local park in Alexandria, Virginia," he said into the phone, clearing his throat. "Jack and I were a few feet away, slouched on a park bench dressed in navy whites acting like wasted sailors sleeping off a binge. Goddamn fool smiled real pretty right into our camera lens," he snickered. "We've got this bastard by the..."

The bathroom door closed shut. Élise had to assume they had their guy by the balls.

Her husband was on round-the clock surveillance, whether on the john, in the shower, or in the closet. His work infiltrated every aspect of his life and, therefore, every aspect of their life. She recalled the blowout they had the day their new bedroom furniture arrived. Though the obvious location for the assembly of the bed was along the lengthy span of wall, Dru insisted he could not sleep in a bed that didn't squarely face the door. It went along with running a background check on our paperboy who delivered the daily *Washington Post* on his bicycle.

A series of muffled, one-sided phone exchanges drifted from the inner closet.

"Forensic evidence... downloads at the lab... indictments... restraints... exhibits... human error... Miranda Rights... custody... profile."

In the five weeks since Jean-Jacques' birth, Dru had spent one Sunday afternoon with the family. He set that time aside because Rose and Patrick O'Neil were driving from Greenwich to meet their new grandson. When the front door opened, and in walked Katy, carrying a giant-sized teddy bear under her arm, Élise was shocked. "I hope you don't mind my tagging along," she said to no one particular; the bear functioning much like a shield to ward off any unnecessary displays of affection.

"Come in! Come in!" Dru welcomed his family. He hadn't shown this much enthusiasm since he was promoted to GS-13. "Great to see you, sis!"

Dru's twenty-four-year-old sister had never been to their Georgetown home. She had shown no interest in her young nephews, and still referred to Élise as her brother's wife. The scholarly economics major, who was working on her postgraduate studies, still lived at home with her parents. She never dated, and never had a boyfriend, unless you counted the life-long infatuation with her first cousin, Andrew.

For the entire afternoon, Dru reverted to a pubescent son and a taunting big brother; belly-laughing at his father's jokes, and smooth-talking his mother, while playfully tormenting his kid sister. He couldn't have been more enthusiastic if he were cheering on his team from front row seats at the World Series.

Like most mothers, Rose assumed she knew her son. However, as is often the case with parents and grown children, she had no idea who he really was, and where his life was headed. In her eyes, Dru was a flawless father and a doting husband. Élise looked at her mother-in-law, wondering if one day she herself would be so easily hoodwinked.

"Dru was right. The baby looks just like you." Rose validated her remark with a hint of regret, turning to Oliver and Will as one might turn to a blood relative in seek of comfort. The hands-off grandmother fixed her eyes on the infant with a cool detachment, as though the child exhibited signs of small pox. The Francophile features of her newest grandchild, and the darkness of his skin, were unsettling to the disapproving woman who had assumed this child would be another blond-haired, blue-eyed bonnie lad. "He's very dark, isn't he?" she said, as if in doubt of his paternity.

"His name is Jean-Jacques? Is that like John…Jack…in English?" asked Patrick, more innocently than derogatively. "No matter," he said, dismissing his own inquiry before Élise could reply. "Whatever you call him, he'll make a fine Marine one day."

The hair on the back of Élise's neck stood up straight in response to the older man's pipe-dream. He didn't need to know that his grandsons were being groomed for Harvard or Princeton, not the halls of Montezuma. That was another exchange she had yet to have with Dru.

Katy barely spoke through dinner, mostly eyeing Jean-Jacques as he swayed back and forth, content in his wind-up swing. She ignored the two older boys whose puerile antics and continuous chatter seemed to only annoy her.

"He's very cute," Katy said, after gathering the empty plates from the table, and carting them into the kitchen, her comment specifically directed toward her brother's wife.

"Well, thank you, Katy. Would you like to hold him?" asked Élise, as if to test the young woman's sincerity.

"Sure," Katy answered. She nestled into the corner living room love seat while Élise placed the gurgling infant into her arms. "Hi there, little fellow," she said gently, rocking the tiny bundle who instinctively nuzzled to her breast. All eyes in the room stared bewildered. Never had the wiry-haired, bespectacled Aunt Katy openly displayed feelings for anyone, least of all a child. Licking her fingers, she slicked down the cowlick which stood straight up atop his crown like a feather in a headdress.

By early evening, Oliver and Will's attempts at gentlemanly behavior transcended into a deafening standoff as they tore through the hallway hailing ninja swords; a personal gift from grandpa O'Neil. At long last, conversations ebbed around the room, as had the food and drinks, as Patrick announced it was time to head on home.

"It's been wonderful seeing all of you," smiled Élise, leaning into Rose O'Neil's obligatory hug.

"I'm glad I came," Katy said to Dru as he handed her a doggy-bag of left-over lemon meringue pie. He hadn't forgotten his sister's neurotic sweet tooth.

"Don't be a stranger," he said, grabbing her, and hugging her tightly. "It's been great to see you, Sis."

Patrick ordered his grandsons, Oliver and Will, to stand at attention against the wall. It was time for a mock inspection of his young recruits. "You could use a spit shine, soldiers" he growled, pointing to their scuffed Nikes.

"Yes sir!" they saluted, giggling as they chased along after him out to the car.

Rose promised to call though she never would for fear Élise might answer. Dru was forced to keep an active landline at home to appease his mother, though she was yet to call or leave a message. "I will never call you on that contraption," she had said, pointing to his cell phone.

As soon as the front door shut, Dru was on his phone. "You're shitting me!" he said. "More than seven hundred electric detonators missing?" he hollered into the phone. "Wait up! I'm on my way."

Élise wondered if he faked these calls. They were so perfectly timed. If so, he should have a mantle filled with Oscars. A call to duty could transform her husband into a man who would sell his family down the river in order to incarcerate one felon. If only his wife and family were nearly so enticing. Crime, to Dru, was seductive as a scantily clad woman to a barroom drunk at closing hour. If only it was a matter of another woman, thought Élise. But the Feds were the temptress and there was no competing. Take away the badge, take away the man.

The irony was, Dru couldn't understand why his wife should be upset as he leaped the stairs to pack his gear, which meant he would not be returning tonight. Thank God, her next meeting with Dr. Katz was only two days away.

12

THE PLAN

Doctor Katz was surprised to hear that his newly referred patient had put together a full-fledged plan since their last session. He slid his rimless glasses from the breast pocket of his English tweed suit jacket, and sank deeply into the high back leather chair. More often than not, patients turned up at his office looking to be rescued. This, however, was not the case with Mrs. O'Neil.

"May I share this with you?" Élise asked, pulling a thick stack of neatly printed text from her saddle bag that appeared to include pie charts, graphs, and graphics.

"Please do," he replied.

Page by page, the young mother of three mapped out a comprehensive strategy detailing exactly how she intended to leave her husband, while keeping him in the dark.

The doctor's knee jerk reaction was that things were moving much too hastily. But he chose to observe and analyze without comment.

"The children are my priority, of course," she assured him.

"Of course," he nodded.

"I'm meeting with my attorney next Tuesday afternoon so I'll have to cancel my appointment with you," she explained, "because…"

"Because you're supposedly at a sculpturing class on Tuesdays," he completed her sentence, to her surprise. Perhaps a break in their sessions was for the best, he reasoned. It would afford time for her to reflect rationally. Running off with three children in tow was, in his opinion, a radical solution with far-reaching consequences.

"I'll have to see you every other week for a while, if that's all right?" Tuesdays would now be a day of juggling therapy, accountants, and attorneys. A glance at the calendar reminded her of a Thursday noon appointment with the actuary to assess Dru's pension plan. She was proceeding methodically and vigilantly, she explained. No need to set life into a tailspin. Her husband could continue his fascination with crime and corruption while she orchestrated her *Mutiny on the Bounty*.

Dru wouldn't fight her over custody of the children since he barely spent a single day a month with any of them. Nothing could have made her happier than to see him taking his sons to the circus and the beach, to the movies, or to their first major league baseball game. They were hardly his priority these days. The thought of Dru as a single dad was difficult to imagine. She'd do what she could to help him adjust to what was likely to be a thorny transition.

As a new single mom, her role shouldn't change much. She would walk the boys home from the bus stop, drive them to play dates or soccer practice, and, in years to come, to the orthodontist. Dru would buy them costly battery-operated submarines and power-driven race cars. She would buy their new jeans, school notebooks, and multi-vitamins. He would answer their every request with *yes*. She would have to be the one to say *no*. It would be the classic good cop, bad cop scenario played out daily in single family homes across America.

"I realize I've been thinking of leaving this marriage for years. Wishing that I could, you know?" she confessed to Dr. Katz.

He nodded with a smile of acknowledgment. "These things never happen overnight. Probably, you hoped things would change, would fix themselves. They seldom do." Having listened without interruption to forty-seven minutes of his patient's self-counseling dialogue, Doctor Katz decided Élise O'Neil was not just another predictable trophy wife with a love story gone awry. He sensed her agent husband's unruffled domestic life had already derailed, and was about to speed full-throttle straight off a cliff. Was it fair? Was it just? Dr. Katz stifled a budding tinge of compassion for her absentee partner, the other half of the O'Neil equation.

"It's my own fault, I know. My husband has grown over the years and I've regressed. Why shouldn't he lose interest?"

The mind can play such tricks, thought Doctor Katz as he considered his patient's perception of herself. Apparently, she has lost touch with how others view her. No conceit. No self-awareness of what a bright and beautiful woman she truly was.

Leaning forward, and flicking a speck of white from his black trouser cuff, he countered, "Frankly, I don't see it as a regression. Might I suggest your values have changed? For example, the high-powered career you once pursued so feverishly is no longer your top priority. But, don't suppose for one moment that the accumulated knowledge and intuitiveness gained in the process was lost or for naught. I see pent up positive energy all around you. What I'd like is for you to see and feel that, too."

Élise felt as though she were sitting across from her wise father but, of course, she couldn't talk to Henri of such things. Her mild-mannered doctor absorbed the flux of human behavior effortlessly as a psychic might read the face of an upturned Tarot card. Dr. Katz had the extraordinary ability to decode each complex thought and irrational action as though by osmosis.

"I can't remember the last time my husband touched me," Élise blurted. "Obviously, we slept together many months ago, which Jean-Jacques can attest to."

The thought lingered, causing Dr. Katz to jot an undisclosed word on his heretofore blank note pad. Interesting to hear her veer toward the bedchamber just as their third session neared its close. The therapist ignored the persistent wristwatch alarm, which summoned the untimely end of their session. "He no longer sleeps with you?" he asked, his voice rising to a notable crescendo.

"Well...when he is home, we share a bed, but not to sleep together in the biblical sense. Middle of the night diaper changes, and nursing a newborn is not exactly a turn-on for either of us," she explained, as though to assume blame.

"Do you two ever talk about it?" he asked, peering over his spectacles.

"We seldom talk about anything," she grimaced. "It's not like he's going to recap his day of disarming explosives from the site of an abortion clinic."

"That's understandable," nodded the psychotherapist, attempting to remain impartial. Half his client base was composed of weary wives, starved for affection, threatening to leave home. Most were not as organized or calculating as the woman sitting before him.

"So, we'll see you in two weeks," she smiled, gathering her belongings, and heading down the hallway.

Dr Katz stood staring at the elevator long after the doors shut tight. Why did this client stand apart from the others? The answer was convincingly clear. It had to do with brain power. If he were Agent Dru O'Neil, he would have worked like hell to keep that woman happy.

13

GOOGLE.com

The fact was, it was grandfather Saint-Cyr who had willed enough funds to his grand-daughter to ensure she would never want for money, nor a home that most might dream of. Yet, on no uncertain terms, Jean-Guy Saint-Cyr had insisted his young heirs pursue advanced educations and career choices. It was so like him to stipulate that Élise and her brother, Símone, be kept uninformed of the generous trust funds they would inherit upon their twenty-fifth birthday. The old gentleman would surely spin in his crypt if he knew his wealth was about to support the undoing of his granddaughter's marriage. Never would he support her decision to break up the family. "Go home, and work it out!" she could hear him say.

The nights flew by as Élise searched website after website exploring real estate postings in the suburbs of Boston. She could only imagine Dru's response to moving the boys out of state. She shuddered, presupposing ugly hurtful scenes reminiscent of *The Taming of the Shrew*. Kicking off her slippers, and curling her legs beneath her, she settled in for another solid night's search, intent on locating a home for her and her sons. For weeks, she scanned locations and properties until her eyes singed from the blue-tinted glare. Like an overextended poker player who'd been dealt too many disappointing hands, she was damned well going to turn this game around.

Typing the words Middlesex County and Massachusetts, she waited impatiently for the listings to appear. Clicking on the letter L with the tap of a finger, she rubbed her weary eyes, and scrolled drowsily down the page. Suddenly, with a jolt, she stopped short. The chair rammed backward into the lamp pole as she sprinted to full attention. "Lexford!" she articulated loud and clear, sounding like a confident contestant in the finals of a state spelling bee. "Of course, Lexford!" With a rapid series of clicks, there it was. Full blown images of the most charming town one could imagine. Her heart was pounding in her chest as she zoomed in on the town lake, church steeple, and the quaint coffee shop. "Perfect!" she said, wishing there was someone nearby to share a victory lap or a high-five with. Squinting at the fine print as it scrolled across the page, she read each word as though it was an email filled with good news from a friend. "Ten miles northeast of Boston. Close enough to my parents in Hyannis, yet far enough from Georgetown."

The view of Lake Wikiup was enough to make her strained neck muscles smile. "Good Lord, a year-round playground for the boys!" Burning with unfamiliar energy, she perched awkwardly over the desktop, nose to nose with the images of lakeside windsurfers. "Swimming, fishing, boating...and its own yacht club!" She scoured the screen surprised by her own girlish laughter. "More than twenty-two thousand people, four neighborhood elementary schools, parks, and biking trails."

Flying across the keyboard, her fingers arrowed to Property Listings. The last time she had been this excited was setting sail for Paris as a college freshman. Boldly, she zeroed in on an attention-grabbing ad:

Three story English Manor stone home on half acre lot, five bedrooms, study, three and a half baths. $985,000.

Activating the on-line video tour, she entered the historic old manor. The creaky wooden floors seemingly audible beneath her bare feet. The camera panned up the stairwell, past the chiseled rosette window, and ultimately zoomed in on the massive fireplace of the second-floor master bedroom. Barely able to breathe, Élise hurriedly saved the site to *favorites* as though to fend off competitive offers until she could call the agency first thing in the morning. The hour was past 2:00 a.m.

For the first time, she was grateful for Dru's long-erratic work hours. This week, he was in Chicago working undercover. Even so, there seemed hardly enough time to sort through the weighty decisions that consumed her days and nights. Like a convict cogitating a break-out, she mulled over each pro and con, fighting the urge to share her plan with someone.

"Cheers!" She winked at the mirror, while ceremoniously raising a goblet of pomegranate juice in a solitary toast. "Life was meant to be celebrated!" her father always said. Henri had instilled that premise in her heart at an early age. That was her objective even if it did mean going through hell and back.

Washington D.C. was never her town. It was Dru's town. Whenever he could, he would escape in running gear, jog past the Treasury buildings, the Capitol, past the White House, and through Lafayette Park. He inhaled the city's power and the thrill of its history. No matter if the streets were flooded with rain, piled high with snow, or drenched in humidity, he ran. He sweated and breathed in the fervor of the metropolis. The man was not without his private passions. They simply excluded his wife.

Boston was less driven, more familiar, and Lexford, the kind of quaint home town setting Élise prayed she'd find. In New England, there were aunts and uncles scattered throughout, along with several favorite cousins she hadn't seen since they were teens, long ago crossed off her Christmas list. Élise was not above humbling herself in order to reinstate such neglected relationships. Social media was a very real option; in some respects, a lost and found department of one's abandoned past.

Too awake to consider sleep, she rested her head on the back of the high back chair. It was easy to envision her Saint-Cyr childhood home in Cambridge, less than a mile from the campus of Harvard University. An easy walk to the end of the street led to the never-ending ivy league collection of red brick buildings. Bustling, book-laden students stared with intent through bottle-thick eye glasses as they hastened about the square. Each appeared to be consumed with a thesis, stepping one foot in front of the other autonomously. This, the city of intellectuals, felt most like home to a woman who'd been gone for far too many years.

The faint sounds of *The Marriage of Figaro* came to its haunting conclusion as the stereo shut itself down. Élise was guaranteed another taxing day of phone calls, baby feedings, carpooling, and delving through financial records and personal files. Manhattan life had never been this harrowing. John Callahan, her attorney, had called late afternoon to confirm Tuesday's appointment. He would need a copy of tax returns, a finalized analysis of Dru's pension from the actuary, pay stubs, check book transactions, mortgage statements, and anything else she could think of that would help him prepare a preliminary proposal for review.

As for finances, Dru neither knew, nor cared, about money. He couldn't balance a checkbook to save his soul, let alone understand the complexities of their joint net worth. The week before their wedding, he had handed over his files like a man relieved to drop off a stray hound at the city pound. Never had he asked the cost of the children's private schools, nor did he question the cost of ripping out the perfectly good Berber carpets throughout the Georgetown house to replace them with imported mahogany wood floors. Bottom lines, balanced accounts, and dispensable income were Dru's shortcomings. To him, finances may well have been written in Greek.

As though to unnerve an evening of euphoria, a voice sounding disturbingly like that of Jean-Guy Saint-Cyr, echoed in her ear. The grandfather she had loved since childhood spoke in his unmistakable broken English. The voice asked its cheerless question. "How can you take three young boys from their father? What kind of mother does that?"

Her head dropped in her hands. There was no answer; simply a question which permeated the room in silent disapproval. Googling the words *divorce* and *children*, page after page of articles, one more disturbing than the next, reeled across the screen. There in black and white, her worst fears… "The Effect of Divorce on Innocent Children." The list was long. Was she selfishly plotting to wreak havoc upon her children's future? Some would say a definitive, *yes*.

14

MIDDLESEX COUNTY

The first call of the day was to Fairmont Banker's realty office in Middlesex County. Élise believed the realtor's forewarning that the property referred to was a new, hot listing that wouldn't be around long. If she was seriously interested, it would mean a trip to Boston this week.

"Is it possible to see it Saturday?" she asked, having no idea how she could possibly pull it off.

"Saturday at 3:00 p.m.?" the agent asked, fingering his electronic calendar.

"I'll be there. Thank you, sir."

Belle was upstairs readying the boys for school. Her Tuesdays, Thursdays, and Fridays were dedicated to the O'Neil household. Jean-Jacques was already bathed, fed, and back to napping in his bassinette. As a sleep deprived mother of a seven-week-old infant, Élise couldn't be more grateful for her loyal housekeeper-nanny.

Élise dialed Henri Saint-Cyr's cell phone. Thank goodness her parents had just returned to the states. "Good morning, Princess," her father answered, delighted to see her name flash across his caller I.D. Relieved by the calm in his voice, she breathed deeply, calculating how much to reveal. He was the one family member she could confide in.

"I wondered if you would be up to a visit from me and the boys? You have a new grandson who is anxious to meet you," she adlibbed.

"Well, of course, darling. When were you thinking?"

"Tomorrow," she stammered. More a question than a statement.

"Tomorrow?" he asked, as though he had somehow misunderstood.

"I know it's short notice. I'll explain when I get there."

Henri was perplexed by his daughter's call but Jacqueline Saint-Cyr gasped at the unwelcome news as though life support itself had shut down. Lady Macbeth's death scene could not have been more dramatic as arms thrust and lashed through the air, pleading for deliverance.

"Cœur sacré! Mais cette maison est un désastre!"

For his wife of nearly forty years, a house devoid of fresh flowers in every room or windows that didn't sparkle inside and out was unthinkable. "Non, non, non, absolument pas! What could that girl be thinking?" she raged in her customary half-French, half-English. "Mon Dieu! You can't just drop by on people. She knows we've been out of the country for six months."

"We are hardly people, my dear. That's our daughter and our grandsons."

"That's not how I raised her!" she ranted, bolting from the breakfast table, clasping her forehead, linen napkin coiled in her hand.

Back in Georgetown, Belle was running the vacuum in the living room when Élise interrupted. "Dear heart, something has come up and I need to drive to Hyannis tomorrow with the boys. Could you help me pack?"

Belle unplugged the cord from the wall, and hauled the heavy machine to the utility room. Her sixth sense told her not to ask the countless questions closeted on the tip of her tongue. Instead, the loyal housekeeper quietly helped roll two monster-sized suitcases up the stairs, setting one in the boys' room and one in the master bedroom.

"Oh, and Belle…Mr. O'Neil doesn't need to know about this yet." The older woman nodded as though she understood, sensing she was in on something bigger than herself.

Since Jean-Jacques' birth, particularly when Mr. O'Neil was not home, his young wife seemed intensely engaged in what appeared to be a personally gratifying, but notably clandestine, undertaking. Nowadays, an impromptu phone call could send her hightailing out the door as though the house was ablaze. Most often, baby Jean-Jacques could be seen buckled in his car seat, happy to accompany his mom on their rounds about town. Belle's eyes welled at the sight, having lost her only son in an auto accident when he was barely five. She had never forgiven herself for being at the wheel. Even now, all these years later, the hurt was unbearable.

Packed bags sat in the hallway and the boys had been sent off to bed by the time Dru walked through the front door.

"What's this?" he asked, pointing to the suitcases.

Élise wasn't looking forward to *this* discussion. She did, however, have his complete attention, which felt oddly powerful.

"I thought I'd take the boys to Hyannis to visit my parents," she answered, as though replying to the question, "How are you?"

"When?"

"Tomorrow."

"And, you're telling me this now?" he asked, unbelievingly.

"I wasn't sure you'd care," she lied.

The old fears began to surface but, today, she would not allow them to take charge. From the corner of her eye, she glanced over the pages of the *Vanity Fair* magazine as her husband approached. Pointing his finger, as a father might do when chastising a misbehaved child, he pronounced each word slowly and deliberately.

"Élise, what the hell are you thinking? You can't just take off with our three kids without talking to me first."

Calmly meeting his stare head on, she let what felt like a full minute pass pretending to be captivated by a Gucci ad. It was simple enough, she explained. Her parents had called, and were dying to see the boys, and especially to meet their new grandbaby. Why not now rather than late summer? She didn't think he'd mind. Nonchalantly, she turned the page.

"Did we have plans?" she asked with convincing bewilderment.

He ran his fingers through his hair, shaking his head. "No, but this is crazy! And you are getting there, how?" he asked, planting his feet firmly with both hands on his hips.

"I'm driving."

"Alone?"

"Of course, alone. I pulled a MapQuest and I have the GPS. It's an eight-hour drive door to door. It's not like we haven't made the drive a hundred times before."

"That's with no stops and your foot pressed to the floorboard. With three kids, it's more like eleven."

He was pacing now. Never a good sign.

"We'll be fine," she said, feigning indifference. "I plan to leave at 2:00 a.m. which should get us there before noon, even with stops. The boys will be asleep most of the trip. Kind of like a red-eye…"

"Just so you know, I don't feel good about this," he said stomping up the stairs, each step heavier than the last.

That had gone better than expected, she thought with a heavy sigh of relief. Showered and dressed for travel in a baggy pullover and stretch pants, she swept and fastened her loose hair up into a ponytail. Sleeping bags, pillows, and thermal ice chest were already in the car, gas tank full, tires checked. All she needed was a few hours sleep on the couch.

Water splashed upstairs as Dru showered and signed off on his customary series of nightly phone calls. By the time he came downstairs, Élise was in the kitchen chopping carrot and celery sticks, and placing them into baggies for travel snacks.

"A little change in travel plans, my dear," he announced. "I called my sister and she's on her way over. She's going with you."

Dropping the knife on the chopping block, Élise leaned against the sink to defray ugly thoughts of other uses for the knife.

"No, that's absurd! Katy is not going anywhere with me."

"It's the only way I'll let you go," he said, picking up the knife with a slight smirk, and beginning to chop the remaining carrots.

"Did you say *let* me leave?"

"Uh huh."

The doorbell rang at 1:15 a.m. Élise could hear Katy's voice as Dru carried her bags in, placing them in the hallway with the others. For now, she would have to go along with his charade. It was the only way to get her children out of the house but she was not without plans of her own. Dru was not in control of her anymore.

15

HOME ALONE

Dru was at the shooting range at 7:00 a.m. when Katy called.

"What the hell do you mean she dropped you off?" he shouted into the phone. The sounds of gunfire blared above his angry protests, making his voice barely audible on the other end of the line.

"I can't hear you, Dru. Call me back," Katy yelled before the line disconnected.

It had been a bizarre night, beginning with Dru's call, pleading with her to make the drive to Hyannis with his wife and children. He led her to believe she was doing Élise a favor so she agreed. Apparently, her brother had not been entirely honest. As she watched him begrudgingly cart luggage down the walkway, and silently place his pajama-clad sons in the back seat, no one need to explain that something stunk in Denmark. Yet, Élise exhibited an earnest show of cheer as the two danced around a visibly awkward goodbye embrace.

Setting a full flask of steamy coffee firmly into the front seat canister, her sister-in-law slid behind the wheel, calmly readjusting the rear-view mirror. For someone about to launch an eight-or-nine-hour non-stop drive with three babies in the backseat, she appeared undauntedly prepared. Over time, Katy had begun to realize what a remarkable woman her brother had married, despite what the elder Mrs. O'Neil had to say.

Serving Thai takeout for Easter Sunday dinner guests was to Rose O'Neil sacrilegious. "Easter dinner is ham and potatoes, not noodles and soy sauce," she had declared under her breath. While everyone but Rose refilled dinner plates with seconds, and moved on to the two-tiered rum cake from La Petite Patisserie, Élise's long-suffering mother-in-law had retreated to the living room feigning indigestion.

Even from the perspective of an inexperienced college girl, Katy fought a constant urge to side with her sister-in-law. Élise admitted she was no cook. Her oven in Manhattan had been used solely as storage space for paper plates and plastic utensils.

"What could be so difficult about baking a cake? A cup of flour, a teaspoon of allspice, an egg..." Dru's mother had nitpicked all the way home from Georgetown to Greenwich. "If it wasn't for the housekeeper, my grandsons wouldn't know what a home baked chocolate chip cookie tasted like."

"What's wrong with Chips Ahoy?" Katy asked, stoking the fire.

The red-headed aspiring scholar had adopted the role of key defender while Patrick O'Neil, brave heart that he was on the battlefront, lay low in the trenches. Even he was at a loss as to why the other O'Neil wives, Kathleen and Lily, dodged the bullet while Élise took the hits. For whatever reason, Dru's wife had drawn the hate card.

"I suppose Jacqueline Saint-Cyr is to blame," Rose reasoned, which was her way of cutting Élise some slack. It would be futile to dissuade Rose that her son had made a terrible mistake in selecting Élise. Convincing her otherwise was as probable as converting the Pope to Judaism. Fortunately, the O'Neil family had dismissed the snarky remarks for what they were; the visceral envy of a woman completely out of touch with today's modern women.

Élise stretched her long legs full-length, and leaned back in the driver's seat.

"This is awfully nice of you, Katy," she began, gently laying the groundwork. It wasn't the young girl's fault she'd been dragged into the midst of her brother's family squabble.

"No problem," the fidgety passenger answered, aimlessly sorting a stack of CDs lodged in the pockets of the side door. So far, things looked dismal...Andrea Bocelli...Barbra Streisand...Josh Groban...Frank Sinatra...Pavarotti.

"We both know your brother. Such a worrier!" Élise said, continuing to build her case. "Truth is, I could make this drive blind-folded and look, the boys are out cold." Katy glanced to the rear where Oliver and Will lay embedded in a mound of downy pillows, arms and legs entwined like twigs on a brambling bush. Both deep asleep while Jean-Jacques snored gently, safely buckled down in his over-sized reclining car seat.

"Please don't take this the wrong way, Katy," Élise paused, aware that she now held the young girl's full attention. "My mother, you do remember my mother, right? I'm embarrassed to say she's nearly hysterical that I'm bringing a guest along. I tried to explain that you are family." With an amplified sigh and shrug, she added, "Dealing with my mother is like talking to a slammed door."

"Oh," blurted a flustered Katy, visualizing the unfriendly and frantic Jacqueline Saint-Cyr. "Maybe this isn't such a good idea, my riding along. Dru said I'd be helping."

"That's Dru, always looking out for us," lied Élise, spinning the driver's wheel to circle the roundabout one more time. "Honestly, it makes no sense involving you like this. I remember my college years. Weekends should be about having fun. To be trapped in a car listening to Nat King Cole tunes on a Friday night is absurd."

Before Katy knew what was happening, she was standing curbside clutching her suitcase and walking up the drive of her parent's home in Greenwich.

Her brother returned her call at noon.

"Dru, calm down! You're scaring me." He was clearly out of control. "Élise assured me she'd be fine. What's the big deal?"

"The big, huge, gigantic, fuckin' deal is I counted on you and God damn you…" Katy clicked off the phone, refusing to tolerate his obscenities. He'd never yelled at her like that before.

Dru hurled his iPhone, sending it clattering to the floor. "Bitch!" he hollered, ramming his foot to the floor of his government issued Chevy Suburban, uncertain who to curse, his sister or his wife. "I don't have time for this," he shouted, just as the bald man at the wheel of a Maserati convertible weaved across his lane.

"You friggin' piece of shit!"

Speeding past rows of government buildings on the far side of Foggy Bottom, Dru ignored all approaching traffic signs. He was late. His team was waiting on him. His personal problems would have to wait. Wasn't he forever working his ass off, and for what? An ungrateful wife who didn't give a rat's ass about him. That's what!

Reeling the vehicle to a halt at the gated entrance, he scanned the cluster of weather-beaten warehouses in the near distance. Flashing credentials at the guard, he drove through the gate. In his rearview mirror a TV News crew tailgated. The driver hung out the window yelling to security, "We're with him!"

The news van barreled through the gate on the heels of the government cruiser, screeching to a halt at the end of the pot-holed lot. Two reporters leaped out of the front seat. Wired and draped with camera equipment, they beat a frenzied path to Dru's vehicle just as he jumped out and slammed the door shut.

"Hey, wait up!" called the female reporter as she shuffled to the lead, her partner trailing behind. "What can you tell us about the explosion?"

Dru walked head down, ignoring the two.

A state police car pulled up, its lights spiraling and flashing. Damn brazen media might have got by security guards but here's where their party crashes. "Sorry, folks. Authorized personnel only," the officer shouted.

"We're friends," they said, pointing to Dru, who shook his head defiantly. He rounded the bend, his mind wrapped around more important matters. Agents Mike Finn and Paul Martin were on the scene, their long-range binoculars in hand. From a safe distance, they were surveying multiple office-sized trash cans covered in silver duct tape propped against a far wall.

"What have we got here, boys?" Dru inquired gruffly with a cursory scan of the surrounding area. One trash can had already exploded, torching the electronic door and melting vinyl siding from the side and rear walls of the structure. There were at least another half dozen cans planted among the adjacent outer buildings.

Mike, a Certified Explosive Specialist, with years of experience on arson cases, continued the briefing. "The PD was making a routine check when they discovered these pretty babies, and alerted the Feds. We got notified from the Resident Agent in Charge, Chuck Connelly, to respond to this location. Looks potentially like a warehouse full of IEDs."

Prince Hal, the trained explosive detection canine, thrust his nose windward as though offended by a foul stench. Mike noticed Dru hadn't showered or shaved. "You look like hell, brother," Mike said, casting a questionable look at his case agent. "You doing alright?"

"I'm fine," Dru replied, annoyed by the questioning. Mike shrugged, unconvinced. Reporting to a disgruntled case agent on a high-profile explosives investigation didn't sit well with him. Not at all.

Agent Rob Taylor rounded the corner, folding a print out. He had been meeting with ATF Public Information Officer, Lou McNally, who was scratching his head, wrestling over which information to withhold from the media collecting at the gate.

"Crazy-ass journalists would sacrifice a limb to score a story for their six o'clock news. Them and their damn Nielsen ratings."

Dru scowled in agreement. "A woman reporter nearly lassoed me as I pulled through the entry gate. Thinks a crime scene is a damn reality show."

"I recognized her. She's that good-looking babe from the local news channel. She's still arm-wrestling with security, demanding to see the agent in charge," reported Rob.

"For Christ's sake, doesn't she have laundry to sort, or a man to take care of?" Mike added, in his condescending tone.

"Enough!" scowled Dru, squinting into the blazing sun. "Fill me in on what you guys know."

Mike spun around, readjusting his gear. "We know these buildings are owned by QEDCO, a subcontractor for the

Federal Aviation Administration. In addition, investigative teams were deployed to the private home of two high-ranking employees where suspicious duct taped trash cans were found concealed in their garages. Local police answered a call out there early this morning."

"Holy Christ," said Dru, donning gloves, and distributing protective gear. "From what I can see from here, it doesn't appear we're looking at IEDs," he said, which he knew had only one purpose and that was to kill. "We're going to move in slowly. But first, I'm calling in a bomb tech to disarm the goddamn thing."

Chuck Connelly had just signed off with headquarters, and was heading out the door when Dru rang. "Got a serious situation out here boss. We're going to need Tim Steele, our Special Agent Bomb Tech, pronto."

"Consider it done," his RAC assured him. "I'll also advise the Special Agent in Charge. You can expect he'll hook up with you and your guys soon as he hears. Prepare for a long day's night."

It was past 1:00 a.m. when Dru wearily swung the nose of his vehicle into the gravel driveway of his Georgetown home. It had been a brutal day. He was so dog-tired that, as the heavy metal door unfurled, revealing the startling sight of an empty garage, his mind registered blank. "What the hell! Where's the Mercedes?" he blurted, hurtling himself out the car door even before coming to a stop. Then he remembered.

His line of work could make him forget everything, everyone. Whenever he strapped on his holster, and headed out the door to face a case, the agency became mother, father, brother, sister, wife, and child. It wasn't easy on any family, he knew that. But, take it or leave it, that was the job.

In the unlit kitchen, the cumbersome home phone blinked twice. Dropping his gear in a heap at his feet, he leaned across the counter, massaging his throbbing neck.

"Hi, it's me," his wife's recorded voice resonated soft and drowsy. "We arrived safely. Talk soon."

Concise and to the point, he thought. He couldn't think of anything that woman could not do if she set her mind to it, evidenced by the fact that he was now standing in their hauntingly dark kitchen alone. And, choosing to leave a message on the damn archaic landline instead of calling him directly on his cell phone…Hell, that's a first!

Flipping on an overhead light, he spotted a neon colored post-it note attached to the microwave, signed by Oliver and Will. Chicken casserole in fridge. Bon Appétit. The kindest words offered him all day. Food and sleep. He could not dispute man's most primal needs. The perfect antidote to the madness of these past few days.

The shower head pounded scalding water down his back, sending shivers to his calves. He was drained. He would call his wife first thing in the morning before heading back on site. In retrospect, their argument had been foolish on his part. All she wanted was a visit with her parents. Nothing wrong with that. A break would do everybody good. Christ almighty, he was such a hotheaded SOB.

Sinking into his side of the bed, he chucked the barrage of monogrammed feather pillows to the floor while checking cell phone messages. Nothing there that couldn't wait.

Staring open-eyed at the silent ceiling, a disturbing question hit him like a car alarm shrieking in the distant night. Had Élise ever mentioned how long she planned to stay in Hyannis with the boys?

16

SULLIVAN PROPERTY

Henri Saint-Cyr was admittedly taken off guard when his daughter took him aside just hours after her arrival to ask if he would take charge of his newest grandson, Jean-Jacques, while she drove to Boston mid-afternoon.

"Of course, sweetheart," he agreed without pause. His daughter plainly had an agenda that she didn't care to discuss. At least not yet. He knew enough to back off, and respect her judgment.

Not surprisingly, Jacqueline Saint-Cyr announced she'd love to lend a hand but had to be excused due to a prior commitment with her bridge club. Henri and his daughter locked eyes knowingly, fully aware that Jacqueline wouldn't know a courtesy bid from a grand slam. She had never played bridge. But, as always, Henri graciously allowed for his wife's unlikely alibi with a smile and an assuring nod. He'd been through this routine a million times.

"Not to worry, ladies. Grandpa Henri is astonishingly capable of caring for his grandson. You two go about your business. We'll be just fine."

The two older boys clamored excitedly into the back seat of the family car, Oliver waving a Boston Red Sox pennant while Will proudly donned his New England Patriots' baseball cap. Grandpa Henri wasted no time branding his grandsons with suitable home team paraphernalia. Élise was noticeably pre-occupied, as if a summit meeting was taking place in her head. She double checked the boys' seat buckles, and turned to offer her father last minute instructions.

"You sure you're up to this?" she asked, as the older man snuggled the child like a practiced wet nurse. Fluffing a layer of blanket into the bed of the stroller, he nestled his grandson into its folds, smiling at the chubby face that turned upward at the sound of his deep baritone voice.

"Off we go," the proud grandfather waved as he wheeled the baby carriage down the hill toward town. First stop would be Joe's barber shop, and then lunch with the locals at Sterling's Diner. Watching her father strut down the road armed with a diaper bag full of pampers and baby bottles, she couldn't help but think, *luckiest daughter in the world.* Élise chuckled to herself as she slowly inched her way down the drive.

The eighty-five-mile drive from Hyannis to Fairmont Realty in Lexford took less than two hours, which included a truck stop luncheon of hamburgers and fries for Oliver and

Will. It was important that the two oldest boys see the property. The fact was, if it didn't suit them, she would keep searching.

Ace Dwight, the real estate agent, greeted his client with a look of poorly concealed skepticism as he escorted the trio into his small back office. He never understood parents who brought young children to a business appointment. Never was it productive.

"So, Mrs. O'Neil, you're ready to look at the Sullivan property?" he asked. His eyes shifted nervously from one boy to the other like a man cornered by thugs. He moved the dish of butterscotch candy from the desktop to the top shelf of the bookcase before sitting down.

"That's why my boys and I are here," she replied.

"And your husband…he'll be joining us later?" he asked, feigning indifference.

"No," she answered, tendering no explanation.

"Well, in that case, let's go take a look," he said, which sounded a lot like, "Let's get this over with, shall we?"

The Sullivan property, as Ace referred to it, sat on a grassy knoll surrounded by a grove of magnificent old shade trees. Pulling up the long steep driveway, Oliver pointed to the deer on the lawn.

"Actually, it's ceramic," Ace scowled, dismissing the joy in the young boy's face.

Opening the lockbox, he followed the mother and children through the side entry, leading into the enormous kitchen. From the twin pantries, to the dumb waiter, to the butcher block countertops, Élise was beyond enchanted.

Every nook and cranny of the historic old house lured her on into the next room where she oohed and aahed like a naïve school girl. Online photos hadn't touched upon the untold charm of the property. One almost expected to see Jane Eyre lolling about the library, or strolling its grounds.

"The house was built in 1897, and is in remarkable condition. It passed a complete appraisal a month ago," the thirty-something realtor explained as he led the way to the second story level. "The Sullivans played an important part in building this community," he continued. "The old man left the property to his only son but it seems young Perry prefers the alternative lifestyle of San Francisco and has no interest in what he refers to as his father's rickety old house."

Oliver and Will scampered room to room, exploring the vast emptiness of the vacated home. They'd never seen anything quite so grand. "Whose mansion is this?" Oliver asked his mother's newest friend, who was reading notes from a tablet.

"You'll have to ask your mother that question," Ace replied, while glancing at the young mother, noticing for the first time she was not wearing a wedding ring.

"Let me ask you boys. Could you imagine living in this house?" she asked, watching their faces light up like two candlelit jack-o-lanterns.

"Yes! Yes!" said Oliver as Will chimed in. "Let's go look some more!" The older boy romped away, leading his brother affectionately in a neck lock.

For more than two hours, the three surveyed the historic old homestead. Ace was exceptionally thorough, baring electrical wiring and copper water pipes. Élise crept up the narrow, crooked stairwell to the third story where the Sullivan's Irish maid had roomed. She laughed at the muted echo of each creaking step, reminding her of eerie sounds imagined on the pages of a well-worn mystery novel. The shuttered windows opened to the greens below. Surely, they clattered with the advent of winter winds. Flashlight in hand, Ace led them into the bowels of the musty basement, then to the shed and old wooden barn in the open field.

Standing before the glass-lined conservatory, which spanned the width of the front of the property, Ace explained how the concrete foundation had been faced with limestone to make the structure look original to the house. By now, he was mildly confident he had a bona fide buyer in hand, though the absentee husband loomed heavy on his mind. It wouldn't be the first time an uninformed spouse emerged like an awakened canker sore to trash a probable sale. He'd deal with that later. Calculating the sizeable commission at stake, even the children's ungainly shrieking had become curiously tolerable, even as he reset the lock on the back entry door.

"Is it possible to drive by the lake on our way back?" Élise asked.

Heading the car back to town, Ace circled Lake Wikiup where people were boating, biking, and fishing. He pointed out the yacht club, and stopped to view the nearby elementary schools, the town library, the church, and the common grounds. Élise kept looking for the chasm, the abyss in the package. Was there such a thing as being too perfect?

As they pulled up in front of his office, the young man knew the time had come to address the inevitable. "We'll probably want to get your husband involved," he said guardedly, inferring that *her man* might want to step in now, rather than later, for any serious money matters and decision making.

"Actually, no sir. I'm a single mom," she said, surprised to hear the words fall so easily from her mouth. "I'm the one buying the house. Let's talk numbers, shall we?"

17

ALL-NIGHTER

Dru was beyond annoyed that his wife wasn't answering her cell phone. But that would have to wait. It was Sunday morning and he was back on the QEDCO case after logging six hours of sleep. They had closed in on a disgruntled employee long known for casting idle threats, and now seemingly bent on keeping good his promises. The arrest hadn't been made though the number of explosive devices had reportedly expanded to five residences, in addition to the multiple warehouses. ATF, the FBI, the state police, along with the bomb squad and fire department were all involved. A variety of loose ends needed to be tied up before moving in to nab their guy, dubbed Trash Man.

Chuck Connelly was poring through case reports when Dru and his team shuffled into the office balancing Starbucks coffee cups. Apparently, the RAC had slept on the office couch as evidenced by his wrinkled trousers and bare feet.

"Some coffee for you, sir," said Dru, setting a steamy cup on the boss's desk, amidst a barrage of strewn paperwork.

"No lemon-tipped pistachio biscotti?" Chuck asked jokingly, clearing a space among the rubble.

"Mocha Frappuccino will have to do," Dru snickered, drawing up a chair near the window. "By the looks of you, boss, we're not the only ones pulling down all-nighters over the QEDCO case."

Connelly had spent the night cozying up with ATF's database, integrating cases to detect ongoing case patterns. "BATS reveals some interesting similarities between our five residential devices and a bombing that occurred January 3rd on the roof of the QEDCO project management office in Syracuse, New York," he informed the men between slurps of coffee. "The Bomb Arson Tracking System was a major tool in assimilating loose ends back then."

Unshaven, Rob Taylor and Mike Finn each claimed a corner of the office sofa to sprawl out on to down their giant fix of caffeine. Agent Paul Martin stood tall in the doorway. No Starbucks for him. "I'll stick to my protein shake," he announced, to a chorus of jeering catcalls.

The boss leaned back in his plush leather chair, assessing his team. The agents instinctively knew their weekend was about to become toast. "Great job guys, but we're nowhere near the finish line," he warned. "Better call the rabbi. Let him know you won't be making it to temple today." It was no secret he demanded a lot from his squads, but no more than he demanded of himself. At this point, no injuries had been reported on the QEDCO case and that's how Chuck Connelly planned to keep it.

Prince Hal remained curled in a fetal position under Mike's desk in the outer office, his paws covering his ears as if in defiance of another all-nighter. A milk bone flavored doggie biscuit lay untouched beneath his chin.

After an hour of brainstorming, the group dispersed, each assuming a specified detail. Dru and Paul headed to the lab to check out results on the dismantled evidence before heading back to the warehouse site.

Juan Mendez, the lab technician hypothesized, "Santa's elves couldn't have packaged these trash cans more lovingly. At first glance, they appear crude and amateurish. But, trust me, these bombs would have caused major destruction if you guys hadn't been at the top of your game."

Paul nodded knowingly. "The clerk at the local hardware store recalls the purchase. Twelve black trash cans, ten rolls of silver duct tape, two cartons of bubble wrap, and a ton of fishing line. It's not your everyday order. He says the guy paid cash, and stood out because he never removed his dark sunglasses, which seemed strange on a blustery, stormy day."

"Lab results suggest he wasn't working entirely alone," reported Juan.

The two agents took note, and left the lab, hyped on zeroing in on their suspect. As their vehicle approached the warehouse gate, Dru recognized the news reporter from yesterday. Her shiny white van with oversized TV antennas sprouting from its rooftop was parked by the roadside like a holiday shopper waiting for the mall to open. The tall blond jumped out of the van as he made the turn.

"Damn!" Dru winced. Reporters were grating as rodents.

"Please, can I talk to you?" she pleaded, the wind whipping at her gold spangled gypsy skirt.

"Lady!" yelled the security guard. "I told you yesterday, this property is sealed off."

Dru eased his foot off the brake, inching forward, while powering down his side window. "I understand that you have a job to do, but so do we."

She kept in step with the moving vehicle, her hand clutching the lowered window. "I'm Liz Summer," she said, handing him a business card. Of course, he recognized her. Half the men in the city fantasized about the six o'clock broadcast journalist who delivered prime time news from their local station.

"I know who you are," he admitted.

The salon-tanned beauty had Paul's attention. "I'll be damned, Liz Summer!" he stammered, flashing a coy smile, for the moment unmindful of his assignment.

Dru leaned on the steering wheel, fingering the card with disinterest.

"Call me. I have some tidbits that might interest you," she solicited before releasing her hand. Stepping back, she watched the government SUV drive through the gate.

"What's with that?" Paul asked, craning his neck in order to steal a second look.

"Just another news anchor trying to earn her way to a bigger market," Dru speculated, tossing her business card into the litter satchel under the dash.

"I read where she graduated from University of San Diego with a degree in civil and environmental engineering. She's more than a reporter." Paul was up to date on the city's most eligible women.

"Maybe she ought to take her brains and beauty, and go build an aqueduct," Dru shrugged, not in the mood to delve in trivia. He had a case to solve.

It was 5:00 a.m. before Dru finished up his day, and headed home. Every bone in his body ached as he bent over to retrieve a stack of weekend newspapers off the front porch. The all-night surveillance of Trash Man's residence, sustained solely by an endless supply of Coke and corn chips, had turned his stomach into a raging war zone. Paul was right. If he stayed on course, this body was doomed. Hell, his hairline was already receding and the bags under his eyes were nearly permanent. Though he hated to admit it, Élise wasn't entirely wrong to remind him there was life beyond work.

Despite utter exhaustion, stepping into the empty house set off a rage that sent his dirt encrusted boots kicking shut the back door with a thunderous blow. "Shit!" he bellowed, with a wildness to his voice he hardly recognized. His cell phone lay dormant. No return call from his wife. Trudging up the stairs, he toppled fully dressed onto the unmade bed, falling instantly into a deep, dark sleep. Later, he didn't hear the home phone ring three times before forwarding to voicemail.

"Hi Dad, it's Oliver. Grandpa Henri is teaching me to pitch and catch the ball. Mom says to tell you we'll call back later." *Dial tone.*

In Hyannis, the early morning kitchen was abuzz with news that Uncle Símone was arriving Monday night. Henri Saint-Cyr had telephoned his son insisting he join the family for an impromptu, overdue reunion.

Predictably, Jacqueline reacted to news of her son's visit with a rash of hysteria, intermingled with French-English wails. "Mais, où dormira-t-il ?" Élise surveyed her father's face for signs of wear. How on earth has this kindly man coped with a lifetime of talking this person off a ledge?

"Relax, mother," the younger woman said with a calming voice. "Símone wouldn't care if he sleeps on the front porch. Stop worrying." It did little good as she stepped aside, and watched her mother scurry down the hallway to check out her fresh linen supply.

The hardest part of this visit was not dealing with an irrational mother. That was a given. It was concealing from her adoring father the true purpose of this trip. Henri had no reason to believe his daughter's marriage was in jeopardy. He certainly had no idea that a property was being held with earnest money while independent inspectors made their final assessment. Not even Henri could be told the truth until the Sullivan home cleared escrow. As far as he knew, she and the boys had visited a college friend named Ace someone. Ace Fairmont, he thought she had said.

Meanwhile, Élise and the boys planned a day of walking the beach, digging for clams, gathering sea shells, and flying Chinese kites. She was determined to enjoy this magical seaside setting, despite the secrecy of underlying business dealings and a ruinous marriage.

The salty aroma of a scrumptious steamy bouillabaisse prepared by Lena, the Saint-Cyr's part-time cook, met them as they stood at the open kitchen door, shaking sand from their shoes. Hunger had everyone clamoring for a seat around the family dinner table and, if her children weren't watching, Élise would have licked the plate.

As the table was being cleared of soup bowls and crusty bread, the house phone rang. Henri held his hand over the mouthpiece and mimed to Élise, "It's Dru."

Breathing deeply, she prepared for the worst as she jostled the phone, and headed toward the sunroom, anticipating what was sure to be a withering cross examination. "We haven't had a free minute since we arrived," she prompted the conversation, awaiting his tone rather than his reply.

"Apparently!" he replied, attempting to remain composed. "Mind if I ask how long you plan to stay?" he asked with stern sarcasm while scribbling circles on the kitchen chalk board with a nearby black magic marker.

"Is there a problem?" she wanted to know.

"No problem. I think I have a right to know. A week? A month?"

"I don't have an answer," she replied, aware of the awkward pause. He swiped the open can of chili off the countertop sending it splattering to the floor, followed by a burst of muttered foul expletives.

"You, okay?" she asked, alarmed.

"Yeah, yeah," he replied. "I dropped something."

Oliver and Will had trailed her voice through the hallway, and were leaping up and down in boisterous refrains of, "Me first! No, me first!"

"The boys want to talk to you," she said, anxious to pass the phone to her oldest son. "Here, honey. Say hello to your dad." Already, she was stage-managing the roles that would be played out in this unfair game of disconnected parents. "I'll be in touch," she offered, handing off the phone to Oliver, and sheepishly leaving the room.

18

LIZ SUMMER

In Washington D.C. the early morning lead story featured a photo of Liz Summer. The camera panned to a live reporter. The backdrop was the QEDCO site.

"News anchor woman, Liz Summer, failed to appear last night for a scheduled evening broadcast, causing concern to those who know her as extremely reliable. It is known that Ms. Summer, for the past week, has been covering a story related to the QEDCO warehouse site. Some suspect she may have uncovered information that the perpetrators construe as damaging. We ask anyone having information to call..."

"Holy Christ!" gasped Dru, just as his cell phone trumpeted its solemn military taps.
"Did you catch the early news?" asked Paul.

"Hard to miss. It's on every network. Jesus," blurted the team leader, "she wasn't bullshitting us."

"You're not going to like this," Paul continued to spill details, knowing Dru was about to go ballistic. "Truth is, I recouped her business card from your litter bag. I didn't think it could hurt to give her a call."

Liz Summer had been surprised to hear the unfamiliar voice introduced as one of the ATF agents she had flagged down in the parking lot at QEDCO days before. Usually, agents weren't so cooperative. The two agreed on an early evening meeting at Old Crosley Grill, one of D.C.'s most famous oyster bars, located steps away from the White House. The notorious hotspot frequented by political insiders, journalists, and theater-goers was for both a familiar stop. She could be there by 7:00 p.m.

Dru held his breath to the count of ten before pounding the refrigerator door, sending Oliver's kindergarten art work toppling to the floor. "This is bullshit, man! Who's in charge of this case? You? What the hell were you thinking?"

"Let me finish," interrupted Paul.

"No, not over the phone. Meet me in twenty minutes on the Capitol steps."

First his wife and, now, his trusted friend. The two people he thought he could rely on were jerking him around like he was a court jester. You don't take my three kids out of state, and not know when you're coming back. And, you don't interview key persons, and not check it out first with the agent in charge. Grabbing the car keys, he bit into a chocolate bar, and stomped a path to the garage. It was ass-kicking time!

"This better be good, pal," he prefaced the derogatory remarks seething beneath his breath as Paul approached.

The two men walked to a corner perch on the east side of the steps.

"To be honest, there's not much to tell," Paul began sheepishly, embarrassed to be caught with his fist plunged arm-deep in the cookie jar. "Funny thing is… she agreed because she thought she was meeting you."

"Me?" a confused Dru kicked at the pesky pigeons underfoot.

"She was expecting *the driver* is what she said. I have to tell you, the woman's face dropped to the deck when I walked in and it was all downhill from there," the agent explained. "We looked like any other couple at the bar, ordering drinks and oysters, and talking for maybe an hour. She was guarded about discussing QEDCO when I brought it up, which was curious. Why else were we even there?"

A number of people had recognized her as they made their way through the crowd to the exit. Paul said he escorted her to the curb, and flagged down a cab when she graciously refused his offer of a ride home. "Maybe she flat out disliked me…or maybe she was keen on you. Hell, we may never know. I do know QEDCO was not up for discussion, at least not with me. If you had showed up, maybe it would have come down differently."

"And, now she's missing. How do you think that looks, you stupid jackass?"

It was 7:00 a.m. as the workforce began to swarm about in formal business wear, bearing bulging leather attaché cases. Cell phones resonated, each chiming its own distinctive refrain, like the sound of an orchestra pit warming up. People nodded to one another. Few smiled. The city of power-driven government employees hustled past with quickened strides and dilated pupils.

Washington was a city with no room at the inn for the less capable. These ego-centered *do-ers* would sooner run a lawn mower over their mother's prize-winning tulip beds than be passed over for the next government level upgrade. Unlike Manhattan, money-spinning was not the driving force. Pride, vanity, and self-intrigue were prerequisites if one were to succeed, and thrive, in D.C.

Élise never bought into it. To her, the serenity of Lexford was far more suitable a place to unleash a meaningful life. Ace Dwight had called to confirm that the appraisal and due diligence inspections were underway and he was aiming for a quick close. He admitted he had never before sold a home whose ownership was to be held in a family trust. He assured a maximum three-week window, assuming all went as expected.

"The town will soon be referring to your place as the O'Neil property," he said laughingly.

His remark sent shivers up her spine...the O'Neil property? No! It would be the Saint-Cyr property, funded solely by her grandfather's trust fund. A volume of documents had been submitted to include required trust papers, with a copy of the prenuptial agreement signed by

Dru. All holdings of the trust were to be held in the sole name of Élise Saint-Cyr. Élise had insisted on a prenuptial, prior to her marriage, per the advice of her grandfather's attorneys.

Up to this moment, it hadn't occurred to her to reclaim her maiden name. Bearing a surname separate from that of her young sons felt somehow disloyal, but necessary. Reverting to her maiden name suddenly became paramount in light of any unforeseen legal discord. *All decisions should be so clear,* she thought, stretching for the phone to make a follow-up call to her attorney.

John Callahan, her friend and counsel, was pleased to report the divorce papers were revised to include edits from her latest e-mail. With a bit of tidying up, he said, they would be ready for a signature by week's end. "Once I receive the signed originals back, we'll serve your husband with papers the following day."

She felt her pulse race. This was really happening.

It was clear she was still in need of therapy to thwart the recurring bouts of self-condemnation. Though normally adverse to telephone therapy, Dr. Katz had agreed only because it was Élise O'Neil. Though a happily married father of four, he admitted, she had a hold on him. For the moment, he wouldn't try to analyze it.

"Shouldn't I be depressed about this whole divorce process?" she asked.

"A failed marriage is a terrible loss. There are stages we go through as we mend; sadness, tears, and depression among them. You've been grieving the loss of this marriage for some time, years perhaps. But, now you're ready to move on. Just be sure to take time to be kind to yourself as you do so."

"So, you don't think I'm heartless, cold, and dastardly?" she asked, half-believing she was all three.

"Absolutely not," he stared at her through the phone. "Are you open to the possibility that perhaps there is no guilty party here? Only disjointed lives wrestling to be free."

His advice rang of a Patsy Cline song.

"So, if I said I'm not sad or remorseful, that's a good thing?" she asked, in hopes of extracting a positive response.

"Divorce doesn't have to be dreadful if the two parties remain civil."

Élise didn't know how civil and respectful Dru was going to be when the divorce papers were served. Five hundred miles wasn't going to be far enough to contain her husband's anger when a stranger walked up, and put him on notice that their less-than- blissful marriage was to become null and void.

"Are you ready for the anger?" Dr. Katz alerted her to the inevitable.

"I'm never good with anger," she answered. Confrontation was not something she handled well, even long distance.

"Let's get clear on what you can expect. You know this man better than most. Will he jump in his car and drive to Hyannis? Will he weep? Go on a drunken binge?"

Élise realized that, after more than seven years of marriage, she had no idea.

"One can never say for sure how another person will react," Dr. Katz filled in the lengthy pause. Élise was grateful for his use of the first-person plural pronoun, as if to reinforce an alliance. "We should prepare ourselves as best we can for the unexpected."

"Ri-i-i-ght," she said, startled by the tremor in her voice.

19

SÍMONE

Oliver and Will didn't know what to expect when Uncle Símone pulled into the driveway in his Jeep Cherokee. They were familiar with their blue-eyed, blond-haired, Greenwich, Connecticut uncles who looked a lot like their dad. At first glance, the dark-haired man walking up the front stairs didn't resemble anyone they had ever known. He wore glasses with heavy rims that made his dark brows appear thicker than bear fur. From beneath a Cubs baseball cap, tufts of black curls twirled below his neckline. Alongside him trotted a short-haired, droopy-eared dachshund who appeared much more friendly than the uncle attached to the end of the leash.

Will hovered behind his older brother cautiously as the strapping man extended a handshake, and introduced himself and his dog in a raspy voice. "I'm your Uncle Símone and this here is Augustus Too Short the III."

"That's a funny name," said Oliver. "Too Short," he added quickly, hoping the long-limbed stranger hadn't taken offense. The lanky man and his short-legged hound were, oddly, physical extremes of each other.

Símone looked as much a stranger to his sister Élise as he did to his nephews. It had been years since they had last seen one another. "Is it really you?" she gushed, not knowing quite what to say. She wasn't certain she would have recognized her only brother if he had come knocking on her door unannounced. But, as if she were still five years old, he lifted her up off her feet, twirling her full circle, triggering a nervous giggle from her two watchful sons.

"Hey, little sister, great to see you!" he said laughingly as he set her down.

Henri hugged his son, yanking off the Cubs hat. "That's not allowed in this house," he chided the six-footer with a scornful smile.

Jacqueline sobbed her way down the staircase, and lunged into her son's arms like a bride on her wedding night. Símone backed off, while Too Short yelped, and began nipping the heels of the shrieking woman, sending Jacqueline pleading for her life.

"Arrêtez-le! Arrêtez-le!"

Augustus Too Short the III was led away to the back porch, head lowered, shuffling his pegged legs like a jailbird in shackles. "It's okay, boy," offered Símone, already questioning this whole impromptu family reunion invite. His mother's melodramatics still sent his blood pressure soaring. It was an instantaneous reaction that the years, unfortunately, had not tempered. Ten minutes in the house, and he was already talking himself out of creating a scene. "Relax, little fella. Hang in there. We're in this together," he reassured the deflated pup.

It was amazing to see his little sister patiently mothering three sons of her own. He wondered how you learn those skills when you've never observed them as a child. After a chilly night curled up on the porch hammock, he and Too Short woke to the aroma of coffee and waffles drifting from the distant kitchen. His parents were asleep but Élise and the boys were dressed, eating, and waiting on Uncle Símone to join them for a jog along the beach.

The brother and sister had years of catching up to do and the boys were anxious to get better acquainted with Too Short, who they looked upon as somewhat of a distant cousin. A romp in the sand would be the perfect forum. Rarely did Símone contemplate marriage and children, but chasing through the marshes with his nephews and dog aroused possibilities. When Élise strapped baby Jean-Jacques onto his back, the warmth of the child's body felt oddly normal as the two melded into one giant stride. These emotional stirrings felt alien, yet welcome, to the gangly bachelor from Chicago.

Growing up in the Saint-Cyr household, it seemed the only thing in life he and his sister ever shared were genetics. In retrospect, he was the class geek, fascinated by test tubes and neurons, while she was the varsity cheerleader, invited to all the parties, and dating first-line athletes. What could they possibly have in common? Their mother flitted from one charity event to the next, from one beauty salon to the next, dutifully surfacing at the six o'clock supper hour, as did Henri. As proper parents, they insisted on a sit-down family dinner, though it was prepared by Lena Beaumont, a neighbor lady who earned extra income through catering. On the few occasions when Jacqueline did cook, it remained questionable whether the main course had been poultry, pork, or beef. There was no way to differentiate one from the other once Jacqueline had her way with a recipe.

Christmas, however, was the family's redeeming grace when the Saint-Cyr household packed suitcases, and set off for Florida, Hawaii, or the Caribbean. More often, they toured Europe. If Símone couldn't recall a family Christmas tree, or a stocking hung on the mantle, he never felt deprived. Standing before the Mona Lisa at the Louvre would always win out when compared to the unwrapping of sox and boxers beneath a tinseled tree.

His father and sister were especially close, which too often cast Símone in the role of third party on a first date. Though his mother bargained for his affection, he remained aloof, turning to mathematical configurations and scientific research for solace. Baseball was Henri's passion, which held zero interest for Símone, whose teenage aptitude did not include sports. When a C- grade in physical education excluded him from the honor roll, he glued his eyes to the tiled floor, and slouched miserably from class to class. Peers snickered, shunned, and eluded him in a way that science and math studies never had. Upon graduation, his choices were clear. A scholarship to MIT and, eventually, a PhD placed him in line for a lucrative job offer in Chicago; a city that held intrigue for the young scholar from New England.

At age twenty-five, when Grandpa Jean-Guy's trust fund was disclosed, Símone was astonished more than grateful, that a grandfather, who had hardly spoken three words to him in his entire life, would leave him such a fortune. What do you say, except *merci?*

20

THE MOVERS

Belle Stevenson wasn't sure how to respond to Élise's request but ultimately agreed. She would let the hired movers into the Georgetown house Tuesday morning as soon as she saw Mr. O'Neil leave for work. Slipping the key into the front door lock, she crept into the empty front room, feeling like a felon revisiting the crime scene. Five weeks had passed since her friend vacated, though it seemed a lifetime.

The housekeeper gasped at the sight of a huge gaping hole in the stained-glass opera doors separating the dining room from the formal living room. "Oh my!" she cringed, tiptoeing through the rainbow of spattered glass stretched across the wooden floor. The china closet doors sprawled open, displaying shattered Waterford goblets and smashed Lenox china. Belle felt her chest tighten at the sight of Mrs. O'Neil's prized Lladró figurine collection splintered beneath the carved legs of the antique armoire.

Angry graffiti-like scribble covered the kitchen memo board; a topless black marker dangled from its cord. A box of cereal spilled onto the countertop next to a half-empty can of Coca-Cola. Mounds of unopened mail, mostly bills, were stacked on the tabletop. In a corner, a stockpile of newspapers lay bound in rubber bands. There were no dirty dishes and no trash, other than scattered candy bar wrappers and a half empty bag of barbecue potato chips.

Upstairs, Belle heard the eerie ticking of the bedside clocks as she walked room to room, scanning an inventory list Élise had compiled as a guide for the movers. In the master bedroom, they were to pack clothes from her closet only; personal items had been removed from the dressers. The bedroom furniture stayed. Throughout the house, the items listed were her inherited antiques, Persian rugs, and irreplaceable valuables. A few items were sentimental, and would mean little to Dru. The boys' bunk beds, tricycles, and toys, including everything in the nursery, were to be boxed for the move.

At 9:00 a.m., the moving van aligned itself by the side door. Two burly men rang the bell. The elder of the two had a stomach like a ponderous front porch, and a cigar hanging lazily from the corner of his mouth. His younger partner resembled a sumo wrestler. Belle handed them a copy of the list, and showed them the layout of the house, from the top floor to the basement. If they had any questions, she'd be downstairs cleaning up the mess in the dining room.

When the men got to the guest room, the elder shouted out for Belle. "We disassembled the bureaus, four poster bed, and bed coverings. We supposed to pack the window draperies?"

"Well, let's see. They aren't listed but they definitely are part of the ensemble." She rubbed her forehead, pacing the room, testing the patience of the two anxious laborers.

"Look, lady, do they stay or do they go? We're about done here so what's it gonna be?" spouted the beefy man who reeked of fetid smoke.

Wanting to do the right thing, she nervously reviewed what would be reasonable and fair. "Oh, damn! Go ahead and take them," she blurted uncharacteristically. Dru O'Neil could get his own window coverings. She had never forgiven him for missing Jean-Jacques' birth.

The truck was packed to the brim, and slowly rolled away from the curb just before noon. Belle Stevenson swallowed her own selfish tears, yet felt relief for her young friend who was strong and alert, and taking back her life. She had watched Élise's emotional decline with the silent lament of a mother mourning a daughter. The older woman knew only too well what it felt like to harbor wasted dreams. Wiping her chapped hands on her apron, Belle dragged the trash bag full of useless china and crystal fragments to the back stoop, and dropped it clattering into the barrel below.

From her open kitchen window, weeks ago, in the early morning, she had witnessed the heartbreaking scene when a stranger approached Dru in the driveway, and served him with legal papers. In disbelief, he had staggered to the brick steps, and read the terms of divorce with slack-jawed horror. "She will not get away with this!" he had shouted, stomping up the stairs, and throwing the door open with enough force to drive the door handle into the wall.

"Pick up the phone, you bitch!" he hollered into the mouthpiece. With every unanswered ring, he smashed another perfectly formed figurine, another Waterford goblet, and another Lenox platter until the shelves lay bare. Tonight was not going to be any easier when he discovered movers had arrived, and emptied out his house.

21

THE ARREST

Trash Man was arrested at 11:00 p.m. amidst a flurry of marked and unmarked police cars that encircled the block of Victorian homes in the historic district of Georgetown. Armed with search and arrest warrants, Dru O'Neil and Mike Finn led the stack of agents as they surrounded the residence of the suspect's parents' home in the dark of night. A porch light flickered on, then off, like a knee jerk reaction activated by the riotous banging on the front door. A brittle, aged man cracked open the heavy-framed door, mumbling incoherently. Instinctively, he attempted to shut the door, stumbling backward as ATF agents flashed credentials, and forced their way through the opening, and into the vestibule.

"We know your son is here," Dru said, pushing past the elderly man who slithered aside, and wrapped his arm around a frail, sobbing woman in a nightdress.

"Worthington!" Mike hollered. "We're armed to the hilt. Don't do anything foolish." He and Dru charged toward the back bedroom where they believed Worthington to be. The other team agents infiltrated the adjacent rooms, scouring under, over, and in between, like a pack of hounds on a royal hunt.

Weapons drawn, Dru and Mike advanced toward the Worthington's bedroom where a muffled voice sounded from a distant hallway. A slender, balding man darted from a storage closet, sprinting down a corridor toward a stairwell, a trail of armed agents in pursuit. A shuffle of agents barricaded through a side door, hurling the wild-eyed man to the floor. Handcuffs forced his flailing wrists to collapse behind his back while fingers meshed together as though in prayer.

From the street below, a slow siren roared like the overture to a hideous concerto, while whirling blue lights cast circles upon the ill-fated scene. Curious neighbors peeped through window blinds. Others stood brazenly on porches or sidewalks, staring at the Worthington home as if a lynching were in the offing.

Curse words spilled from the man's raunchy, twisted mouth.

"Don't be a jerk, Worthington. Haven't you caused your folks enough grief?" From the corner of his eye, Dru caught sight of the frightened parents peering at their son, sprawled spread eagle on the cold stone kitchen floor.

"You have the right to remain silent," Mike began to recite the Miranda Rights. The man thrashed about like a newly landed halibut on a ship deck. "Anything you say can be used against you in a court of law." As the man was led to the front room, head hung limp like a deflated soccer ball, he spoke not a word to either parent.

At the door, Dru apologized to the fretful parents for their pain. The shrunken woman reached out, and asked, "What happened to your hand?"

Dru had forgotten his bandages. Sweet mother of God. Her son is being led away in handcuffs and his mother is worried about my hand!

"Oh, this? A minor cut is all," he answered, awkwardly discomfited by the sign of compassion as he watched his agents surround the captive man, and force him into the rear seat of a cruiser. "We'll take care of your boy," Dru said, deliberately turning broadside to obstruct her view of the army of flashing lights of police cars and ambulance on stand-by. He could do nothing to shroud the drone of the helicopters hovering overhead.

"He's in a lot of trouble, isn't he?" she asked, moving closer to her husband, who shivered noticeably.

"Yes, Mrs. Worthington. I'm afraid your son is in a lot of trouble."

Trash Man, aka Daniel Worthington, worked for QEDCO for more than ten years until being dismissed in early January. His wife and children had been concerned by his incessant talk of retaliation, but never suspected the church-going head of their family to act on it. They were completely unaware he knew anything about explosives.

Police Chief Dwayne Goodwin released a statement:
We are thrilled that the cooperation between ATF and local law enforcement resulted in a timely arrest of Mr. Worthington before he harmed anyone.

Officials believed co-conspirators were likely involved. This arrest could only bring authorities closer to apprehending others who may now be on the run.

Across town, Chuck Connelly stomped back and forth, irate with one of his own. Paul Martin had been removed from the QEDCO case following his antics in approaching Liz Summer without authorization. The police had interrogated the seasoned agent concerning the woman's disappearance, but determined he was simply another skirt-chaser. The fact that he was a federal agent didn't help the reputation of the agency at large.

"What kind of idiot are you?" the supervisor shouted, shaking his head in disbelief over his agent's juvenile poor judgment. "All the women in the city and you have to chase this one?"

"In retrospect, it was sheer stupidity, sir," Paul admitted, chastising himself for his own foolhardiness.

"You're lucky you're only on suspension," Chuck warned. "I can only protect you so far. Next time, I'll throw your ass to the wolves so fast that even little Red Riding Hood couldn't save you."

"There won't be a next time, I promise you that," Paul swore to it, just as Dru arrived, leading his team of disheveled agents through the supervisor's office door.

"What the hell is that on your hand?" asked a stunned Chuck, pointing to the bandaged right hand of his top agent. "Worthington get the best of you?"

"No, sir. His sorry ass is tucked in down at the county jail, waiting to be transferred to the federal court house," he answered, ignoring the inquiry into his aching hand.

"One down…" Paul joined in, attempting to allay the thorny position he had created among himself and his peers. Dru ignored the comment and the others silently shifted eyes toward the window. Not a good idea to screw with your federal brothers. None of them were ready to offer him a pardon just yet. Follow the rules, shit head.

Chuck inspected his weary looking crew. "You guys did a great job but you look like hell. How about we call it a day. Go home, get some rest." Glancing at the wall clock, he bellowed a deep sigh. "Let's see, it's 0200 hours. I'll need to see you all back here by 0700."

"You're all heart, boss," said Rob Taylor, rubbing his eyes, and stretching his huge frame like an alley cat. "That gives me time to drive home, feed the hamster, shower, and drive back."

"Sorry, but we're going to heed the advice of my dearly-departed, saintly grandmother who always said, strike when the iron is hot. We're not nearly done here, boys. The lab techs insist Worthington had at least one, if not two, accomplices. Lots more to be done. I'll be here waiting on you band-of-brothers with a sack of warm bagels."

Chuck laid his hand on Dru's shoulder as he rose to exit with the others. "Got a minute?" asked the supervisor, with a look that suggested there was but one answer. Dru slumped back down, massaging his throbbing hand. Paul left the room, closing the door behind him. He was off the hook for now.

"Hannah tells me there is trouble in paradise." Chuck opened the conversation straightforward, grabbing two bottles of Perrier from the corner refrigerator. "Want to talk about it?"

"I have a choice?" Dru relented, squirming boyishly. "To be honest, I've hardly had time to digest it all myself but, in a nutshell, Élise bailed. Took the three kids and headed to New England."

"For late spring break, maybe?" the boss asked, not wanting to sound bleak.

"A break would be accurate. You see, the little misses served me with divorce papers. I went a little crazy," he said, holding up his clubbed hand as evidence. "Tore up the house a little."

"Is there another guy involved?" Chuck inquired, in which case, he could identify with the self-inflicted injuries. In his lustier days, the commanding supervisor had been known to throw a few punches into walls over a woman; a side of himself he would rather forget.

"Nothing as simple as that. Truth is, this whole ATF business, the endless hours, the secrecy, the whole disruptive family life, apparently didn't fit her American dream. Hell, I know it's no picnic in the park, but to slip out of town in the middle of the night with my three kids. That's the shits!" He winced as he smacked his bandaged hand against the edge of the desk in frustration.

"No need to explain," his boss calmly added, lighting a cigarette. "Hannah has threatened to leave me so many times I've lost count, but she's still here. Probably because she didn't have the guts to do otherwise. Not all women have the chutzpah of Élise. There's a compliment in there somewhere," he chuckled. Chuck and his wife adored Élise, and hated the thought of these two good people splitting. "If you need time off to go work this out with your family, I'll take over QEDCO," Chuck offered.

"No, I won't do that!" Dru defiantly sprinted from the chair heading to the door. "I'm in the middle of a friggin' case. I don't need bullshit. See you in a couple of hours, boss." The office door slammed shut behind him.

Chuck never felt good at times like this. How many agents, including himself, had reduced their marriage to rubble for the sake of cracking yet another hard case. Élise wasn't the first, and wouldn't be the last to finally say, "enough," and seek the services of a divorce attorney. He feared he was looking at another protégé who might live to regret his decisions.

Unfortunately, he knew that men like Dru wouldn't listen to reason in the heat of the moment. Too often, agents saw themselves as modern day warriors; every jailed villain a conquered empire. Except one day, he wakes up with failing vision, dentures floating in a glass next to the bed, a second wife in the kitchen brewing coffee, and wishing he could have made it right, way back then.

Even now, nearly 20 years later, Chuck would have raced, not walked, to reclaim his former life with his three-year-old twin daughters. But it was too late. They were grown now. Estranged from him and, most days, he was able to convince himself he wasn't that unhappy.

22

MOVING DAY

"Quite a set-up you got here, ma'am," said the hired mover, tossing his full-length blond hair over his shoulder, and flexing his bulging muscles. Oliver and Will jumped up and down as they watched the gruffer, older man puffing a cigar while rolling their bicycles down the ramp of the huge trailer truck. It felt like Christmas morning to the young O'Neil boys as they watched the pair of scruffy Santas uncrating and carting the truck load of furnishings into their new house.

"Keep out of the way, boys," cautioned Élise as she directed the men toward the winding stairwell. With each step, they huffed, twisted, and turned, taking great care not to damage the heavy, cherry-wood four poster bed.

"Perfect," said Élise as the men positioned the headboard to face the marble fireplace. If Dru had been here, the bed would have to face the door, and block the magnificent floor-to-ceiling window. No need for firearms on the bedside table and no mug shots posted in the walk-in closet. It felt good to be in charge.

"Great view from up here," coughed the elder man taking in the scene below.

"Isn't it grand?" she agreed. From the distant hallway, she could hear the laughter of the boys playfully rolling about on their unmade beds while Jean-Jacques slept soundly in the nearby room. Weeks worth of unpacked boxes lined the walls of each room; a reminder of the hurdles ahead. *One day at a time,* she reminded herself.

Élise knew she worked best alone. When her father insisted he drive down from Hyannis to help with the move, she stood her ground. Once his daughter made up her mind, it was cast in stone. Her *'no'* was as solid as Plymouth Rock sitting in the bay.

Henri Saint-Cyr had come to inspect the Sullivan property the day after closing. He stood staring at the magnificent old home in disbelief. How on earth could she have pulled this off without my knowledge? The unsettling announcement of a pending divorce from Dru O'Neil was even more shocking. Good lord, divorce! Marital difficulties would have been the furthest thing from his mind. He had not an inkling. His mind immediately flashed to the storm ahead when he would have to explain all this to Jacqueline. His ears were already abuzz in anticipation of his wife's judgments, opinions, and condemnations. But, at the moment, his grandsons were leading him up the front steps to the tune of "Grandpa, look at this. Grandpa, look at that!"

Élise had scurried up the stairs, holding open the door with a wide-eyed smile he hadn't seen in a very long time. "Don't you worry. It will all be just fine," she had reassured him with an oversized hug.

The movers were still jostling with the assembly and realigning of the dressers in the master bedroom when Élise suddenly stopped short. Clearly, that was the front doorbell ringing. "Who on earth can that be?" she asked no one in particular. Fluffing her straggly hair, and mopping her brow on her sleeve, she hustled downstairs toward the front room. Flinging open the massive oak door, she stood frozen, face to face with Paul Martin.

"What the hell are *you* doing here?" she barked out the words.

"Everybody has to be somewhere," he said. "I thought I'd check in on my favorite girl." After an awkward silence, he asked, "May I come in? I've been driving since 4:00 a.m."

Élise was stunned, forgetful of her usual impeccable manners. "I'm sorry, of course, of course. Come in." He stepped in, feasting on the beauty of the grand old home.

"Dru sent you I suppose?" she surmised, trying to rationalize.

"No! He has no idea I'm here," the agent said, quick to clarify. Élise arched a suspicious eyebrow.

Oliver and Will sailed down the banister, singing out, "Uncle Paul!" It wasn't their dad, but close enough to appease their puzzled minds. Their innocence and trust were a stabilizing force when doubt and misgivings slithered into her mind, threatening to destroy her resolve. Oh, to be a child again.

"Hey, there they are!" shouted their broad-shouldered friend with his eyes lit up and arms stretched wide. He scooped their young bodies high into the air as they yelped, giggled, and group hugged. Élise looked on, befuddled. Not that she wasn't thrilled to see a familiar face but this was madness!

Just then the internet service van pulled up the long drive, raising dust and spewing rocks before parking adjacent to the leaning wood shed. "It's insane here today," she apologized while guarding the doorway, and waving the service man through the back gate.

"Don't worry about me. Go do your thing. We'll talk later," Paul said as his young tour guides tugged, and led him through the house. She was sure there was a reasonable explanation for his unannounced arrival but, for now, it was the movers and service man who needed attention.

By dinner hour, the moving truck had left and the house, though chaotic, was taking on the look of a home. A couch and lamps in the living room. Rugs laid. The dining room table, though stacked high with cartons, stood in its rightful place. Boxes boldly marked KITCHEN covered the stone floor of the enormous room. A rocking chair cozied up to a shuttered window, which framed the wooded backyard.

As the sun set, they settled on packing the children into Paul's Jeep, and driving downtown to test out the local Thai restaurant. All five were hungry, tired, and beyond caring why it was they found themselves sitting around a table being waited on by two kindly Asian women with broad, toothy smiles. Élise sipped a lemony cup of steaming green tea. For now, she was enjoying Paul's being here, for whatever unlikely reason. Baby Jean-Jacques was cranky, which was highly unusual. Bouncing him on her knee, she felt his forehead. Oh no, did he feel a bit feverish? Oliver and Will sat tall in corner chairs, artfully working chopsticks to the bewilderment of Paul, who was struggling clumsily with the awkward sticks and a dish of Pad Thai.

"I'll teach you later," promised Oliver, while handing his fatherly friend a fork.

"Thanks, kid. I think the American plan is best for me," said Paul.

As everyone lapped their platters clean, Paul detailed the circumstances surrounding his suspension. "It would have blown over as simply a case of incredibly bad judgment on my part if it hadn't been for the disappearance of the prominent local news anchor. When the police called me in for questioning, I knew I was in the hot seat."

"Liz Summer is missing?" A surprised Élise had no idea.

"For more than a month now," he answered.

"I knew Liz fairly well," said the young mother, obvious concern written in her eyes. "She was keynote speaker at a charity ball which I chaired a few years ago. We hit it off and she called from time to time. I was honored she remembered me at all. In fact, she dropped off a baby gift to the house when Jean-Jacques was born."

"You're kidding?" said the astonished Paul. "So why is it Dru didn't mention that when we ran into her at the QEDCO site?" He directed the question more to himself than to Élise.

"I doubt he noticed," she said, remembering her husband barely showed a shred of interest in much of anything that occurred at home in the days before her leaving.

"It's not like you forget Liz Summer dropping by!" replied Paul, wiping his chin with the oversized cloth napkin.

Oliver and Will began to fidget in their chairs now that their fortune cookies were unraveled and devoured. Jean-Jacques' benevolence had extended its limit and he began to wail his discontent. The two women servers scurried to the table to help the children down from their seats as Paul swayed the baby car seat to and fro, attempting to soothe the howling child. He signed the credit card bill, and soaked in the hostess's congratulations on his beautiful wife and children.

"Let's go, dear," he said with a wink, placing his hand in the small of Élise's back, and escorting her and the boys out the door. He could only wish.

23

PAUL

Dru lost it when Oliver innocently told his father that Uncle Paul didn't know how to use chopsticks. "Son, put your mother back on the line," the enraged father scowled over the phone, trying to camouflage the quiver in his throat. The confused six- year-old dismally delivered the phone back to his mom.

"What the hell is Oliver talking about? Paul Martin is *there?*" he shouted with open rage. "That son of a…"

"Calm down," his wife said, picturing the veins of her husband's neck knotting up as he paced feral-like through their Georgetown home. Élise flashed on Belle's description of shattered Lenox, Waterford, and Lladró collections spilled across the dining room floor. It was less surprising than disheartening to imagine Dru in such a state.

In their nearly eight years together, Élise experienced her husband's wrath on two isolated occasions. The first, when he backed her into the corner kitchen cabinet, twisting her arm behind her back until she screamed for him to stop. She was six months pregnant with Oliver, and had defiantly rejected the idea that Dru's sister, Katy, move in with them. He was incensed by his wife's selfishness. The second occurrence struck her as accidental. *But, was it?* After a surprise happy birthday phone call from a former male co-worker, Dru followed her upstairs, ranting jealous innuendos before shoving her into the bed post, bruising her eye. She shuddered every time she relived his yelling at the top of his lungs, "Tell that bastard to never call here again!" Neither time did he apologize, nor demonstrate the slightest remorse. It simply was never mentioned again.

"Chuck and Hannah were concerned," she explained. "They got my new address from Belle, who passed it on to Paul. Friends looking out for friends is all."

"Who gave Chuck Connelly permission to interfere in my personal business?" he shouted. "And, you can tell Paul to…"

"Why can't you understand that people are trying to help?" she shouted back, barely recognizing the vindictive voice of her estranged husband. The O'Neil brothers of Greenwich, Connecticut hardly drank, cursed, or got into brawls. Dru, the wholesome, former altar boy, boasted of the abuse he withstood from his fellow Marines for making Pepsi, rather than beer, his beverage of choice.

"I don't need any goddamn help!" Dru shrieked, followed by a loud thud as he swiped a row of tabletop books to the floor.

"Dru, stop it! Pull yourself together if you expect me to talk to you," she said, grateful for the miles that stretched between them.

Dr. Katz's words rang in her ear, "Are you ready for the anger?"

This is exactly why her leaving Georgetown was staged under pretense of a family get-away. Some couples could have *the talk,* and keep their wits intact. But, Élise knew that was not going to be possible with Dru. He would go ballistic at the thought of divorce. Deceit and secrecy were not part of her makeup but it became a last resort. She hated herself for it.

"I have a right to see my sons!" he demanded.

"Absolutely," she agreed. "Our attorneys will work that out…"

"You've thought of everything, haven't you?" he scorned flippantly. "My attorney and your attorney can just figure this whole goddamn mess out, huh? Well, let me tell you something, you ungrateful…"

"Dru, I'm sorry but this conversation is officially over," she said, hanging up the phone. There standing before her, looking confused if not wounded, stood Oliver and Will. No time to throw herself a pity party. Instead, she wrapped her arms around the two, and ushered them out the door to make good on a Reggie's hamburger run. As young as they were, she knew the time had come for the daddy-isn't-going-to-be-living-with-us-anymore talk.

On the way home, they stopped at the town library on Main Street in hopes that Dr. Seuss would have a book of rhymes to explain away divorce. Apparently not, so the boys opted for Seuss's tale, *Oh the Places You'll Go*. Élise would have to find a way to weave the fragile message through tonight's bedtime storyline.

"Just like us," she said light-heartedly, interspersing her reasoning into the verses, and reverting to the silly illustrations when words became too sober. Oliver and Will hung on every word, asking 'Why? How come? What if?' Jean-Jacques was luckiest of all in his safe little world of babyhood. Worn out, the three youngsters dozed off, oblivious to the haunting draft in the room, or the eerie rattling of copper pipes from the basement below.

During Paul's unexpected four-day visit, Élise realized how safe her friend made her feel. They talked till early morning, which was something she and Dru had stopped doing years ago. While it became convincingly clear that his interest in the Liz Summer case was more than a passing fancy, Élise wasn't sure where he was heading with this. He was involved in a twisted sort of way, being one of the last to see her before her mysterious disappearance. Unfortunately, Liz was the catalyst for his suspension and why his future was now under scrutiny by the agency. With time on his hands, the Summer's case had lodged a permanent campsite in his head. He needed answers.

Sitting at the kitchen table, Paul looked up from his laptop. He had been tapping and clicking keys with the focus of an inspired pianist. "Someone has to know something!" he clamored, draining the final dregs of beer from a chilled glass mug he supposed had belonged to Dru.

"I actually got to know Liz quite well," the young mother recalled, lazily stirring a pot of beef chili simmering on the stove. "We logged a great deal of time together working the charity scene in D.C."

Paul's ears snapped to attention. "Did she ever share anything unusual, anything at all? Something she might have said that would give reason to one day pick up and vanish without a word?"

Élise was reminded of the many lengthy discussions shared with Liz Summer. "I'm not exactly sure why she opened up to me the way she did. There are things that were told to me in confidence. Things I wouldn't feel right repeating."

"Like what, Élise? You have to tell me!" He rose from the table, and took the wooden spoon from her hand. "Look, call me crazy, but my gut senses Liz is in danger and, damn it, you just might hold the key to lead us to her. No one walks away from an illustrious life like Liz Summer's unless a dragon is hot on her heels."

Slowly, and carefully, the story unfolded in the dim light of the early morning hours. Guided by his probing skills, her agent friend listened with eyes, ears, and an open mind to every word, reading meaning into each inflection. "What I do know is that if one of my sons was in danger, there is nothing

I wouldn't do to save him," she said, with conviction that left no room for questioning.

"Including vanishing?" he asked.

As a teenager, Liz Summer had given birth to a child out of wedlock. It broke her heart, the news reporter had told Élise, when her parents arranged to place the child with distant relatives; cousins, who were more than willing to raise the baby boy as their own. Liz was graciously invited to spend vacations with her son's family each year, though the child remained unaware she was anything other than a family friend. The nineteen-year- old father of the baby, Stan Crowe, suspected his child had been given away and not aborted as he had been told. The Summers did not approve of the hell-raising Crowe boy or his family, who would surely have interfered if the truth were known. So, Liz faked an abortion, and left town to spend a nine-month hiatus with the adopting family.

"So, her disappearance could be related to the child? Or, with this Crowe fellow?" Paul's mind was churning.

"Could be," shrugged Élise.

"Liz has to be about thirty-four, which makes her son about fourteen, fifteen? Did she say where these relatives lived? What the boy's name was? Anything about the family?" He was firing questions faster than she could respond.

"Arizona," she remembered. "Scottsdale, Arizona." The adopted father was an orthopedic surgeon, Liz had told her. The family name was Ost. "I remember because she emphasized that it was pronounced like toast." The family had been so kind, allowing the young girl to name her baby. "She called him Devon. Devon Ost."

Paul's eyes bounced back and forth from her face to the keyboard like a Wimbledon spectator as he keyed data fast and furious. He jotted concise notes into a black leather ledger as if working a crossword puzzle, the empty cubes filling in faster than most could skim the clues. "Have you any idea, my darling, how much help you've been?" he asked, bouncing to his feet to give her a bear hug.

Élise was concerned that Liz's privacy be protected. Had she mishandled her friend's trust by divulging the story? Paul read the guilt written on her face.

"Look at me," he whispered, lifting her chin up to face him. "If she or her boy is in trouble and you could help, you would, right?"

"Of course," she mumbled in response.

Early the next morning found Uncle Paul cooking bacon and eggs for the boys while their mom rocked Jean-Jacques through his bottle in a corner chair. Sliding the lever on the dishwasher to the locked position, the visitor explained to the boys that he had to go back to the city this morning, and catch bad guys, but would always, always, always, be just a phone call away.

Picking up Jean-Jacques with a big smile, he said, "And you, young man, keep growing big and strong till I return. Deal?" The chunky baby gurgled, and clapped his fat little hands. Instructing the boys to cart his tote bag out to the jeep, Paul asked them specifically to take a look at his tires.

"Be sure they're well inflated. I've got a long ride ahead," he quipped, as they chased each other out the back door.

"You know you can call me anytime, gorgeous," he said, taking Élise by the hand. "That's what friends are for."

She avoided eye contact, allowing her mane of morning hair to flow over and around her face. Last thing he needed to know was how much she dreaded to see him go. His surprise visit had been more reassuring than she cared to admit.

Paul thanked her, and promised to keep her abreast of his findings on the Summer's case. "We're in this together," he reminded her with a wink. With names, dates, and cities to follow up on, he had ample work cut out, even if unofficially from the sidelines.

Driving away, he waved to the sounds of his blaring horn, already thinking how he would handle his next encounter with Dru O'Neil.

24

KATY

Rose O'Neil was quick to detect the seriousness in her son's telephone voice the minute she heard, "Hi, ma. Got a minute?" Dru took a deep breath before drawling out his gloomy news. "Fact is, Élise and I are getting divorced." The stunned woman didn't muster a word though, subliminally, he could hear *I told you* so in each labored exhale of his mother's silence. "I take it Katy has not yet mentioned I've invited her to move in with me?" he segued. "I think it would be good for both of us."

Dru assured his sister he would make the call, and drop the bomb that was sure to detonate Rose's O'Neil's colitis to new highs. He held the phone from his ear to muffle the wheeze that would surely follow. While Dru continued a one-sided conversation, his mother shook her head, attempting to shake the dreaded notion that her only daughter might even consider moving from home. "That's ridiculous! Katy would never move from home to Georgetown," Rose chided.

Meanwhile, Katy was upstairs in her room, transferring the contents of her closet into oversized Glad bags. Her dream of severing twenty-four years of overly-protective parental ties was about to materialize. As ungrateful as she felt dissembling the bookcases that lined the bedroom walls, it could not undermine the riotous elation taking place in her head. Her cell phone blared just as she tied up another bag's worth of belongings to hear Dru blurt in her ear, "Ball's in your court. She knows."

Simultaneously, Rose O'Neil opened the bedroom door; her face transfixed into a frightening death stare, her body rigid as fossilized stone. Without a word, the sullen woman lowered her head, and trudged away with a heart that had plunged to the depths of a waterless well.

Patrick O'Neil entered the room, and wrapped his arms around his daughter. "Your mother thinks of you as her baby," the old veteran spoke softly. He always knew this day would come and, without instruction, reached for the nearby screwdriver, and quietly began to detach the iron headboard from its metal bedframe. Patrick knew his wife best be left to herself to fester over what she would later express to the world as a kick in the teeth.

Katy's move to the Georgetown house brought balance to her brother's otherwise misconstrued world. It's amazing how the smell of burnt toast, and the taste of too-strong coffee, can satisfy a void. Dru accepted the clutter that trailed his novice housemate room to room. When it should have grated on his nerves, the disorder brought a calming in an uncanny sort of way. The toe-thongs left by the front door, the umbrella dripping on the costly oriental rug, and the cyclic rap music vibrating through the walls; all signs of life in an otherwise murky world.

God, he despised attorneys. Did he want them to look more closely into possible spousal rights to his wife's inheritance? "Hell no!" he advised them. He wanted no part of it. "What I want is for this divorce business to be put to bed as quickly and simply as possible. That's what I want. Can you do that?" he asked curtly, abruptly ending the call. What he didn't want was any more damn headaches.

He glared at a stack of unopened household bills, piled high on the kitchen table, as if they were activated grenades. And, quite frankly, to him, they were. Christ, he hardly knew how to write a personal check anymore. Élise was the financial wizard. When his bank informed him that his account was overdrawn by thirty-four hundred dollars, he considered jumping into his truck, and driving straight through to Lexford and begging, absolutely begging, his wife to come home. How the hell was he supposed to know his government deposits wouldn't automatically transfer to a newly opened personal account without a signature? Hovering over his checkbook, he squinted helplessly in an attempt to decipher his wretched chicken scratched entries. "Does that look like a five or an eight?" he asked Katy, who answered with an indecisive shrug.

And, why did Livingston, Livingston & Livingston, Attorneys at Law, find it necessary to call nearly every other day? Was he considering claiming custody of the children? "I could do that?" he sputtered like a naïve law school freshman. That option had never crossed his mind.

Just then, Katy came barreling through the back door, carting a paper sack overflowing with sweet smelling hot pepper and sausage hero sandwiches. "Dinner is served!" she announced. Best words he'd heard all day. It was hard to imagine his daily dependency on his crazy kid sister was evolving into his saving grace.

The QEDCO case was nearly put to bed with a second arrest made three days after that of Worthington. The disgruntled employee had succeeded in setting off a total of four blasts at private residences of his former management team. The wife and child of his immediate supervisor were hospitalized with severe head injuries. Two others were treated for burns and cuts.

Dru was right about Worthington. He caved after the first few hours of interrogation, blowing the whistle on a neighbor who provided the brain power behind the vicious plot. The college-aged neighbor confessed, "Building explosives, it's what I know." He told police that Worthington boasted of the injuries caused by their joint effort. Two other accomplices had joined them. "We got high setting up bombing devices under Worthington's direction," he bragged, like a quarterback singing his own praises. "Kinda like playing a deadly video game, only for real," the young student said displaying a sick smile.

"I knew Worthington was a coward the minute I laid eyes on him," Dru told Chuck as he sat facing his supervisor.

He did his best these days to dodge one-on-one discussions with his boss, fearing the conversation would ultimately turn to Élise or himself, neither of which was any of his damn business.

"Doing okay?" Chuck would ask.

Here it comes, thought Dru, sitting upright. "I'm fine," he lied, diverting eye contact.

"You look like shit," the boss observed, boldly staring his agent down. "Hey man, you need to know I'm not the enemy," he added. "Beside the fact that the mocha frappe latté deliveries have fallen off, I'm worried about you."

"Is there a problem with my work?" Dru asked flippantly.

"Your work is exemplary," Chuck replied.

Dru had stood to his full six feet. "So, we're done?"

The disheartened boss wanted to shake his lost friend into oblivion but, instead, nodded agreement, and watched the young man turn, and walk away.

25

MOTHER TO MOTHER

Élise couldn't believe what she was hearing when attorney John Callahan called to warn her that Dru was talking shared custody of his sons. "He wants them every summer," he informed her.

"The man hasn't spent a full day with any one of his children in the past two years!" she shrieked into the phone, contesting like an impaled bull.

"That may be true but your husband has every right to demand shared custody," he told her as gently as he knew how. "To be honest, I expect he's been advised he could create havoc with your taking his boys out of state under false pretense."

Élise's hands shook as she rang Paul's number. She had to talk to someone. Paul had become a crutch, never pretending to have answers but always making time to offer an upbeat ear to his friend's quandaries. "Hell, what do I know?" he would preface his comments. "Never been married. No kids that I know of..." his voice would trail off with a laugh. For all his lack of experience with family life, she could always count on his manly viewpoint to fill the gaps, and afford balance. "Despite my many inadequacies, I am a good listener," he would tell her. "Fire away!"

Two weeks passed yet Paul hadn't returned her call. She knew he had problems of his own. He made it clear that Dru's friendship meant a great deal to him, and was set on making it right. "You can't make old friends," he told her. Her mind rallied with likely and unlikely explanations, all of which made her feel a lesser human being. She feared he was distancing himself. Regretting his recent visit. Trumpeting fears was hardly an attractive attribute, she reminded herself with a self-deprecating shrug. It explained why therapists prospered so handsomely, empathizing in closed door meetings in exchange for outlandish fees. As if on cue, she reached for a note pad, and scribbled *CALL DR KATZ* across the page in large print.

It was dinner hour and Will was stabbing a pile of carrots he had sectioned off in a corner of his dish. "I hate carrots," he complained a little too assertively, causing his mother to raise an eyebrow.

Swallowing a carrot slice, Oliver offered a bit of big brotherly advice, "My teacher says they are good for our eyes."

"I see good without carrots," argued Will.

"But, can you see in the dark?" the older brother asked, causing the offender to reconsider, and hesitantly fork a slice into his mouth.

Élise, who as a rule ignored phone calls at family dinner hour, hungrily leaped over the potato bin when she caught sight of Paul's name flash across her cell phone.

"Where are you? I've been so worried about you," she said, quickly realizing that's what mothers tell neglectful children who stay away too long.

His voice was low and focused. "I found Liz Summer," he announced. "I need you to take a deep breath, and listen carefully to what I have to say."

"Thank God! But what are…?"

"Just listen," he cut her off. "You were exactly right. Her disappearance has everything to do with her son." It seems Dr. Ost contacted Liz late at night, apologizing for the hour, but said he felt uneasy about a man who visited his medical complex earlier in the day. The man acted strange, and was asking a few too many questions. As soon as the doctor added, "Does the name Stan Crowe mean anything to you?" Liz leaped out of bed and, without a second's pause, said she would be on the next flight leaving D.C.

"Good Lord, so that explains it!" Élise gasped, dashing to the kitchen table to break up a butterknife dueling match.

"Behave!" she hollered. "Oh…sorry. No, not you, Paul."

"So, you are where?" she asked, knowing the answer before the question left her mouth.

"I'm in Arizona. I'll explain later in detail, but for now, no one can know about this." He quickly added, "Absolutely no one."

The ATF agent was already on probation for his prior involvement with Liz Summer. If the bureau caught wind of any of this at this stage, he was dead meat. "I know what I'm doing. You are going to have to trust me on this," he murmured in a slow, even, knowing voice. "Here comes the heavy part," he charged on cautiously. Élise took a deep breath, frightened by what might be coming next. "Liz is asking if she could send her son to stay at your place."

"You mean here? Paul, you can't be serious!" she heard herself shouting. "You know I'd like to help but..." Élise sprung to the table just as Will knocked over a tumbler full of milk. Ripping off a handful of paper towels as she balanced the phone in the crux of her neck, she began to mop at the spilt milk, watching it flood the table, and seep onto the stone floor. Oliver continued to mash his potatoes into a pool of ketchup.

"So, the answer is yes?" he asked. "Look, Liz is out of options. She's truly going mad trying to keep the boy safe from a destructive, crazed man. It's okay to say no," he paused, "but I told her we could ask. She is right here. Would you talk with her?" he asked as kindly as if he were about to put his ailing grandmother on the line.

"I don't know, Paul..." she stammered.

"Élise, it's me, Liz. I'm so sorry to get you mixed up in this but you are one of the few who knows I have a son. I wouldn't ask this for myself. It's just that my child is in serious danger and I'm desperate to keep him safe somehow. Mother to mother, I'm begging you," she sobbed into the phone.

Paul was back on the line. "I'm truly sorry to put you on the spot like this," he said. And, yes, he did realize what he was asking of his friend, who was buried with her own mountain of troubles.

"How would he get here?" Élise asked, realizing she was wavering.

"I would drive him myself. It would take about four days," he added.

She was frightened out of her mind but how could she refuse? Stan Crowe was, from all accounts, unstable, and a potential threat to Liz's son. The harried young mother of three hung up the phone disbelieving what she had just agreed to. Faced with the possibility of her own sons being taken from her three months a year, how could she take on housing a stow-a-way teenage boy? Was that even legal?

Élise had no idea she had just linked up with Paul Martin and Liz Summer in one of the biggest news stories to hit D.C.

26

BREAKING NEWS

Dru stormed through the front door, cursing like a sailor facing dishonorable discharge. "Physical abuse, my ass!" he ranted, dropping his weighty holster onto the dining room chair. "That bitch should know better than to threaten me!"

Katy's triple-tiered mouthful of bologna-provolone-sprouts-on-rye lodged deep in her throat as her brother banged his fist to the wall. She choked, swallowed, and coughed her way to the sink. "What now?" she hollered between gulps of water. Her self-assured, doting brother had been replaced by an angry and vengeful cursing machine. She stood motionless, awaiting his next move.

"My insane wife, your idol, says she'll press physical abuse charges if I pursue shared custody. I never touched that damn woman!"

The way he recalled the two incidents cited by her attorney could hardly be called physical abuse. Replaying it in his head, he had barely shoved his wife when she brushed against the bed post. It was nothing. Callahan claims there is a photo on file taken by a friend that clearly displays a bruised eye, and a friend who says she'll come forward if necessary. "Goddamn Hannah!"

Dru had no choice but to back off the custody battle, he told Ron Livingston. It was one thing to lose his family but another to jeopardize his career. The bureau would toss him and the bathwater out the window at the mere mention of wife abuse, even if it never happened. Once again, she wins! So far, he was scoreless.

If that wasn't bad enough, in the office this morning, Paul Martin, *his wife's new best friend*, was being silently heralded as an off-duty hero for directing authorities to the missing news anchor. "*LIZ SUMMER SURFACES*!" headlined every newspaper in town. Video clips of a red-headed Liz Summer donning a butch haircut reeled across television airwaves coast to coast. The story became all the more intriguing by the presence of an unidentified black man glued to her arm as the two were filmed scurrying from an oversized black Hummer.

"We are ecstatic to report that well known news anchor, Liz Summer, has been found safe. Details will be disclosed as they become available," the news reporter announced, with a close up that showcased his perfectly aligned white teeth.

"What the hell?" Chuck Connelly snarled as he inched his nose closer to the screen. "That's Paul Martin on her arm!" he hollered loud enough that the early morning staff came rushing to his office door.

"You, okay?" his assistant, Karin, asked, setting a stack of files atop his desk.

"Fine, fine. Everything is fine," he assured his workers, sending them back to their cubicles. For the first time in all his years as supervisor, he was baffled. Should he defend or demonize his agent's position when the higher-ups begin to call? After all, wasn't Agent Martin doing what any self-righteous ATF agent on probation would do? Solving the biggest missing person case in D.C.!

"Christ, I'll be under the gun myself on this one!" Chuck muttered as he kicked the litter bin, watching it spill its wasted donut crumbs and coffee dregs across the floor.

Paul had called Élise at 11:40 p.m. to forewarn her that the Summer's story would likely be airing on every network come morning. Huddled in her oversized bed, she punched remote control buttons with the dexterity of a teen hooked on Xbox. The screen flickered from FOX, to CNN, to local affiliates lighting up the otherwise darkened room. While the rest of the house slumbered, she nervously dress rehearsed how best to coach her fourteen-year-old house guest, Devon Ost, through what was sure to be a dreadfully fragile day. Ready or not, this is the day the crap hits the fan, her disheveled mirrored image preached to her from above the mantle. No turning back now, the image frowned mockingly.

The tanned young boy with sun-bleached hair had settled effortlessly into the O'Neil household as if his arrival had long been arranged. Oliver and Will had never heard of their teenage *cousin* until Uncle Paul dropped him in the driveway weeks ago, lugging two overstuffed duffle bags behind him. To them, having Devon around was like unearthing a buried treasure, as he never ran out of innovative ideas. When Élise agreed to drive him and the boys to the lake to set up a telescope in the dark of night to survey the skies, they were ecstatic. From the library, he would check out books on astrology, zoology, and anthropology. This was the kid you pictured winning the national spelling bee, but without the horn-rimmed glasses.

The four-day drive from Arizona to Massachusetts allowed Paul time to minister to the confused young man. In the course of a day, Devon had discovered *Aunt Liz* was actually his birth mother and that his real father was some surfer dude from San Diego named Crowe. In an instant, you are no longer the son of a prominent physician. Your mother isn't your mother? So, who are you then?

He had nodded to his sobbing parents that he understood the secrecy surrounding their sending him to New England for his own safety. The why, when, and how of this madness would have to play itself out like the Harry Potter mysteries packed in his satchel. Gambling on uncertainties was a lot to ask of a boy of fourteen whose immediate concern for the journey ahead would be calculating average miles per hour to meet an ETA. That's how his young mind worked as it attempted to console itself.

"You like burgers?" asked Paul, thinking fries and a chocolate shake might offer a quick fix for his young travel companion. At least that's what the bachelor was banking on as he pulled up to the take-out window. He might not be able to keep up with the mental prowess of his young passenger but a juicy hamburger could be counted on to bridge the generation gap.

"Your mom is a really big deal in D.C.," Paul explained. "So, when this story unravels, her picture, your picture... they're going to be splashed on every newspaper and television screen in town. It's going to be a lot to take in, but your mom, me and Mrs. O'Neil, we've got your back. You gonna be okay with all this?"

"Yes, sir," he promised, slurping the remains of his shake, and wolfing down his second double cheeseburger.

As predicted, the news media didn't disappoint. Their dusk till dawn frenzy didn't let up for weeks on end. In D.C., the city of elites, fans demanded answers from their notorious news anchor who resurfaced looking, freakishly, like a pop rock star on speed. Horrified by news clips of the shorn red-headed, halter-topped vixen claiming to be Liz Summer, her conservative-based audience was appalled. News commentator Cameron Frost signed off with a politically incorrect Cuban impersonation of Ricky Ricardo.

"Liz, you got a lot of 'splaining' to do," he quipped as the cameras faded away.

Paul also had a lot of questions for the megastar journalist, who many had written off as abducted, if not worse. Surprisingly, it hadn't taken much effort for him to locate her. But, convincing her to meet him for a cup of coffee in downtown Scottsdale took nearly a week. He would never have recognized her if she hadn't motioned to him from the window seat booth. Needless to say, she was stunned to learn he was in town, and wanting to meet with her. "How do I know I should trust you?" she demanded guardedly.

"I'd say you could stand to have a friend about now. I'm here to help," he pledged convincingly, carefully reading her every expression.

A question had baffled him since the day she hailed him and his partner at the QEDCO warehouse site. Maybe he was paranoid but, clearly, Ms. Summer had her sights set on meeting up later with Dru. Was he right?

"Well, yeah," she explained. "Mr. O'Neil's wife, Élise, once mentioned at a charity event that her husband was with the FBI? CIA? Secret Service? One of those…" she continued on as though they were one and the same.

"A-T-F," Paul clarified. "The Bureau of Alcohol, Tobacco, Firearms and Explosives," he frowned aloud. *Hell, no one ever got it right.*

"When rumors began to surface that my college boyfriend was convinced he had a son, and was determined to find the boy, I thought immediately of Agent O'Neil. Maybe he would have some advice, purely off the record," she made clear. "I was, in a roundabout way, a friend. I didn't want to file reports, or take legal steps. My initial concerns were based on sheer rumor so I definitely didn't want to create any kind of public scene."

"Well, that didn't work now, did it?" he snickered sarcastically.

"So, when a tall black man showed up at the Old Crosley Grille that night instead of Dru O'Neil…"

"That was a disappointment, to say the least," she said, finishing his sentence unapologetically.

"Ouch!" cringed Agent Martin.

"Yeah, well, keep in mind that reaching out to Agent O'Neil that day in the parking lot had nothing to do with the QEDCO case," she added. "It was deceptive. I hoped he would understand." The famous face had aged ten years in just a few weeks. Darkened circles underlining her eyes, and hollowed cheeks, exposed the fright that had taken its toll.

Dr. Ost was providing twenty-four-hour security at his Paradise Valley home for his adopted son, but it couldn't go on indefinitely. Liz was scared out of her mind at the danger associated with the thought of trying to remove the boy on her own. Stan Crowe was in town; she knew that much. She had unnamed sources.

"We have to get your boy out of town," Paul had said, leaving no room for argument. "And, you're going to have to trust someone. I suggest that someone be me." He laid out his current situation with the heads of the ATF Bureau. She had no idea he had been placed on suspension due to their meeting the evening of her disappearance.

Unraveling the tarnished, napkin-bundled silverware set before him, Paul clasped a fork upright in one fist, and a steak knife in the other, as though laying bare his credentials.

"I've got two things you need. Time on my hands, and knowledge of how the criminal mind thinks."

Liz's hands shook as she lifted the coffee mug to her quivering lips. "What do you propose?"

"Élise O'Neil could be the answer," he said, speed dialing the Lexford number even though it was dinner hour on the East coast.

27

STAN CROWE

An armed Stan Crowe waited patiently at the base of the foothills in Paradise Valley, Arizona, in a battered pickup truck with Oregon license plates. His son had certainly done well for himself from the looks of the colossal panoramic adobe home clinging ominously to the side of the mountain, overlooking the magnificent valley of the sun. After weeks of scouring directories, and questioning neighbors under the guise of a handyman who had lost his way, he zeroed in on the unmarked palatial residence owned by Dr. Ost. From behind the brush, just beyond the lengthy drive leading up the steep incline to the home, he parked and observed the daily comings and goings of the Ost family.

A Mercedes heaved its cloud of dust and gravel skyward as it descended the serpentine drive facing into the blaring mid-noon sun. Through the tinted glass, six silhouettes emerged; a woman driver accompanied by five passengers. Squinting behind darkened sunglasses, the sweltering onlooker could make out the twisting forms of what appeared to be two adolescent girls seated in the front, and three teenage boys in the rear. Crowe crouched lower, his head level with the crack in the windshield. His heart pounded beneath a tank top clammy with sweat. Any one of the three boys in the back seat could be his son. The story that Liz Summer fabricated fourteen years ago about aborting his child never registered as truth. Call it a sixth sense, call it what you will, he always knew there was a child; a son.

The grey-green SUV poked its nose from the drive, and slithered onto the roadway, turning east toward town. Crowe edged his white pickup out from behind the brush, allowing a second car to fall in line. A black Volvo sedan with Minnesota plates separated him from his own flesh and blood. The labored breathing he heard was his own as the rattling truck slowly twisted its way along the silent, rubberized pavement. Saguaros, ocotillos, and an endless span of desert bordered the winding roadway. He sat up tall, craning his neck like an ostrich so as not to lose sight of the Ost van. Turning left, then right, and over a crest, the caravan descended into a town center which clustered at the foot of the gully. Traffic lights, overpasses, billboards, department stores, restaurants, office buildings, parking garages, and shuttle buses burst onto the scene as if Babylon had dropped from the sky. Crowe tagged behind, pulling into the parking lot of an expansive movie theater.

From a short distance, he watched as the automatic car doors slid open, and tanned limbs of varying lengths and bulk unfurled from every direction, like a centipede stretching its multitude of legs.

Shit! The neighbors said there were five kids. How do I know which one is mine?

At the sight of the boys' hairless bronzed chests, curly blond hair, knee length Hawaiian flowered shorts, and neon flip-flops, Crowe sickened with disgust. Goddamn bunch of fairies. These were exactly the type of prissy young men he and his construction buddies loathed. *My son is a friggin' pansy!* All three hovered around the hood of the vehicle as though connected by umbilical cords. The rage of fourteen years loomed in the gruff man's gut like a bull taunted by matadors in red tights. Tightening his hold around the loose door handle, he bit into his lower lip and counted to ten... twenty... thirty... as his teeth sank into flesh.

It was hard to know if the two Ost girls standing in the group were twelve or eighteen by the sensuous way they tossed their blond-streaked hair about in the sun. For that matter, the doctor's old lady was eye candy herself in short shorts, a halter top, and high heeled shoes. Standing in the midst of her children, she whispered something to each child while delving out crisp dollar bills. Life as the child of a prominent surgeon was a whole hell of a lot different than growing up in the backwoods of Gold Beach, Oregon.

Thirty-five-year-old Stan Crowe lived in a rented cabin overlooking the Pacific Ocean on the outskirts of Gold Beach, Oregon. In his wooded retreat, the air was clear; the people earthy, and life real. Nights were silent except for the owls, and the baying sounds of the forest animals conversing. Days were uninhibited. Not like this airless desert rat hole, polluted by noise, congestion, and stifling hordes of people living plastic lives. The North Pacific coast was a place where young boys matured into sturdy men, unlike the eunuchs of this glorified wasteland. All the more reason to bring my boy home.

Staring down the facial features of each of the three boys only confused Crowe more. No identifying upturned Crowe nose that he could tell. He watched as the group waved cell phones, synchronized watches, and flocked away, merging into the crowd of what seemed an army of clones. For now, he must focus on the rattling truck, idling like a panting buffalo, its overheated engine chugging defiantly as it eased from the parking lot in pursuit of the moving van. The boy would be his soon enough.

Without signaling, the Ost's Mercedes pulled back into traffic and, several traffic lights later, turned into a strip mall, stopping in front of Saguaro Foods, an upscale grocery market. Slinking out of the front seat the way a steamed oyster slides from its shell, Beth Ost glided across the parking lot, her body engaged in a cell phone conversation. She looked behind her before hurrying into the store, her lilting laughter trailing behind.

He'd waited long enough to get Beth Ost alone. It was time to end his stay in this hotbed of hell they called Paradise Valley. Within ten minutes the unsuspecting mother exited the market carrying a parcel in each arm. Crowe listened for the front door of the SUV to automatically unlock before rounding the front bumper. As the two bodies nearly collided, a silent shriek filled the air as both bundles flailed to the ground. Splattering eggs and liquid yogurt curdled in puddles coating the feet of the startled woman like a soured milkshake. Stan Crowe met his foe face to face.

"Forgive me," he said dropping to one knee apologetically. "I'm so sorry. Let me help you with that."

The frazzled woman froze, dripping with frustration at her own clumsiness. She hesitated before stooping low to grab hold of the torn bags. As she leaned forward, Crowe kicked the sacks and placed his hand over her mouth, thrusting his handgun into her side.

"Nice and easy, Beth," he whispered in her ear. "I don't want to hurt you." The woman's eyes filled with terror at the sound of her name.

Grabbing her purse, the unkempt man muscled his prey to the floor of the truck. Taping her mouth and strapping her feet and hands together, he wedged her into the corner while he climbed over her to the driver's side. The frightened woman's whimpers reminded him of a wounded bear cub he had trapped on his last hunting trip.

"I'm sorry I have to do this to you," he said. "But, you see, you have something of mine."

28

BIKERS

Within twenty minutes, Crowe's truck pulled off the road onto a rocky trail, and came to a stop. He dragged the woman and her purse through a desert area, and set her down at the opening of a cave-like formation. Boulders, piled one on top of another, reached sky high as far as the eye could see, resembling a fiendish moonscape. Not a twig in sight; just rock, and dirt, and evil. Digging the cell phone from her leather satchel, he held the gun to her forehead. He explained he was about to remove the tape from her mouth.

"No screaming," he instructed, as though a living soul were within miles.

He explained he was the biological father of the boy she had raised as her own.

"I just want my son back. You can understand that, can't you?" he asked, searching out signs of mercy within the mother's screaming eyes. Trying not to notice her heaving synthetic breasts, he scanned the cell phone index.

"Now, it's time we call your loving husband," he informed her, while fumbling through the speed dial options.

No answer.

"Where could the good doctor be?" he asked mockingly, his wit wasted by barefaced insolence. "Let's try a page," he said, pushing *4* followed by the # sign. "This qualifies as an emergency, wouldn't you say?"

Dr. Ost stepped out of the operating room at the Mayo Clinic at his usual quickened pace, and scanned his list of calls. His wife paging him? That was unusual.

At the first strains of the bell tone, Stan Crowe flipped open the phone, and spoke directly into the speaker. "Good day, Doctor Ost. Listen, and listen carefully," he began his well-practiced monologue. Beth Ost wept into the speaker. Yes, her husband should follow the caller's directions or she would be harmed. The physician was to drive the boy to a lookout just outside of town.

"I want the boy drugged." Crowe dug his heel into the rock, shaking loose rocks and thistle from his deeply grooved soles. "Also, a set of syringes and enough drugs to keep the boy *calm* for a week or more." No one would be hurt as long as everyone did their part. Once he and the boy had a running start out of town, Dr. Ost would be led to his wife.

"No cops. No fuck ups," he admonished.

"Understood," the doctor replied, staggering with disbelief as he weaved through the maze of hallways toward his corner office.

Neither the surgeon nor his wife disclosed the fact that Devon had been placed into the safe hands of Paul Martin more than two weeks prior. He was wisely removed from the Paradise Valley home for his own protection. When their son hugged them goodbye, and followed the stranger out the door into the dark of night, Beth thought that had to be the worst day of her life. With Crowe's hand gun positioned at her forehead, and with his malicious bad breath in her face, she sobbed, pleading for mercy.

Liz Summer had convinced Beth and her husband that Devon's life was in danger. They were told the boy's biological father was frantically searching for his son, and would likely find him. Only days before Devon's departure, Beth got wind that a curious looking man had been questioning neighbors about the Ost family. The family knew what they had to do. After Devon was whisked away, they would have to carry on as though nothing had changed to avert any suspicions.

Crowe lowered his gun, and replaced the duct tape around his captive's mouth before driving away, leaving the frightened woman lodged in the hollow of an encrusted rock formation near the broad span of mountainside.

The one-hundred-and-fourteen-degree heat was still brutal by 6:00 p.m. as Stan Crowe stepped out of his truck at the secluded lookout north of town where he was to meet Dr. Ost and the boy. Slugging down a pint of bottled water the way a sports fan would a chilled beer, he scanned the skyline, wondering how all these sons-a-bitches could afford these cliff-hanging mansions. They can't all be surgeons, he reasoned. Infrequently, a breeze blew up as a car whizzed by. No one seemed to notice him peering through binoculars at the vast landscape below. The beauty of the desert was wasted on him as his mind walked through the scene about to take place. His stand-still world was disrupted when, suddenly, two bikers noisily roared into the isolated graveled spot and parked to the far side of the scruffy white truck.

"Shit!" Crowe blurted.

"Hey, partner," said the one, wiping sweat from his brow with a crumpled bandana after making a pit stop behind a decaying saguaro. The other cowboy biker scraped clogs of dirt from the bottom of his high-heeled boots while puttering around the front wheel of his Harley-Davidson, checking air pressure.

"You from these parts?" asked the overly-friendly biker, drumming up small talk. He pulled an orange from a side bag, and began to peel it with his teeth.

"No," Crowe answered, walking away, shaking his shoulders with annoyance. He felt his teeth grind involuntarily the way they sometimes did when he woke from a violent dream.

"Or-a-gone, huh?" shouted the biker, reading off the tarnished license plate, and reaching out to offer up a slice of orange. It was irritating as hell when people mispronounced the name of his home state.

"Asshole!" Crowe thought.

"Real pur-r-ty state. Lots cooler there," exclaimed the biker, as the juice drooled down his chin, and lodged in his scruffy beard. "What the hell you doin' in the desert in these blistering temperatures when you could be in cool, breezy Or-a-gone?" he asked, plunging another massive chunk of fruit into his mouth. "Doesn't make sense," he added, having come to his own conclusion.

Crowe didn't answer, hoping rudeness would read as disinterest.

"Real pretty this time of day, idn't it?" said the biker, following after Crowe and pointing to the desert sun. "Sure you don't want any?" asked the bothersome intruder, holding out a dripping piece of orange as though it were a sirloin off the grill.

"No thanks," Crowe answered, wiping sweat from the back of his neck.

The more subdued biker adjusted a digital camera, and began snapping photos. Crowe was sure he was in at least one head shot. Bastard! Last thing he needed was to be photographed. Both men wore holstered guns but that wasn't unusual in Arizona where even grandma packed a pistol.

"Mind taking a picture of me and my buddy?" the photographer biker asked, approaching Crowe while pointing to the flash button. Both men threw their arms around each other, and smiled cheek to cheek like they were a lot closer than brothers.

"That's real nice," the biker said to his friend approvingly as they viewed the image in the lens, and giggled like teenage girls. "What do they say? That's a keeper, right?"

Up the roadway, a black BMW purred round the bend, and slowly pulled into the gravel area. Its darkened windows blurred the shape of a single figure behind the wheel of the compact car as it backed into a side lane, its backside to the sun. As the bikers and Crowe stared, Dr. Ost climbed out of the front seat, and walked cautiously toward the strange lot of gaping men.

"Where's my son?" Crowe asked straightforward, while walking directly toward the distinguished silver-haired physician. The two bikers turned their backs, and politely strolled away as if embarrassed by being caught in a domestic quarrel.

"Where's my wife?" demanded Ben Ost, in retaliation.

"The conditions weren't clear enough for you?" Crowe growled, grabbing the doctor's arm, and leading him to the far side of the truck. "No boy. No wife!" he mouthed, displaying his gun as the two onlookers rounded the corner.

Before Crowe knew what hit him, the two bikers rushed him from behind, thrusting his face into the steamy, hot Arizona dirt. "Told you ya' shouda' stayed in Or-a-gone!" slurped the undercover ATF Agent, still reeking of orange peels, while his partner slapped handcuffs on the would-be abductor, and pulled him to his feet.

Four police cars sirened into the parking lot, and flocked around the disoriented Crowe, who was no newcomer to the Miranda Rights. He scowled as the officers began, "You have the right to remain silent…"

"Thank God, your wife is safe," the agents said as they approached the terribly shaken Dr. Ost. "Your contact, Agent Paul Martin, alerted us. We were able to trace the cellular telephone tower that led us to the deserted area beyond The

Granite View Resort. Crowe technically hung himself with the push of a button!"

Apparently, Paul Martin had been working overtime on the Summer's case from behind the scenes until the time was right to close in on Crowe. Unrelenting, he was determined to see the dirt-bag put away. Doctor Ost could not have been more thankful.

Ost watched as the ruffian was led away, looking like a snorting piglet with his sun-burnt face dripping beads of sweat and grime. "Say goodbye to Oregon's pride and joy," said the biker agent as he turned the grisly offender over to the officer, who escorted the prisoner to the squad car.

"What about my truck?" asked Crowe.

"You won't be needing it where you're going," spouted one of the officers.

"Maybe it can be part of your son's inheritance," the undercover agent shouted, kicking its patched rear tire, setting the truck to wobbling side-to-side, reminiscent of a fleshy old man enjoying a hearty belly-laugh.

29

LEO'S PLACE

> THE AGENT'S WIFE: A NATIONAL HERO
> A Lexford resident, the new owner of the Sullivan property on Longwood Lane, is being lauded as a hero in the nationally publicized case of the D.C. missing news anchor, Liz Summer. The newly divorced wife of a United States ATF Agent, Élise O'Neil, played a key role in solving the mystery involving the planned abduction of a young boy that spanned the nation from the District of Columbia to Phoenix, Arizona.

Élise gasped in disbelief at a paparazzi-like photo of herself splashed across the cover page of the morning edition of the *Lexford Minuteman*. The picture was snapped surreptitiously with Jean-Jacques strapped to her back as she hustled from the dry cleaners early yesterday morning. "Good Lord ...!" she yelped, ogling the sight of her own backside glaring back at her. Unbelievingly, the media had hyped her minor-league role in the arrest of the now infamous Stan Crowe into a play-by-play World Series with her as MVP. Amazing how they do that!

In downtown Lexford, at Leo's Place, the trendy local coffee house on the corner of Union and Main, Marge Maitland swiped her sweaty brow as she bustled booth to booth, managing to spill as much coffee on the floor as in the cups. Jam packed with regulars, the shop buzzed like a nest of underfed hummingbirds, each familiar face probing a contradictory view of the morning headline.

"Can you imagine?" slurped Mrs. Petricone to her friend Hazel Bloom, pointing to the front-page photo of the young woman clad in body-hugging yoga pants with a baby perched on her back. "Why, to think she has been secretly harboring that teenage boy under our very noses!" Slathering a hefty slab of butter across the face of a crusty English muffin, she side-eyed her peers seated at the neighboring table in a feeble attempt to harvest condemnation. No one at the nearby table paid her any mind. "Mark my words, she is nothing but trouble," she decided, topping her poached eggs with a swirl of freshly ground black pepper. Hazel quietly nodded her agreement while buttering her toast.

Marge whisked on by, avoiding eye contact while balancing a tray of eggs-over-easy with multiple sides of fries. Experience taught her long ago to cold shoulder gossipmongers, and keep the omelets and freshly baked scones moving.

The feast of morning kibitzers continued their fixation on the newest resident of their picturesque community with a rash of unwarranted disapproval though, admittedly, most had yet to meet Élise O'Neil. One would think the commune of Lexford was an exclusive private club whose house membership had been flagrantly compromised. *Did she really think she could settle in amongst them without giving notice?*

Élise overlooked the frosty, if not sanctimonious, behavior of the longstanding town folks who chose to snub her as a newcomer. It wasn't personal. They had no idea that she herself was born and raised a stone's throw from the campus of Harvard University, and fully understood their standoffish ways. Prudence and discretion made perfectly good sense. In fact, it was their blatant disregard that had granted her the necessary privacy to house teenaged Devon Ost, unharmed and undetected. For that, she was grateful.

Retired church choir director, Ned Joslin, ceremoniously paused to wipe his mustache free of residual biscuits and gravy before rendering his outtake. "They say a divorced woman with three children bought the old house on the hill," he announced, as though unraveling something unknown. Eyeballing his table full of gassy, silver-haired men, his enunciation of the word *d-ee-vorced* hovered as if it reeked of compost. The group grunted a seasoned acknowledgment, jointly, pronouncing divorce a misdemeanor at very least.

"I have to ask, what would a single woman want with an oversized ten-room house?" muttered a balding, meticulously groomed man seated at the counter next to a bosomy, blonde woman he failed to recognize. The roomful of regulars all turned collectively as if awaiting an answer. She shrugged her shoulders as if obliged to respond.

Marge noisily emptied a filter full of soggy coffee grains against the stainless-steel sink, banging metal against metal far longer than necessary. She, herself, a divorced single mother, took offence to the tone of this morning's *holier than thou* breakfast crowd. She had yet to meet Élise O'Neil, but was beginning to think she might like her.

"You couldn't pay me to live in that huge, spooky house!" piped a larger-than-life sized woman, shifting her bulk to one side of the left leaning bar stool. A festoon of curly, red hair spiraled from a tightly braided bun at the nape of her neck. "Does anyone really know what's going on up on the hill?" she asked no one in particular. Aimlessly dropping four sugar cubes into her coffee, she offered a high-pitched assessment that her two-bedroom bungalow adjacent to the lake was far more preferable.

No one bothered to agree or disagree.

From the far corner of the room, seated in the back booth, Elizabeth Frost, the town librarian, looked up, and spoke out in a calming, assertive tone. "Actually, the former Mrs. O'Neil was married to a federal agent." All eyes turned to the back booth with prying looks of an inquisition. "She, in fact, gave up an illustrious Wall Street career to move to D.C. to become an agent's wife. I see her often. She comes into the library with the little ones at least once a week."

"Really! A federal agent's wife?" shouted Jessica Marley, as if she had mistakenly heard 'rock star's wife.'

"Moreover," explained Elizabeth, clearly relishing the attention, "the handsome man, whose face is all over the news, the one accompanying the formerly missing news anchor Liz Summer, he, too, is an agent. He's a friend of Élise O'Neil, and has been to the library several times with her and the boys. Seemingly, all very nice people," she concluded, readjusting her Italian framed progressives that had slipped down her nose. With that, she toasted the roomful of diners with a flute of freshly squeezed orange juice, and returned her attention to the morning obituaries.

Silence.

"Bacon on rye!" yelled café owner Leo Albany from the kitchen. Amid the rattle of pots and pans, he slithered a sandwich plate across the open countertop to Marge. Out the broad, front store window he caught sight of a caravan of television vans circling the rotary like a fully grown caterpillar on the prowl. With a loud, two-fingered wolf whistle, he pointed toward the window. "Looks like we're on the map folks!" he announced in a coarse, deep-throated voice that begged attention.

All heads spun in unison to witness the trail of vehicles creeping at a snail's pace up the hill, toward the Sullivan house on Longwood Lane. Leo edged his way to the front door, opening it wide, wiping his reddened, dish panned hands against the grease splattered bib of his oversized apron. Standing tall, hands-on hips, like a sea captain surveying far off coastal land, he watched till the last van disappeared round the bend.

Overnight, the town of less than eight square miles was overrun with inquisitive, abrasive, out of town reporters, all in search of the Sullivan property.

Head down and without another word, Leo hoofed it back to the kitchen focused on one thing. Surely, all this hoopla was sure to be good for business!

30

DEVON

Young Devon Ost and Liz Summer sat, heads locked, deeply engrossed in the *Boston Globe*'s front-page story, silently mouthing each word of a tale that signaled mutual gloom.

An armed Stan Crowe was arrested for a bungled abduction plot of his biological son at a roadside pullout near an exclusive Paradise Valley resort. Beth Ost, the adoptive mother of the boy, and wife of the well-respected Dr. Benjamin Ost, was gagged and battered before being abandoned in an undisclosed desert location. The orthopedic surgeon responded to Crowe's threatening call as he stepped from the Mayo Clinic operating room by calling D.C. Agent Paul Martin, who then notified authorities who responded immediately.

The boy had fidgeted through a long and emotional telephone call the previous evening with his mom, Beth Ost. With heart lodged in her throat, she assured him, "I'm okay." Still recovering from an unspeakably, frightening abduction by Stan Crowe, it was all she could do to accept the fact that her son was three thousand miles away.

Devon was her child as much as any she had birthed. How she had celebrated the arrival of that child! The afternoon Liz went into labor, anyone would have thought Beth were the one about to give birth as tears of joy streamed down her face. In stark contrast, the adolescent mother-to-be bleakly had hauled her heavy hearted, bloated body out the side door of the family SUV. Liz could not have felt more terrified or defeated if she were heading to the scaffolds for her own beheading. Each timed and pain ridden contraction would only bring her closer to the most dreaded moment of her life; the moment this child would no longer be her own.

The young college girl had little say in the matter. Her family had arranged everything. Lucy Summer, her mother, emphasized how *grateful* she should feel to the Osts for adopting the child. "Soon, it will all be over," her mother spoke softly into the phone. "You'll begin anew." Despite how thankful everyone told her she should be, she felt robbed. Her baby was too beautiful to just forget he existed. Never could she forget he was her child, her son.

Now it was Beth Ost stifling unimagined sorrow, and biting hard on her lower lip to quell the quivering. With the cell phone pasted to her ear, she listened to Devon explain his plan to stay back east. "It's amazing here, Mom!" he gushed.

"Mrs. O'Neil took me to a science exposition at Harvard University last week. Ever think I'd be hanging out at Harvard?"

"Harvard, wow!" she replied through a forced telephone smile. "You know, sweetheart, your dad and I are one hundred percent behind you with whatever you decide," uttered Beth while her maternal impulses screamed, "*NO!!!*"

Liz turned to her son, running her hands through the soft golden curls that toppled about his head, and spilled to his shoulders. "It will get better, I promise," her morning smile coated in gut-felt guilt. *Sometimes you have no choice but to own the misery you've caused. It wasn't for herself she was worried. It was her boy she cared about now.* Before draining her second cup of coffee, she had already labeled herself incompetent, pathetic, and bordering on appalling. No one else need condemn her. The jury was in.

Rightly or wrongly, Devon had never been told the true circumstances of his birth. The Osts had glossed over details, careful to guard his history until the time proved right. Why complicate life for a perfectly well-adjusted, happy kid? He got along with his siblings, and had tons of friends. No one ever questioned he was anything but another Ost kid. Beth found herself chuckling the many times strangers pointed out her son looked just like her. Same nose, same cheekbones. Even now, glancing at the family photo propped on the mantelpiece, she could see it. "One day, we'll tell him everything," she would say to her husband. "Not just yet."

You're woken in the middle of the night and told to pack a bag while an armed federal agent waits in the living room to escort you from your home, and drive you cross country. *It's friggin' insane!* Worse yet, you're told your mother isn't your mother. Your distant 'aunt' is your real mother. *Some kind of crazy stuff, man*! Five days later, you find yourself settled into a three-story New England country manor house with perfect strangers and your own room at the top of the stairs.

Seems Mrs. O'Neil, owner of the home, and friend of Agent Paul Martin, knows Aunt Liz somehow. Paul explained how Mrs. O'Neil recently relocated from D.C. to the historic old house with her three little kids. "She's moving on," was what Paul said. "It's complicated," he had added, and left it at that.

I'm a kid, so, you know, whatever!

Everything was going swimmingly until Aunt Liz arrived. Her endless attention made him feel like a swarm of hornets had come to nest, torching his every nerve. Why did she always have to hug him *every time* he walked into a room? Instinctively, he would pull away, wanting to swat her hand as she approached. And, what's with the fingers running through my hair? It's all too weird! She wasn't his mother. Beth Ost was. *Please, please, make her back off*, he heard his mind shriek. Maybe he should just go home. He knew he still could. He would call his mom back; say he'd changed his mind.

And, this crazy news story being blasted all over the media about how the well-known news anchor, Liz Summer, had gotten herself *in trouble* years ago, and screwed up her otherwise perfect life. *And clearly, you come to realize you are that now famous screw up they are alluding to!* That's the news story staring back at him this morning.

Wait, it gets worse.

The refined, well-respected surgeon, Doctor Ost *...as the news article so lovingly pointed out...*is not your dad. Your dad is some crazy dude rattling around in a mangled pickup truck. *Total humiliation for the whole world to see!* This was the moment Devon sprung upright, fighting back angry tears, and slamming the tabletop with closed fists. Liz grabbed the corner of the wooden table, coffee splattering onto the white linen tablecloth, and silverware clattering noisily to the floor. The teenager bolted up the stairwell to his room with the fierceness of a young buck spotted in a hunter's lens, the door slamming behind him with a thunderous thud.

Paul had been sauntering about the kitchen, listening, watching, and examining the interaction of the reunited mother and son. He dropped yet another slice of kiwi into the gaping mouth of the juicer as the drama played itself out. Silently, he raked his hand across his face as he watched Devon sprint from the room, and escape up the stairs.

Pulling up a chair in slow motion, he took the hands of a visibly shaken Liz.

"He's just a boy," he sputtered, searching out the right words. "Look, I'm not the one to be giving parental advice," he hesitated awkwardly, "but, I'd say he needs time…and so do you." He watched as Liz bowed her head, and closed her eyes. "Let him be for a while."

'He hates me," she groaned, brushing an unflattering clump of shorn, carrot red hair off her forehead. "Can you blame him? Look at me!"

"Nah! He doesn't hate you but you have to admit this is some heavy-duty crapshoot for a kid to handle, you know? It's going to take time to sort itself out."

Devon sprawled face down on the oversized canopy bed, wishing he was anywhere but here. His mind awhirl, like an oversized fidget-spinner he once owned. "What a royal dick, I am!" He had never acted out like that, not ever!

It was hard to fathom Aunt Liz as an east coast television phenomenon, though every newspaper and TV anchor were praising her safe return as if it were the second coming. Paul had tried to forewarn him about the hype and the media coverage sure to follow. All Devon saw was a desperate woman wanting to be liked, most especially by him. This whole *mom* thing was not happening for him. He didn't see how it ever could.

That's how it seemed as he tunneled his head deep within the feather pillow. New England was amazing. He wanted to stay though he had no idea how, or if, it could work out. He had probably blown it downstairs with his crazed, childish tantrum down in the kitchen. He could picture Liz, Paul, and Élise right now, huddled around the kitchen table, brainstorming the cheapest, quickest way to send him home. Embarrassed by his outburst, he could hardly face himself when Paul came knocking on the bedroom door.

"Sorry," the boy offered dourly, like one who had been caught red-handed lighting fire to the family barn.

"It's okay. No need to apologize," Paul said placidly, heading to a replica of a B17-G model airplane halfway built sitting on the desktop. "Didn't know you were into airplanes," he acknowledged. "A bomber, huh? My friend's dad flew one of these in WWII," he said, closing in on the detailed cockpit. "Courageous men, those pilots. Sitting ducks soaring over hostile skies. Hard to imagine!"

"The motor is over there, still in the box," Devon pointed out. "Flying them is the best part."

"Way cool," said Paul, trying to be *way cool*. "I'd love to see it take flight when it's ready. Deal?"

"Deal," replied the boy while his attention moved to a grinding sound outside the curtained window. "What the heck?" he gasped. "Who are all those people at the end of our driveway?"

Paul glanced out. "Holy Christ!" he heard himself shout out just as he spied Élise take to the stairwell by leaps and bounds. The boys followed, shrieking, stomping, and pretending to be elephants. Baby Jean-Jacques joined the fracas as he dangled like a dead weight off his mother's hip. Approaching the grand bay window, Élise couldn't believe her eyes!

"Oh my God!" she hollered, causing everyone to rush to the front room for a better view. Outside, at the bottom of the drive, hordes of television reporters jostled sophisticated camera equipment in circus style while focusing high powered lenses directly at the majestic old home atop the hill.

"Awesome!" shouted Devon as he landed feet first with a thud, vaulting from the stairwell, greeting Oliver and Will with animated high-fives. "There's an army of paparazzi out there!" he announced, as if a UFO had descended on the front lawn. The teenager had rebounded from the heaviness of the morning's outburst, hooting and hollering at the commotion down below.

And that's a good thing thought his mother as she winked knowingly at Paul.

"He thinks we're famous," Paul whispered in her ear. "Let him enjoy the madness. He'll grow up soon enough." He smiled as they all peered through the glazed-gilded glass at the gathering crowd.

"What do they think they're going to see?" Élise had to ask.

"Haven't a clue," Paul said, pulling shut the shutters surrounding the expansive solarium. "What I do know is, me and my boys, we have a Patriots game about to start any minute. Right guys?" He was a master of diversion.

"Yes, sir," answered Devon, seemingly relieved to get on with being a kid.

Oliver and Will dived under the grand piano in the middle of the grand room, giddy to be included in the invite. "Yea!" they shouted, as they followed Paul toward the big screen TV in the game room.

"Kick off time!" Paul announced, as though proclaiming it a national holiday. "See, no matter how life treats you, there's always football," he chirped. *Always the philosopher*. "How about it, ladies. You in on this?"

"Why not," Liz chimed in, wadding the stack of morning newspapers into tightfisted balls, and tossing them into the fireplace for kindling. "What a bunch of clowns!" she declared, glancing out the front window at her cohorts, seeing the media for the first time from an outsider's perspective.

Devon struck a match and lit the papers, sneaking a sheepish look at Liz, as if hoping to clear the air between them as he set the provocative morning article ablaze. Liz watched approvingly, realizing she had volumes to learn about raising a child. Whatever it took, she was game.

31

THE AGENT'S WIFE

"The Agent's Wife is what the locals call me," Élise scowled across the room as her father leaned over the kitchen skillet, frying bacon. "I moved five hundred miles from Georgetown hoping to leave my past behind." She growled in an undertone that would have been deafening had it not been stifled by rage. "But here it sits, parked on my door stoop, like a difficult house guest who hasn't yet determined how long they plan to stay."

With an overly ambitious stroke she drew her fingers through her long, tangled hair. "I can't leave the house without people pointing at me with their frosty probing stares, whether at the supermarket, the bookstore, or even at the local park. For God's sake, what's wrong with these people?"

Knowing full well not to interrupt his daughter's one-sided conversations, Henri Saint-Cyr gingerly continued to slice, arrange, and garnish a plateful of fresh garden tomatoes he bought at the market earlier in the day. Inevitably, he knew she would arrive at her own conclusions without his interference. "Mayonnaise?" he inquired, layering the final piece of toasted herbal bread atop the BLT.

"When friends need help, you help, right?" she stammered without a pause. "It's what you always taught me. So, when Paul Martin called to say Liz Summer needed a safe place to send her son, how could I say no? But now, here I am, slam-dunk caught in the midst of this crazy fiasco. I'd do it all again," she added. "It was the right thing to do."

"Eat. You'll feel better," her father gestured toward the luncheon plate he placed before her on the sturdy wooden table.

"Here, listen to this," she said, alluding to the incriminating news article clutched in her hand. She began to read aloud as one who returns unwillingly to the site of a gruesome roadside wreck for a final glimpse.

"It's been said the former Wall Street investment advisor, divorced mother of three, abandoned her agent husband, vying for a more idyllic life to raise her young sons."

"Abandoned my husband…!"

Henri bit into his three-tiered sandwich without a word, swallowing a generous sip of sweetened jasmine tea. It wasn't the first time he had turned himself into a human sounding board. He had called his daughter last night to say he was free to drive down from Hyannis for the day. Élise was thrilled since a visit with Henri was always welcome, and long overdue.

The boys were at school and baby Jean-Jacques was down for his late morning nap and, quite honestly, with Devon gone, the house felt bigger, emptier, and admittedly, lonelier. As soon as Liz Summer had reclaimed her illustrious news anchor position, she wasted no time in sending for her son. Using her powerful connections, she was able to enroll Devon at the elite St. Anselm's all boys prep school. That was enough to lure him into packing his belongings, and following her to Washington, D.C.

Élise's attention returned to her father, who was painstakingly unwrapping the homemade apple pie he had baked the night before. "So, your mother and I were wondering about the holidays," said Henri as he sliced the pie into larger-than-life portions. "Any thoughts as to how that will play out this year?"

With Christmas less than seven weeks away, she had not only given it a lot of thought but had taken matters into her own hands. "At first pass, this might sound a preposterous idea," she began warily. "You see, I've extended an invite to Dru and his sister Katy to join us here at the house for the Christmas holiday. It's been months since the boys have seen their dad. I think it's only fair…"

"What did Dru think about that?" Henri asked, discreetly clearing his throat.

"I don't know if that's such a good idea!" was what Dru had said.

"It's up to you," she had replied. *No pressure there.*

"Think about it why don't you? Get back to me in a few days," she had suggested. "The boys would love it if you would come. They miss you."

Surprisingly, Dru called back two days later, seemingly ecstatic about the invitation. "You're right. It's time I put the boys first and, yes, it has been way too long since I've seen them." Work was relentless, he told her. He'd been working primarily undercover assignments, and traveling a lot, handling some gang-buster cases.

"How exciting for you! You like that, right?" she ventured her support.

This was the first 'real' *conversation* she and Dru had exchanged since their unpleasant, ugly divorce. His weekly Friday evening phone calls to Oliver and Will, school photos, and art projects posted on his refrigerator door were the only contact he had with his three sons, or with her for that matter. Perhaps, going forward, they could parent like quasi-civilized adults.

Then, she dropped the bomb!

"Oh, and Paul Martin will also be here for Christmas," she added, dropping the news as though it were an afterthought.

"What the hell!" Dru gripped hold of the phone as if it had grown talons, and had quickly turned on him.

Élise was quick to cut him off, and begin walking through the logic. "Please hear me out," she said gently.

Dru's instincts said, *hang up now before you say things you'll regret.* But, instead, he took a deep breath, counting backwards from ten…nine…eight…seven… The first rule in anger management.

"You have to admit it would be terribly awkward, just you and I with the boys." Élise resumed building her case. "You can see that, right?"

Silence.

She continued, "Which is why I thought if Katy and Paul could join us, it might make things less…"

"…dreadful?" he offered.

"Yes, less dreadful," she agreed. "Perhaps, even joyful."

"So, you're thinking two alpha males, an ex-wife, a sister-in-law, and three little kids singing carols round the Christmas tree will make everything merry and bright?"

"I'm willing to give it a try. Are you?" she responded.

Dru was not entirely convinced that Paul and his ex-wife weren't *doing it* though his friend repeatedly denied any such thing was going on. But, now, Dru had to admit he'd be damned if he'd let his suspicions keep him from his own children.

"For the sake of the children, I'll give it a try," he said hesitantly. It was time he got hold of himself. Apparently, his ex was getting along fine. She made it seem easy but, for him, it was a struggle.

Upon hanging up, the thought occurred to Dru that, once again, he would play the villain, obliged to inform Rose O'Neil that neither he nor Katy would be coming to Greenwich, Connecticut for Christmas. It wasn't like his mother had yet forgiven him for taking Katy away. Now, this!

The phone call to Rose O'Neil later that week went just as expected. Did he know his father had developed a troubling, lingering cough? As for herself, she has not been sleeping well. The water heater had given out last week and the car transmission was about to go. A distraught Rose filled him in on every facet of family news as though the knowing would surely convince him and his sister to alter their holiday plans. His brothers, David and Dennis, would be there, his mother would remind him. Both always at the ready. A mere phone call away. That much, at least, gave her solace.

Katy broke out into all smiles at the thought of Christmas in New England as she ran off to scan her closet, considering what she could possibly wear. It had been *forever* since she had been anywhere. She tried to imagine what Christmas would be like without Rose O'Neil's inflexible house rules. No Scottish tea-pouring rituals or rose-shaped linen napkins to fold. And, dinner wine served without being given the evil eye. She shouldn't feel so gleeful but, truthfully, it would be wonderful seeing Élise and the boys in their new house. She couldn't wait!

Élise reached across the table, and touched her father's hand, hoping he was not too awfully disappointed about her plans. "Of course, you, Símone, and mom are more than welcome to join us. There is plenty of room for everyone," she offered, knowing Jacqueline Saint-Cyr would be horrified with such an arrangement.

"I'll talk it over with your mother," Henri softly replied, scooping an extra-large serving of vanilla ice cream atop a second piece of pie. He knew full well the outcome of *that* discussion. It goes without saying, she'd be appalled.

32

HOME FOR THE HOLIDAYS

Oliver and Will screamed, and jumped up and down at the sight of Uncle Paul setting down his luggage on the staircase. Yet, four hours later, the two brothers, who'd spent weeks asking, "When does our dad get here?" huddled together in the front hall like cautious bear cubs when Dru's car pulled up into the drive. Élise's heart thumped in her chest as she opened the door wide, prodding the two boys in the direction of their father.

"Go give your dad a big hug," she instructed them gently as they uncharacteristically clung to her side. "Sorry," she blurted to the man who essentially had become *the voice* on the other end of the phone. *A rocky start to be sure.*

"It's okay," Dru shrugged sheepishly. "How 'bout a high-five, guys?"

With that, they stepped forward with hand slaps and wide-eyed smiles. "Wow! Quite an impressive bungalow you got here," Dru said, as he took in the majestic property in one full sweep.

Katy echoed, "Wow!" as she stepped into the vast entryway, clinging to the handle of her roll-away bag whose wheels continued to spin as if questioning their welcome. She hadn't seen or talked to her ex-sister-in-law since the night Élise left her standing in her parents' Connecticut driveway, and sped off into the night.

"I'm so glad you're both here," Élise gushed, wrapping both arms around the young college girl, and making her way toward Dru for a brisk exchange of hugs. *She supposed it's how it should be done.*

"You look amazing!" spouted Élise, stepping back to view the hardly recognizable Aunt Katy. Gone was the frizzy red hair, which now lay sleek and stylish in flattering shoulder-length layers. The schoolgirl thick eyeglasses had been replaced with Italian tinted sunglasses and the floppy penny-loafers traded for fur-lined knee-high boots. And, where were the freckles? Katy had obviously reinvented herself since moving to Georgetown. Élise, of course, had no idea how much she, too, had changed in the eyes of her guests as they greeted one another in her elegant new surroundings.

Dru's scraggly-faced beard, and hair grown past his shirt collar, startled Élise. *Hadn't expected that!* The ever-meticulous Dru O'Neil appeared…slipshod, almost negligent, as he dropped his duffle bag inside the door. The changes might explain the boys' unexpected standoff; their puzzled faces shrieking, 'This isn't our dad.' Somehow, we expect people to stay exactly as we left them, forgetting life goes on.

As if on cue, Paul sauntered into the foyer. "Dru, you made it man!" he smiled, grasping hold of his colleague's hand, and offering a 'Merry Christmas' around the room. "And, this lovely lady must be the beautiful Aunt Katy I've heard so much about." Flashing his brilliant smile, he continued to address Katy. "I'm Paul Martin. Here, let me take your coat, and get that luggage for you."

Paul, sensing a stalemate as the vestibule grew silent, turned to the boys. "Hey, guys, what do you say we show your dad and Aunt Katy round the place?" Everyone looked relieved to follow orders from the one person amongst them not overwrought by emotion. "Oliver, grab your dad's bag. Will, help me with Aunt Katy's luggage." Nodding to Dru and Katy, he led the entourage up the winding stairs to show them to the guestrooms.

"Make yourselves at home!" Élise hollered as she watched them turn the corner. Hanging her head, she found herself taking in a deep-seated breath. She could hear Paul's baritone voice in the upper foyer, pointing out the shower rooms and fresh supply of towels and toiletries as if he were the hired help.

Dru's eyes scoured the massive walls and ceilings as Paul and the boys showed their two guests through the roomy old manor. How strangely intimidating to find yourself surrounded by roomfuls of once familiar furnishings; like the desk he once wrote his daily reports on, the wall of bookcases where his stack of law books once stood, the boys' bunk beds, rocking chair, and wooden toy chests. All sadly remote, not unlike the rush of feelings that had surfaced when he first saw Élise standing at her front door. What really stung was to see the boys, timid and shy, as if frightened at the mere sight of him.

He hadn't expected a cheeky faceoff from his own sons. And, Christ, where did Paul Martin fit in? Walking around like he owns the place. Not twenty minutes into it and Dru was wishing he could turn around and leave. What a blasted mistake coming here was. *How's this gonna work?*

As the door to the nursery opened, Jean-Jacques rolled over in his crib, holding onto the bars, jabbering undistinguishable gibberish. The scowl he grimaced, before turning his back on his visitors, and nestling back into the security of his eider down blanket, spoke volumes. Paul quietly closed the door, retracing his steps. "Maybe we should let him be for now. He can be grumpy when he first wakes up."

Was it his imagination or could he feel Dru *hating on him* as they clambered up the rickety third floor stairs with the two boys hot on his heels? Can't say I blame the guy, Paul thought. Hell, if roles were reversed, I'd feel the same. It was a virtual catch-twenty-two attempting to remain loyal to both parties of a newly broken marriage. You do your best to remain impartial, fly under the radar. But, in the end, you come up short. He should have backed out the night Élise called begging *please, please* come for Christmas. *It would make things so much easier* is how she phrased it. Well, not for him, that's for damn sure! That was his chance to nip this thing in the bud. But, how could he say no after the whole Liz Summer affair when Élise had stepped up to the plate, opening her home, and taking in the kid. So, here we are.

"Need any help?" Dru asked as he entered the kitchen after showering and settling in. "Katy's taking a short nap after our long drive through the night."

The look on his face brought back memories of the first agonizing Christmas she had spent with the O'Neils in Connecticut. Way back then, before she mastered the art of not caring what Rose O'Neil said or thought. Hands dredged elbow deep in a bag of flour, Élise smiled as she rolled out a perfect pie crust on the butcherblock countertop. A bowl of blueberries the boys had picked last season sat covered in powdered sugar and cinnamon. Dru couldn't help but stare as he watched her roll, pinch, knead, and sift, all the while trying to not look astonished.

When had she learned to cook?

"You could take the boys for a short walk around the neighborhood if you're up to it," she suggested.

"Great idea!" Dru replied, eyeing the boys, who looked at one another as if they'd been asked to clean the litterbox, or some other distasteful chore. With hats, mittens, scarfs, and boots in place, Oliver and Will set out through the mudroom, pointing out Othello, their resident cat, snoring noisily in his wicker basket.

"He's mean, but he catches mice so we keep him," Will explained.

"I see," said Dru, recalling his ex-wife's aversion to cats.

"He's not mean. He's a fearless general like his namesake, Othello, also known as The Moor," Oliver clarified. Dru threw back his head in laughter. It appeared he'd best brush up on his Shakespeare if he wanted to keep up with his six-year-old son…or had he already turned seven? Damn, he couldn't remember.

By late afternoon, the house was filled with tantalizing homecooked aromas as Élise flitted about the kitchen, checking the timing of the pork roast, yams, and breads. From the corner of her eye, she could see Dru in the far room fingering the sterling silver ornaments that hung from the upper branches of the seven-foot fir tree in the grand room; each globe-shaped decoration engraved with an individual name: Élise, Oliver, Will, Jean-Jacques, Dru. On top of the grand old tree was the Waterford crystal star, a wedding gift. The Lenox baby shoes with Oliver's date of birth hung on a solitary branch next to Will's framed baby picture. She shook her head, surprised to feel tears flooding her eyes. She wasn't expecting emotions to be riding at such a high.

"Look, Dad. This present is from me to you," she heard Oliver say.

"And, this one's from me," shouted Will, hauling a package across the room with the pride of an artisan who had just completed a custom order. Paul had brought Jean-Jacques downstairs, and quickly disappeared out back to stack firewood, making himself as scarce as possible. Jean-Jacques hugged on Katy, flirting as only baby boys can do when being cuddled by a strikingly pretty woman. If one didn't know, you'd think this was an ordinary household celebrating the holiday, rather than a family in search of itself.

The candles were lit as everyone gathered around the table, spread with roasted pork loin, green beans, yams, creamed potatoes, home-made apple-cranberry sauce, and oven baked whole grain bread. Élise's efforts experimenting with untried recipes this past year were paying off. She invited Dru to sit at the head of the table, and Paul at the other, while everyone else scurried to find their place.

"Cheers," said Dru, raising a glass of wine, and offering special praise to the chef. "This is amazing!"

As the heated plates were passed across the table, and everyone reached out for seconds, any former tensions were long forgotten. Funny how breaking bread together around a table filled with good food does that to people. Will needed help cutting his meat while Oliver had moved past any shyness, and was talking up a storm. Jean-Jacques chomped on a piece of hard crusted bread while Paul refilled water glasses and Katy stirred the candle-lit gravy boat.

Just as Dru reached for yet another helping of Élise's home-made cranberry preserves, the two exchanged eye contact, and a smile that lingered just a bit too long.

The kind of exchange that, for a sliver of a moment, sets one's mind to elusive thoughts... 'Had they even tried to save their marriage? Should they have given it a second try?' *NO. DO NOT GO THERE!*

Within the passing of a second, Élise brusquely turned to wipe Jean-Jacques' chin. She stretched to readjust him, and her thoughts, as the baby boy slouched awkwardly in the refurbished antique wooden high-chair.

"So, Katy," she said, taking a deep breath, "do you see much of your neighbor Belle? Gosh, I miss her so." Élise felt badly, having been lax in keeping tabs on her dear friend. Katy's face lit up at the mention of Belle Stevenson.

"Actually, Belle has turned out to be a lifesaver for both Dru and I. Of course, she sends her love to all of you."

Dru, with a mouthful, nodded agreement as he buttered another slice of warm bread. "What with keeping the house clean, even cooking for us from time to time, she's remarkable!" It had taken courage, if not utter desperation, for him to swallow his pride, and pick up the phone to ask if she would consider helping out. "She has a key, and checks in nearly every day. She changes bed linens and towels, polishes the floors, and keeps a sense of home alive. Wouldn't you say, sis?"

As a bonus, Katy had found a much-needed friend in Belle. She and the elder woman had developed the relationship Katy wished she could have had with her own mother.

Come evening, it was beyond wonderful to see the boys reconnecting with their dad enough to romp about on the floor, just as they had as toddlers. As for Jean-Jacques, he hadn't left Katy's side, cooing like a lovesick poet to this woman he claimed as his own. Paul tended to the several fireplaces, intermittingly keying Christmas carols softly on the staid, grand piano while Élise scurried about, camera in hand, flashing photos as moms do at times like these.

She could not recall a more memorable Christmas eve, despite its shaky beginnings. Some might caption such a gathering as dysfunctional. Call it what you will but, at this moment, attorney settlements, angry phone exchanges, embittered in-laws, or unforgiving betrayals had been long cast aside. The only thing that mattered was this night of family-loving-family in a home that, for the moment, found no fault, no disappointment, and no disagreement.

When Élise suggested Dru take the boys up to bed, Will jumped on his back while Oliver scrambled up the stairs. Even Jean-Jacques jumped into his arms, wanting to be carted off to his crib. Oh, holy night!

33

GOT YOU COVERED

Paul walked Élise to the driveway at noon on Christmas Day, placing her overnight bag into the oversized trunk. Slamming it shut, he assured her, "Not to worry! Uncle Paul's got you covered." He, Katy, and Dru were adamant that she leave them in charge, and drive to Hyannis to spend the balance of the day and overnight with Henri and Jacqueline Saint-Cyr, as planned.

"They're not getting any younger. You really should go," they all agreed. "We'll be fine." The boys were blissfully engaged with an overload of male attention, and a roomful of new toys, while Jean-Jacques continued his infatuation with Aunt Katy. Élise had a holiday turkey dinner with all the trimmings ordered from the local food mart, to be delivered by two o'clock. "Get going," they all chimed in, all but helping to pack her bags.

"Your dad's in charge," she announced to the boys as she watched Dru's face light up like a rookie drill sergeant assigned his first round of recruits.

Élise had promised her father she would try to join the family for dinner, and a possible overnight if all was in order at the house. The boys and Dru were interacting just like old times and Katy and Paul seemed to be enjoying their adopted role as second tier in the scheme of things. Still, the house appeared solemnly cheerless in the rear-view mirror as she drove down the hill and turned round the bend. Alone in the driver's seat, just herself and an empty backseat, no children squabbling, no diaper bags, no cookie crumbs, and no spilled sippy cups to clean up after. Somehow, it felt very wrong. So, this was what it felt like to be a divorced parent. Suddenly, she felt very sorry for Dru. *How does he bear it?* she thought. Accelerating, and heading to the interstate, she glanced in the mirror only to see a guilt-ridden ogre staring back. She hadn't meant to create such hurt.

Henri Saint-Cyr stood on the front porch with his heavy lined hood drawn over his head to shield the cold as he spotted his daughter's silver Mercedes maneuvering its way up the drive. "She's here!" he hollered, his breath hanging in the icy salt air.

Her brother, Símone, appeared in shirt sleeves, waving wildly while his little dog, Augustus Too Short the III, scampered about, wagging his stump of a tail as if to keep it from freezing. "Merry Christmas," they wailed, excited as Santa's elves welcoming him back to the workshop after a hard night's run.

Kicking off her boots before entering the warmth of the gracious family homestead, Élise stopped in her tracks, hardly believing her eyes. A splendidly decorated Christmas tree dominated the entire living room, towering to the height of the sky-high ceiling. Stockings hung from the fireplace mantle, pine cones spilled from ribboned baskets, and red poinsettias smiled from every table top. Never had the Saint-Cyr home looked like this on Christmas day! More normal would be to see heaps of luggage piled in the front hall with a super shuttle purring in the driveway, waiting to usher the family of four to the nearest airport. It was as if she was in the wrong house. Overwhelmed, she fought the urge to bawl like a child, and run to her father to be picked up.

Mother Jacqueline rose from the corner sofa, and allowed herself to be hugged, immediately apologizing for the disarray, though the house appeared sterilized. "How wonderful to see all of you!" Élise gushed, feeling more like a school girl home on spring break instead of a mother of three. Jacqueline returned to the sofa to continue her work on a piece of needlepoint, as aloof as if she had been interrupted by a cold caller at dinner hour.

In stark contrast, Henri all but danced around the tree. "Well, this is certainly a first!" he declared, taking hold of both siblings in his arms. "It took all these many years to celebrate the holiday at home with just our little family." Glancing at his wife, it registered how disassociated she was from her own children, as though they were imposters rather than her own flesh and blood. Well, perhaps not so much with Símone. Without apology, Jacqueline had always made it clear her son was her favorite child. Símone never understood why.

Élise hugged her brother, so glad to see him. Amazing, it had taken half a lifetime to get to actually know him or, more importantly, to like him. They would have a lot of catching up to do after settling in. Like a spoiled only child, Too Short unabashedly weaved in and out between her feet, insisting he not be ignored. "I think he missed you," smiled Símone.

Mrs. Beaumont rang the backdoor bell punctually at dinner hour, arms stacked with urns of steaming hot food, enough to feed a legion. Hard to believe the elder Lena Beaumont was still alive, let alone still stuffing turkeys. She'd been baking, stewing, and delivering meals to the Saint-Cyrs since Élise was a child. Like a scene from *Our Town,* Henri and his grown children offered a helping hand, carting in trays full of homemade breads, sweet potato pies, and colorful vegetable platters while Jacqueline hurled orders from her sewing corner.

"Wonderful to see you again, dear," Lena smiled at Élise with twinkling eyes and a lilt in her bent step. "Are you married yet?" she asked unknowingly, confused with age.

"Not yet, Mrs. Beaumont," Élise retorted with a gentle smile, continuing to pour a round of dinner wine into Grandpa Saint-Cyr's long-stem antique goblets. It was easier to say no than to explain.

"Don't worry," the aged woman said, embracing the young woman warmly. "One day, Mr. Right will come along."

Símone raised a dinner toast to their first family Christmas together in Hyannis. As glasses clinked loudly in unison, Too Short scurried beneath the table linen, alarmed by what he determined to be friendly-fire. Hovering discreetly beneath the table, he knew he could count on his master to offhandedly drop him treats. He didn't ever like to beg.

Throughout the meal, Jacqueline hardly spoke, except for an occasional *merci* and *s'il te plait*. There was a time Élise would have allowed her mother's distant behavior to dampen the moment but Dr. Katz's therapy sessions had changed all that. She no longer pandered to the thought that, in some ghastly way, she was liable for Jacqueline's state of unpleasantness. "It's her game," he had explained. "Senseless as it seems, some parents feel threatened by their own offspring. They feel *less than* when a child becomes a better athlete, smarter, prettier, or more successful. Resentments can arise." He suspected Jacqueline's insecurities were in place long before her daughter was born. "Unfortunately, you are her number one target. Nothing to do with you." He had paused, staring at the floor, letting that sink in.

Glancing across the room to the head of the table was Henri, truly living in the moment without a care, smiling and laughing as if he were hosting his best friend's retirement roast. Ever the rock of this disconnected family, he could make all that seemed wrong feel right.

After dinner, Élise called home for the second time before heading out with Símone to not only walk the dog, but to work off the high caloric meal. Bundled up to face the frigid night air, the brother and sister welcomed the chance to be alone to catch up on each other's news.

"So, Dru is finally reconciled to the divorce?" Símone asked.

"Well, let's say he and I are now trying to work it out together," she replied. "There's only so long you can live with raging anger, you know? Sooner or later, you have to come to terms with what is. We couldn't go on the way it was. Well, I couldn't," she added.

The sound of the roaring ocean filled the open sky, ablaze with multi-colored holiday lights. It was a perfect picture-postcard night.

"And, you and the boys are liking your new home?"

"It's wonderful. You have to come visit!" she gloated. "I think you know D.C. was never my home," she continued, cautiously side stepping a rut in the winding road. "Marble monuments and stuffy chambers were never my thing," she laughed.

"Probably had a lot more to do with what was going on behind closed doors at your place," he offered, fully aware he knew nothing about what made for a happy home. His life was simple. No wife. No kids. Just him and his dog. Not wanting to come off pessimistic, he gently reminded her, "You do have your work cut out for you raising three boys alone."

"Ironically," she countered, "it feels less difficult now that I'm on my own. I always knew I was destined to be a mom, but not necessarily a wife. At least, not a good wife."

"Well, maybe not an agent's wife," Símone added jokingly.

"True!" She couldn't dispute that.

Símone talked about his life in Chicago. Career wise, he had four scientific patents under his belt, a hefty pay raise, and a substantial promotion being the end result. A date here and there, but no real love life. He seemed okay with that. Convinced that no woman could or would deal with his disproportionate need for alone-time, he didn't see it happening. Thinking, calculating, and unearthing was what he did for fun. Admittedly, he had a yearning for children, a son. But that would entail making room for a woman…so no.

"Never say never," uttered Élise with a puckered brow. "I'm no spokesperson for marital bliss but it does exist, they tell me. But, for the unforeseeable future, I'm liking my newfound freedom."

The seriousness of the moment was broken when Too Short's little legs skated across the rink-like sidewalk as he attempted an abrupt stop, causing him to skid, swirl, and twirl about like a novice ballerina. He looked up pleadingly, ears drooping, refusing to budge. Símone picked him up, carrying him the rest of the way home, nestling him in his arms as any God-fearing, nurturing father would. "I know, little buddy. It's been a long day for me, too."

34

M.I.A.

"What do you mean he left!" Élise heard herself holler into the phone.

"Well," Paul proceeded in his all too familiar mediator voice, "a call came in about eleven last night. Dru took it in the other room. It was short-lived. When he came back, he said he couldn't discuss details, not even with me. He was going to have to leave right away. He stopped to write you a note, gathered his stuff, and, just like that, he was gone."

"It's Christmas, for God's sake! Where is his head? Where is his heart? Why didn't you call me?" She fired off a barrage of questions one might use when addressing an incompetent staff member.

"And, *what exactly* could you have done at that late hour?" Paul ignored the incriminating tone, knowing she would chastise herself a thousand times over after hanging up.

"I'm such a shrew," she'd say apologetically to him later. He'd agree and they would laugh it off.

"Look, stay put. Everyone here is fine. The boys are out back with Katy, waxing their new snowboards, and I'm here hanging out with the little guy. Enjoy your day with the folks. When you get back tonight, we'll hash it out. Really, it's all good."

Henri knew his daughter well enough to recognize the ashen look on her face as she reentered the living room. "Everything okay, honey?" he asked. When they heard Dru upped and left late last night to return to D.C., the room fell silent. Even Jacqueline looked concerned, waiting for her daughter to elaborate. "Oh!" is all Henri could muster, as though the Grinch had stolen his Christmas.

Within the hour, Élise was behind the wheel, steering her way back to Lexford, a heavy foot on the floor pedal, her mind clouded in chaotic disbelief.

How does a man make such self-filled choices?

Not that she was squared away by any means; there was still so much to set right in order to call herself whole. But, Dru's actions of last night were the final nail in their marital coffin. It was the blessed *kiss-off* to any and all connection to his loathsome gun raids, mug shots, and bomb dogs, and the unending fallout of life as an agent's wife. There was a certain level of relief in it all, as if a final curtain had been drawn, leaving no wiggle room for questions or regrets. Perhaps he was owed a standing ovation for cementing the end to their doomed marriage with such an improvised final exit.

Frank Sinatra was singing *My Way* on the radio in his lounge room style as she sped along the outer lane. She found herself harmonizing the heartfelt lyrics written for those who've had regrets too few to mention. Abruptly, she snapped the dial off. She'd heard enough.

She could hear the voice of Dr. Katz playing inside her head in his gentle supportive tone: "You tried to work it out, until you no longer could," he had told her.

No one could deny her marriage had been a life of interruptions, of unpredictable days and nights. She remembered the night Dru broke the news that he had to go to Montana.

"Okay," she had said haphazardly.

"For four months," he added, waiting for the axe to fall. "It's my turn on the rotation. No one wants these assignments but it's part of the job," he explained to a fretful Élise, who was then three months pregnant with Will.

And, how many plans had been derailed by last minute *calls to duty*? Too many to count. Her heart would sink at the sound of Dru's government phone belching its needy plea at the most inopportune times, knowing full well that she, his family, his friends, and every living thing was about to be deemed irrelevant. An air raid siren couldn't have been more dreaded.

She remembered his disastrous thirtieth birthday; a night she had spent weeks preparing for. *The call* came in just as a caravan of guests made its way up the walkway, laden with armfuls of bottled wine, boxes of Belgian chocolates, and festively decorated packages of every shape and size. "Sorry" was all he could rally as he bowed out the back door, leaving herself and a houseful of party-goers to dance the night away. Back then, their marriage was young enough to shrug it off as simply *unfortunate*. They'd kiss, and make up, until the next go-round.

Not so for the three-hundred-dollar-a-plate New Year's Eve gala several years later when he bailed before midnight. "Gotta go," Dru had whispered in her ear while the bread baskets and salad bowls were being passed to the left. There she stood, solo, unable to forgive or forget, as the clock struck twelve, in a floor length designer evening gown, hailing down a taxi back to the Ritz Carlton.

"I could write a book!" she grimaced aloud to an indifferent city sand truck.

The traffic was light and free-flowing heading into the morning sun. Most people were where they were meant to be on this glorious holiday weekend. Few were chasing down the freeway to put out yet another family fire. That's what life felt like since she left Wall Street to marry Dru O'Neil; one giant, eternal firestorm.

As her mind drifted in its state of admitted self-pity, a beer-hauling semi delivery truck jerked his mile-long rig in front of her, mud flaps spitting gravel like an angered hissing cat. "Nice going pal!" she sputtered, flashing her headlights off and on, as if its driver might notice or care. His *'How is my driving?'* bumper sticker hung sidewise, tattered and worn, the 1-800 phone number faint and unreadable in the glaring sun. Veering off at the next exit ramp, she refreshed her mindset with a Starbucks sugarized fix, and a scroll through the latest news postings on her new smart phone; a Christmas gift from her techie brother, Símone. Once again behind the wheel, dodging the snowbanks piled sky high along the freeway exit ramps, she was soon back on track, and more than halfway home.

"Mommy, mommy!" shrieked the two older boys when a bedraggled Élise entered the candlelit library. With no makeup, and hair tied up in an unseemly, quirky bun, she looked as if she'd flown in on a red-eye. Jean-Jacques yelped, hurling his bottle across the room in what could best be interpreted as an unchecked display of affection. Katy, smiling, spun around from the fireplace, grasping hold of a rod stacked with smoldering marshmallows as Paul glanced up from a silver fondue pot of melting chocolate.

"So much for not hurrying home!" he cried out, dropping the wooden spoon, and rushing to welcome her with a man-sized bear hug alongside Oliver and Will. Paul was right. Everyone was fine. He and Katy had taken care of everything. The boys hustled back to the fireplace to finger the gooey marshmallows with Katy every bit in control. Jean-Jacques resumed sucking his retrieved baby jug, gurgling at Élise as she kissed his rosy cheeks. '*I'm good*' he seemed to say.

"Come on," Paul said as he shuffled Élise down the hall and into his favorite room in the house, the kitchen. He had spent enough days and nights here to feel attached to the farmhouse sink, potbelly stove, and brightly polished copper pots. His theory was, no matter how many rooms in a sprawling household, the core of family life always played itself out at the kitchen table. Tea, coffee, expresso, hot chocolate; the choice was immaterial. Without asking, he began to brew a fresh pot of chamomile tea.

While unwrapping and tossing her heavy winter coat and scarf in a heap on the corner rocker, she posed the expected question. "So, what can you tell me?"

"Not much," Paul answered, handing over a sealed envelope. "I'm as much in the dark as you but, hey, he did stop to write you a note," he chimed, as if proposing a softer sentence for his buddy. She recognized the handwriting. Too perfect for a man, each letter carefully crafted; worthy of a wedding invite. While Élise silently began to read, Paul ducked into the pantry. He would give her a moment alone while he aimlessly shifted dishes back and forth in the stain-glassed hutch.

Dru's first paragraph was non-frilled:

Had to leave. Can't say why. Thank you for everything.
It was great to see you and the boys.

"Paul," she shouted in a droning, low-pitched voice, much like that used by his mother when she needed help on a troublesome task. "You are not going to believe this!"

Paul stuck his head around the corner, holding up two china tea cups. "I'm all ears," he said, pulling up a chair.

Unfolding the note, she began to recite the second paragraph aloud in brusque, staccato-like sentences. "Élise, that would be me," she jested, not amused. "Please take the boys to the pound on North Street to pick up the dog I have arranged for. He needs to be picked up by noon Monday. It is my Christmas gift to them. It's a Golden Labrador puppy I've named Argos. I'm hoping you will share with them the Greek tale of war hero Ulysses and his devoted dog, Argos. Love Dru."

Paul let out a loud whistle, and an, "Oh boy!"

"Is he crazy? I do not need a damn dog! Can you believe he even gave it a name?" More amazed than enraged, she couldn't fathom how he would think it okay to add another member to the household without even a discussion. "Figures!" she huffed, sipping cautiously from the steamy hot china cup, which threatened to burn her lower lip. Dru never did understand boundaries. It was unlikely Will and Oliver knew anything about the dog. She would simply give a pass to the whole pound fiasco. Maybe get a hamster instead.

Katy entered the kitchen with Jean-Jacques riding her hip, the boys tagging close behind. Oliver and Will snuggled up to their mom as though suddenly realizing she was home. "I'm sorry about my brother," Katy offered as an aside.

"Oh, Katy, honey, not your fault," Élise insisted as Jean-Jacques reached out to thrust his little arms around his mother's neck. The fat-legged baby wrapped himself around her waist like a tight-fitting corset, chomping his fist, surprising himself with a man-sized hiccup. "You and Paul have been absolute lifesavers. I can't thank you enough," she said, snuggling her baby boy.

"Dad says he bought us a special Christmas present," piped Oliver. "He said we can go get it on Monday. It's a big,

big surprise!" he shouted, stretching his arms spread eagle, as wide as they would go.

"Uh-huh," said Élise, hugging on him, with an *"oh shit!"* almost escaping her lips.

"And...what's the pound?" he asked, scratching his head.

"Dad had to leave," Will informed his mom, while wedging Oliver out of his way, allowing a delayed reprisal to the pound inquiry.

"I know sweetheart," she offered, pulling him close. "It's okay. You guys had lots of fun though, right?" The young boy stood limp, disheartened, looking like a forgotten middle-child, clutching an oversized, green stuffed frog larger than his four-year old self.

"Yes," he said, as though suddenly remembering. "We wrestled and I won!" he boasted. Everyone cheered, which brought a huge tooth-missing smile to his face. "Dad brought me this frog," he added while tossing 'Mr. Green Jeans' in the air. Paul playfully tossed Will and the frog in the air. The room filled with laughter as baby, boys, man and the two women joined in the silliness.

The fact that her ex-husband, father of her three children was technically M.I.A. would have to work itself out as it always had, given time. Just another soap-opera-like-day in the life of Élise Saint-Cyr, a name she was beginning to reidentify with more and more. As Dickens would say: *It was the best of times, it was the worst of times.*

35

HOW? WHERE? WHEN?

Paul took the early morning call. "Chuck, hey, my man. What's up?" he hailed the chief in his usual high-spirited manner, but was confused when his boss curtly asked, "Is Élise there?" Paul shrugged his shoulders in an *'I haven't got a clue'* gesture, while handing off his phone to Élise. They had both been up all hours of the night with the newly acquired, whimpering pup, Argos, who was now pleasantly wrestling with a rag toy between his stub-like teeth.

"What kind of terrible news, Chuck?" she stammered, clutching her nightrobe as if to fend off what was to come. Paul watched the young mother as she nodded in silence, listening to an unusually longwinded, one-sided conversation. "Oh my God," she whispered in interims, closing her eyes, and slouching her way to a nearby seat. "Of course, Chuck," she uttered, her eyes intent upon every word, too stunned to even know what she was hearing, thinking, or saying. "The boys and I will be there by tomorrow morning," she said, her hands shaking as they tugged on a mass of tangled bed hair. "Thank you, I will," she mumbled before ending the call.

How many nights had she lived and relived this moment? At least a thousand times when Dru was on the streets, while she lay in bed, the digital clock scrolling through its timely night watch, in fear of this very call. Did all agents' wives have such a premonition or did her imagination dictate the outcome until it became reality? She never really believed it could happen. Like swimming in the ocean, you knew of its unthinkable dangers; sharks circling, ready to lop off an arm or a leg. But, never did you really believe they would come after you. It was always someone else's catastrophe. Never yours.

Paul immediately called back Chuck, his coffee-colored skin ashen as he gathered the horrific facts. "Fuck!" he heard himself spout in glowering anger.

Hanging up, Paul and Élise fell into the comfort of each other's arms. Neither spoke because there were no words. The pup took on a sulky, melancholy stare, more from exhaustion than of understanding, huddling at their feet. Together, like a grief-stricken triumvirate, the threesome mounted the stairs to awaken Dru's sister, Katy.

36

AGENT DOWN

POLICE IN DESPERATE SEARCH FOR SUSPECTS WHO SHOT UNDERCOVER AGENT

More than 100 local and federal officials are combing parts of Philadelphia today as authorities try to track down the people responsible for shooting at undercover agents in the early morning hours. "The actions of the offenders in this were barbaric," Philadelphia Police Superintendent Steve Anderson said today. This is the fifth law enforcement officer in a year that's been shot over in that area.

According to Leonard Steele, the Special Agent in Charge for The Bureau of Alcohol, Tobacco, Firearms and Explosives, the agent was "ambushed" at approximately 3:00 a.m. today.

He said the injured agent had been carrying out an operation to intercept illegal guns when individuals opened fire, striking Agent Dru O'Neil in the face. Fellow officers put the agent into a silver SUV, and rushed him to a hospital where he was pronounced dead on arrival.

Steele said he had a message for the suspects: "We will knock on every door, talk to every witness, watch every piece of video, and analyze every piece of evidence. Believe me, you will not get away with this."

37

THE GODMOTHER

Rose O'Neil would always believe Élise caused her son's horrific death. It was written in bold caps across the furrowed lines of her stern, grieving face as she sat in the aisle across from the Saint-Cyr family. The folding chairs were aligned graveside, the two women in full view of one another as the preacher spoke his condolences. Élise had tried to approach Rose, to no avail. The mournful mother, who had aged drastically since her only daughter left home, seemed to be withering away with each agonizing breath. The once-spirited eyes, now steel-grey, pierced the air that surrounded her reviled ex-daughter-in-law; the one who had destroyed the O'Neil family.

Patrick O'Neil, the father of his now dead son, sat motionless, like an overly disciplined child, staring blindly at the flag-draped casket, in private communion with himself.

He blamed no one for his son's death. The retired colonel would be the first to tell you Dru savored every minute of his life as a federal agent. He would say danger was the risk of the job his son signed up for. For many an agent, putting themselves out there, facing harm's way, seemed to feed an unquenchable thirst for whatever made their adrenaline surge. With each new case, they found themselves begging for more…more…more. Why that is, only they could know. The old man swiped dry his eyes with his pocket handkerchief, bowing his head in genuflection, grasping hold of his thread-worn family Bible. From her adjacent seat, Katy, his precious daughter, realized she had never seen her father, the man who never complained, not ever, fully shattered.

Élise hadn't seen Dennis or David since the divorce. Both they and their wives discreetly greeted her cordially at the preceding church services, hugging the boys, and offering any help they could give. But, as they returned to take their assigned places beside their mother, each took on the compulsory posture of embittered in-law.

"Let us bow our heads in prayer," the preacher directed the crowd. The army of ATF agents stood motionless in the back row. Dru's boss, Chuck Connelly, and his wife Hannah, remained gracious, reminding Élise of their endless support.

Oliver and Will sat wedged between their mother and Paul, leaning one against the other, shoulder to shoulder; innocent children attempting to understand what death entailed. "Do you get to Heaven by airplane?" Will asked his mother.

The black-veiled, tearful young mother couldn't help but feel a forgery, a counterfeit prop, clasping her hands in prayer before her once-husband's stately casket. Though her heart ached as deeply as any newly bereaved widow, she recognized her diminished status. She was now the in-law that everyone prayed would not attend the annual family barbecue; the ex-wife, which, to Rose O'Neil, was on par with outlaw. Over and over, she had to ask herself, *"Would Dru be alive today if I hadn't run off the way I did?"*

The Saint-Cyrs, Henri, Jacqueline and Símone, sat behind her and the boys, shocked as everyone to find themselves attending Dru's funeral. This scene had been played out a thousand times around the globe with nameless other families gathered in sorrow to celebrate the life of a loved one. Yet, even as a flurry of white balloons and doves airlifted into the open sky, Élise could not conceive the concept of celebration. You never know what death is going to feel like. Not until it's you in the black dress, explaining to your children that Daddy is in heaven with the angels, but will always be with you. How do you explain something like that when you're not even sure what you yourself believe?

As the crowd dispersed, Élise, from the corner of her eye, caught sight of the elder Mrs. O'Neil approaching with family in tow, marching in cadence, as one. The quasi-widowed young mother took a deep breath as one might in preparation of a knock-down brawl. '*Here it comes*!' she thought, bracing herself, clasping arms tightly around baby Jean-Jacques, as if he were a shield of armor. The dogmatic, grey-haired mother stretched herself tall to establish eye-to-eye contact so as to best hurl her final fatal barb. Henri Saint-Cyr watched the scene with trepidation as though it were being re-enacted in slow motion while Símone stepped forward, taking a stand abreast of his sister, not knowing what to expect as the two women faced off.

Élise never took her eyes from the granite-faced woman who spit out the numbing, malicious words, "I hope you're happy!" Her icy tone hung airborne like a mushroom cloud to be inhaled upon her departure, leaving her ex-daughter-in-law speechless rather than angered. The young mother of three could only feel immense sorrow for the enraged, broken-hearted woman who staggered away on the arm of her mortified soldier husband. The O'Neil entourage followed in what looked like a poorly choreographed scene from *The Godfather*, but this time more appropriately entitled *The Godmother*.

Only Katy remained behind, joining Élise, Paul, and the Saint-Cyrs to greet relatives, friends, and the troop of agents who had come to pay homage to one of their own, each expressing his and her heartwarming concern as they hugged the woman they knew as Dru's wife, and shook the hand of the three young O'Neil boys. Élise told the agents Dru had always thought of them as brothers, a term from the heart, and just how much it meant to see them here today.

Élise and the boys would be staying on at the Georgetown house with Katy for a time. There were many details to tend to in the coming weeks. The house would be sold. Katy was seriously contemplating her sister-in-law's offer to move to

Lexford to continue her studies in New England. So many changes were all happening so fast.

Belle Stevenson was at the house, waving from the front porch when everyone arrived back to Georgetown, tired and hungry. Oliver and Will, not a bit shy to run to the elder neighbor woman, hugging her in a way forever foreign to either of their grandmothers. What a wonderful yet tearful reunion that was!

Everyone was eager to sit down to a hearty, home-cooked dinner prepared by Belle, and to catch up on news. How sad to learn Belle's husband was now living in a nearby nursing home. "*Not doing very well at all.*" Yet, amidst such sadness was heartfelt happiness as they reminisced on life and better days. The reality of Dru's death had not caught up with any of them yet. Since that terrible morning, when the phone call from Chuck Connelly came in, life was running purely on auto pilot, simply putting one foot in front of the other. Amongst surges of tears, and utter breakdowns, the horror of it all felt completely surreal to Élise and the others as they moved about the house she and Dru had once called home.

That night, she curled up on the couch with a crocheted cover and a discolored sponge pillow found stashed away in an upstairs closet. Lying still, emotionally drained, and longing for a good night's sleep, she found herself wide-eyed, panicky, and over-wrought. In the stillness of the early morning hours, her mind rambled on. *I simply wanted out of a bad situation. But at what cost? An amazing man, my once-upon-a-time husband, is dead.* Still unable to wrap her mind around that thought, her heart kept pounding its nagging, ruthless sense of blame. Maybe Rose O'Neil was right.

And what would she have done without Paul? Not that she looked to him as a partner, not now or ever. But he was her strong-arm. Fortunately for her, a very comfortably, confirmed bachelor friend. He loved her children. She knew that much. And, that was huge. He was the kind of man a woman longed for. She sat up, appalled, shaking off the blanket and the thought. *What kind of woman dwells on another man on the evening of her husband's funeral!*

Staring into the darkness, she could hear that bothersome, overused cliché, *Life can change in an instant.* There is no happy ending to burying a loved one. The finality of it immeasurable. There is no going back, not to the way it was, or the way you wished it could have been. You move forward, guardedly, at a snail's pace, with a newly acquired wakefulness.

Throwing the pillows aside, and discarding the worn cover, she placed her bare feet on the chilled wooden floor, and headed to the kitchen. Never one for leftovers, she nevertheless flung open the refrigerator, and stared down her options. Slicing off a piece of cold turkey, she poured herself a glass of milk. The kitchen didn't seem all that different since she'd been gone. Same dishes, same silverware, and the same Welch's grape-jelly glasses. Dru hadn't been much on household upgrades. Opening the 'junk drawer' that every kitchen has, she filtered through heaps of coins. He never liked to carry coins so would empty his pockets here every night. Keys of all sorts, some on chains, and some on paperclips. For sure, he had no idea what any one of them opened or locked. She began to laugh at the memory through the onslaught of tears before slumping to the floor, head in hands, sobbing uncontrollably. "Oh God, Dru! I'm so sorry."

Despite the cold night air, she huddled on the floor for hours, knees to her chin, trying to rationalize how this could have happened. Never had she imagined it would end like this. People divorce all the time. They go on, and make new lives. She had actually prayed Dru might meet someone new. But that isn't how it all worked out. He was dead. That's how it all worked out.

Suddenly she, and she alone, would be wholly responsible for the lives of three minor children. Why was that so much more frightening than being a divorcee with an estranged ex-husband living hundreds of miles away? On the surface, her day-to-day life hadn't changed. Yet, going forward, everything about life had changed. Her children had no father and that made all the difference.

38

CARRY ON

Chuck Connelly prided himself in never having lost an agent. Until today. Seldom was he at a loss for words, but this morning counted as one of those times. Crouched over his office desk, surrounded by a roomful of forlorn agents, he eyed Dru O'Neil's badge and open file, which lay on his desk as if they had life still in them. Sitting across from him was Agent Paul Martin, who slouched uncharacteristically, reduced to a solitary man. The RAC was aware of the underlying tension over the past year between his two prized agents, Dru O'Neil and Paul Martin. Early on, Chuck had made the decision to treat the conflict as a personal matter between two employees. As long as their working partnership remained intact and professional, he'd stay out of it. Rumor had it their differences stemmed from Paul's reaching out to Dru's estranged wife and children. As supervisor, Connelly was not about to step foot into such a delicate, private affair; not unless ethics or performance dictated, in which case, without reservation, he would intervene.

Both Paul and Chuck, more than the others in the woeful room, knew Dru had not always been his rational self in these latter days. The divorce and separation from his children had been a shock which, in retrospect, clearly left him a changed man, despite his insistence that he was *over it*. "Being single isn't all that bad," he had told his boss, looking convincingly happy when he said it, recalled Chuck.

But Chuck knew better, and would forever question himself on his decision to stay impartial. And, Paul would forever take himself to the river for his out-and-out backing of Élise. He should have stayed out of it, and minded his own business. Had both men contributed to Dru's demise? His death? Neither would speak of it but the questions lay before them like the stench of cat piss on a family heirloom carpet.

Mike Finn, the Certified Explosive Specialist who had worked with Dru on the not so long-ago QEDCO case, arrived with an armload of the boss's favorite beverages. Designer lattes for all. The room remained silent except for the opening of cream and sugar packets, and wooden stir sticks loudly echoing down the hallway. "Isn't this the shits?" sputtered Agent Rob Taylor, waving his cup at Chuck, hoping to rouse words of wisdom, or even an empowering shrug. He got neither so he returned to his corner seat among his distraught fellow coworkers.

The roomful of men had all attended the funeral the day before. They had seen the casket, heard the prayers, and offered up their condolences to the family in mourning and, yet, it seemed inconceivable that Dru O'Neil could possibly be dead. Gone, in the shake of a pig's tail. "Fucking bastards," said Lou McNally, ATF Public Information Officer, as he downed a second Krispy Kreme scoffed from the nearby box. Granted it was 5:30 a.m., no time for a gab fest, but no one had within them more than two-word sentences to console themselves or the somber group of coffee drinkers. Tim Steele, the Special Agent Bomb Tech, lit a cigarette, despite the fact that there was no smoking allowed on the premises. He then drained his latte in one fell swoop.

"Sooooo," said Chuck Connelly, running his hands through his slicked down hair. "You're probably all thinking, that could have been me, or maybe that should have been me, or next time it will be me, and you could be right. But it wasn't you; not this time anyway. So, guess what? It's up to us to carry on. We're the whole team, minus one."

The men shifted nervously in their seats, wanting to regroup, with no inkling how. It wasn't just another day in the field. It would be asinine to pretend nothing had happened. One of their own was murdered in cold blood, like an animal, while the suspects were lulling about in a nearby jail cell on a somewhat uncomfortable steel cot, rethinking alibis, and concocting crock-of-bull storylines. Their sole purpose, to persuade a court appointed attorney to unearth any-and-all loopholes that might get their scum of the earth asses off the hook. May they rot in hell!

Each of the agents in the room had families at home; terrified families, traumatized by the brutality of Dru's death.

"I hate to admit it," voiced Agent Rob Taylor, "but I felt like a traitor this morning buckling on my holster and leaving the house." He looked around the room for acknowledgment, an unspoken *'yeah, me too.'* There were none. "Hey man," he continued, "I'm not fearful for myself but I am for my wife, my children...for them. But you know what? I'm here. Come hell or high water, I'm here. This is what I signed up for, what we all signed on for, and by God I'm going to do my part, and do it just as goddamn well as I'm able."

The collection of dour agents nodded, making eye contact with one another for the first time since arriving at daybreak. Outside the second story window, they caught a glimpse of the dim, yellowed lights in the adjacent parking garage as they flashed once, then shut down for the night. A police siren could be heard in the near distance and the sound of rain, as if to make this day a little more bleak.

"What happened is horrendous," Chuck Connelly began, picking up where Rob Taylor left off. "Fucking breaks my heart. Just like each of you, I looked into the eyes of Dru's mother and father, his three young children, his wife...well, technically speaking, his ex-wife. Nevertheless, there's no denying, it hurts like hell."

Taking a deep breath, he rose to his feet. "Just know that when you shed our brother's blood on our doorstep, it appalls us. It enrages us. But, you know what? Not only will we carry on. We will come back stronger, wiser, and with an unforgiving vengeance!" He was beginning to feel and sound like the leader he knew he was. "Let's remember the oath we swore to, shall we?" he added, scanning the room.

"Dru O'Neil will always be our hero, a brother, among our finest. Let's not forget him or his sacrifice. Not ever."

"Here, here!" spouted Mike Finn as the others raised their oversized cups, and clumsily spilled donut drippings onto the cold, hard floor in a unified cheer. In attendance was Prince Hal, awakened by the revival surrounding him. He rose on all fours from his corner and, on command, strolled to his master to receive a morning treat and an, *'atta boy.'* Rest assured, man's best friend was on board.

"We ready to move on?" Chuck wanted to know, fully cognizant of the wrenching hurt confronting each man as they jointly scattered to face yet another day. "I love you, man!" shouted Chuck to his team in a half-joking fashion, but meaning every word, watching as they filed one by one from the room. All but Paul.

39

GERMANY

"Heidelberg!" Élise heard herself cry out when Paul broke the news. "You're leaving for Heidelberg, Germany. Oh my God, when?"

More than a week had passed since the funeral and Paul had been keeping Argos at his place while Élise tended to the many issues facing her since Dru's passing. "Come here, boy," she squatted to her knees to welcome the frisky golden lab who ran to her, tail wagging, jumping as if he'd been offered a walk in the woods. "We missed you!" she admitted, rubbing his ears, and hugging him while he leaned against her seemingly relieved to hear it. "The boys are out and about with Katy. They'll be ecstatic to see you both," she confided while Argos cocked his head from side to side as if he understood.

"He's been a great house guest," Paul assured her, removing the leash from around the dog's neck. "However, I'm guessing he'd rather get back to his life in the countryside with you guys. Locked up all day in an apartment in the city is hardly great fun for a puppy."

"So, what's this about Germany?" Élise asked. "For how long? A few weeks?"

"Actually," he said, pausing to take in her reaction, "more like a few months."

"Months!" spouted Élise, catching herself sounding regrettably like a disgruntled spouse. Quickly, she tried to cover with a forced smile and a, "Wow, lucky you! Care to tell me all about it over a cup of coffee?" *There was always cappuccino to turn to when all else fell short.* Paul followed her to the kitchen with Argos in tow.

Seated at the table Paul recounted his meeting from the other day with Chuck Connelly. He admitted, he arrived that morning with a signed letter of resignation in his vest pocket. How could he go back out in the field like it was just another day after what happened to Dru? "I just can't do it anymore," he told his boss.

What he couldn't bring himself to tell Élise was that he needed to back off from her and the boys for a while. If he was honest, he cared about them way too much. Maybe, just maybe, if he had been there to back his long-time friend, Dru would be alive today. He couldn't shake the blame game rattling around in his head night and day. So, when Chuck proposed an alternative, an undercover case that would take him to Heidelberg, Germany, Paul's ears perked up. At the very least, it would buy time to re-evaluate his future.

"The fact you've got a law degree makes this case an easy fit," Chuck reasoned. "You'd be working undercover as an assistant law professor on campus at Der Staat University. They have an impressive, extensive exchange program for American law students in their criminal justice program."

"Well, wow!" Élise said, pretending to be thrilled with what appeared to be a great opportunity for him. Afterall, Paul owed her nothing; had zero obligation to her. She realized that. "It'll be wonderful," she smiled, holding up a plateful of Belle's homemade chocolate brownies.

"There's a lot of *stuff* going down over there. Bad stuff! Which is where I come in. Criminals everywhere!" he joked, walking to the stove to refill his cup. "Chuck told me to sleep on it. The case is mine for the asking but, if I take it, I'll be leaving Monday."

This week had been a plethora of emotions. Paul's leaving was yet another heaped on the mounding pile. The boys would be confused. First, their father is gone forever and, now, their best man-friend was about to leave them, too. Big worries for such little minds. Life was throwing curve balls right and left, stealing their innocence when they were just trying to be little boys.

"Katy and the boys should be back soon. Can you maybe stay for dinner?" she offered.

"Better yet, how about I take all of you out for dinner tonight? A sort of farewell party. What do you say?"

"Sure," Élise agreed, though *party* was not part of her vernacular these days. It would give Paul a chance to talk to the boys himself, and explain why he, too, had to leave. Why was it that her paranoid-self couldn't help but feel his rash decision somehow had to do with her?

40

OTHELLO

With divorce, there are no public announcements. The grim news simply filters furtively through the grapevine. No need to explain to others the *why, how, where, or when* of the untimely breakup; it's a private matter after all. Not so with the death of a loved one. For, in the midst of suffering, while your heart is splattered at your feet, you must dress up, show up, and present yourself to the world. Only after the ceremonies are complete, and your loved one is laid to rest, are you free to crumble in the comfort of your own home.

Élise was relieved to return to Lexford after what amounted to a grueling two weeks in Georgetown. Preparing the house for realtor viewing, and helping sort through Dru's personal effects, had left her with a gaping hole in her chest, and feeling inadequate to face yet another day. The trauma of divorce seemed trivial, if not wretchedly petty, compared to the grief of the here and now.

Dropping the mounds of luggage in the front hall, she watched as the boys scurried about the house, excited and inquisitive, as if they were newly moving in. Argos scampered happily underfoot as though he, too, understood he was home at last. A flood of messages had been left on her iPhone, along with a heap of sympathy cards now amassed on the hallway table. She would sort these out in the days ahead. Most surprising, over the next few days, were the many offerings from locals dropping by, tendering kind words, freshly baked cookies, and homegrown flowers and house plants. The very folks who never voiced a friendly *hello* since she and the boys moved in were now waving, and inviting her to morning coffee. Why is it that it should take something so dreadful as a death to bring out the best in people?

With the boys returning to school, life began to take on a sense of normalcy. There was laundry to wash, dinners to prepare, errands to run, and Jean-Jacques to tend to. Slowly, the days morphed into weeks, and weeks into months. In no time at all, Oliver and Will were propped up at the dining room table, surrounded by stacks of Valentine cards to be signed and addressed; one for each classmate. Normally, Élise would be baking heart-shaped cupcakes with colorful sprinkles in pretty ruffled party cups. But she didn't have it in her this year. She doubted Saint Patrick's Day would fare much better. Would these humdrum feelings never end?

Flinging open the endless span of windows in the front room conservatory on the first day of April, she took in a breath of the fresh morning scent of budding trees, rooting berries, and wildflowers clustered below. Springtime represented new life which, in itself, was enough to stir the glummest of souls into action. *Wallowing about in a funk was not helping anything or anyone*, she thought. Glancing at the upper corners of the immense room, she spotted an oversized black spider hard at work weaving an intricate system of connecting webs. He appeared to have a well-thought plan in place as he scaled the lofty ceiling. "Good grief!" she shrieked. Enough excuses! It was time she herself set to work. Armed with a long-handled dustmop and a can of bug spray, she began to scale the rickety wooden stepladder found hidden in the attic. From outside the open window, she could hear the laughter of her two older sons as they raced across the front lawn. They had certainly come to grips with their new life with nary a whimper. Perhaps, she should learn from them.

Oh my, she thought, looking down at the dire state of the grass below and its bare-faced dirt patches. She supposed it was in need of reseeding, fertilizing, or whatever it takes to make a lawn green and luscious. *Time to find a handyman...*

When the phone rang and she heard her brother Símone's voice saying he would like to pay a visit over Easter break, she literally jumped for joy. "Tell the boys I'm bringing fishing rods," he added. "Maybe teach my nephews how to hook a worm!" he joked. "And, your new puppy, Argos. He'll be okay with Augustus Too Short tagging along?"

"He'll be fine!" she assured him, actually more concerned with how her ill-humored member of the clan, a cat named

Othello, might handle the intrusion. Cats, she was learning, were extremely territorial. At least it was so with this robust feline.

"I thought you didn't like cats?" recollected her brother.

"I didn't... I don't!" Élise admitted. She was never a cat person...until the day she spotted a nest of baby mice hovering behind the washer in the basement. That very afternoon, she rounded up the boys, and headed to the pound. They chose a dark-faced, long-haired, Maine Coon cat who looked not entirely mean but was, irrefutably, not a lap cat. He turned out to be an avid hunter, taking care of the mouse invasion with little coaxing. So, here she was, a divorced *widow-of-sorts* with three kids, a dog, and a cat, living in her own country manor atop a hill. Something she would never have foreseen in her years as a high-profile Wall Street broker. If they could see me now, she admonished herself, glimpsing down at her scuffed-up running shoes and threadbare Yankees t-shirt.

Katy, who kept close contact with Élise, had stayed in D.C. to continue her studies, and moved in with neighbor Belle Stevenson, much to the chagrin of Rose O'Neil. "Why on earth would you want to live with a stranger?" the elder Mrs. O'Neil alleged accusingly. It was beyond trying to explain the *why* to her mother. It turned out to be the perfect arrangement, especially since Belle had been rattling about alone in her oversized, four-bedroom house ever since her husband was moved to the nursing home. She and her new young roommate kept each other company in a sweet, workable relationship that Rose O'Neil could only dream of.

Word from Paul Martin in Heidelberg came sparingly, if and when at all. A few hastily written lines here and there, scrawled on a postcard, which mystified Élise. *Had she overstepped the boundaries of their friendship one too many times?* "Apparently so!" she muttered to herself as she carted the hefty laundry basket up the cellar stairs. It was a huge adjustment not having Paul a phone call away. She guessed he'd had enough of her, of the boys, and of their unending quandaries. What else was there to think?

When Oliver and Will would ask, "When is Uncle Paul coming back?" she was at a loss for words. 'People come, people go' was on the tip of her tongue, but that hardly seemed a kind enough answer.

"Maybe he forgot about us," Will said, head down, sullen, in the manner of an abandoned Dickens street urchin.

"Of course not!" his mother was quick to assure him with a huge bear hug. "How could anyone ever forget either of you? I'm certain Uncle Paul is so busy chasing bad guys that he barely has time to tie his shoes!" That would fetch giggles long enough to divert their attention. "How about let's take Argos for a walk, shall we?" was always a healthy alternative. In fact, she was not certain of anything Paul was thinking. Damn him!

The boys were intrigued with their new-found friend, Jack Andrews, a local workman Élise hired to take on the countless home maintenance projects sprouting up around the old manor house. From a safe distance, they watched gleefully as he fertilized and reseeded the grass, swept out the chimneys, checked the furnace, and replaced roof shingles blown loose by winter winds. Jack was a treasure of information who came up with the name of a nearby housekeeper he knew of named Sarah Austin. "Give her a call," he said, jotting down her number on a scrap of pocket paper. "Tell her you're a friend of mine."

Within a week, Sarah was on-site, polishing wood floors, changing linen, and happily spending time with the boys whenever Élise had errands to run. Baby Jean-Jacques adored Sarah, who tirelessly read storybooks and sang nursery rhymes with him even as she worked. The sprightly, middle-aged woman would arrive with a tin filled with home-baked treats for the boys. Today, it was cookies in the shapes of trucks and cars, which set off an outburst of laughter. "Look mom, it's a pickup truck!" squealed Will.

Élise could be counted on to whip up a batch of peanut butter fudge from time to time, but never could she match the creativity of her new housekeeper. Sarah fit perfectly into their lively household, like a New England version of Belle, graciously answering every need with her distinctly patented Boston accent. "How come Sarah calls these caaaas?" Oliver wanted to know, holding up his cookie in the shape of a race car.

Jean-Jacques O'Neil was growing faster than Élise liked, acting less like her baby and more like a toddler as his first birthday approached. His hearty, infectious laughter made him sound as if he had just heard the funniest punch line. It was in these times her thoughts turned to Dru. This child, more than the others, reminded her daily of the senseless loss that had fallen upon them as a family. This precious little boy would always be her *fatherless child*. A sad thought in itself. Oliver and Will would have countless memories to draw on that Jean-Jacques never would. There were times she would overhear the two speaking of Dru as their little minds worked through their innocent grieving process. "Can he see us?" Will would ask.

"Don't be silly," Oliver would answer with authority. "He's dead!"

Instinctively, it was difficult to fight the need to intervene but Élise was learning that she could not shield them forever. At some level, they would have to sort it out between themselves. Children, she was discovering, were more resilient than we give them credit for. And so, today, for the first time in months, she was feeling cheerful, looking forward to a visit from Símone because, ready or not, life goes on.

41

HALLO, MEIN FREUND

Paul lay on his bed rereading Élise's letter for the umpteenth time.

Dear Paul, she wrote…
Hope all is going well for you on your new assignment. You know my only wish is for you to be happy, wherever that might lead. Just want you to know how much we appreciate all you've done for me and the boys over the past year and we will always think of you as our dear friend…
p.s. Oliver, Will and Jean-Jacques send their love.

"Scheisse!" he uttered, folding the letter, and shoving it to the back of his German dictionary on the adjacent bed stand. He had been in Heidelberg going on five months with little end in sight, which wasn't a bad thing. Life in a foreign land kept him finely honed as he crafted his way into the inner workings of this rare assignment he'd been handed. It was exactly what he needed, he convinced himself each morning as he set off to the campus of Der Staat University. For starters, it was different wearing a coat and tie to work, which was necessary for his undercover role posing as a visiting assistant law professor. "I always knew that law degree would come in handy one day," he droned.

It was almost disappointing to find how many students, and German citizens in general, spoke perfect English. He feared one day, sooner than anyone thought, the Germanic language could become extinct, as have others of ancient history. But, for now, he found it a kick to stumble his way through the native language, putting it to the test every chance he got, viewing it as yet another personal growth opportunity.

"Ein bier bitte," he confidently placed his order at the local tavern, only to have the server reply back in English.

"Will that be on tap, sir?"

"Ja, auf abruf." Paul was determined to stand his ground. "Ein menu auch," he added casually, without looking up. The server gently slipped a menu on the table with an all-English translation. It was like being in a linguistic duel with the barista, unlike in Paris where a simple "bonjour" conjured a polite, "Vous parlez très bien français, monsieur."

His first week in Germany, Paul found himself preregistered for a two-week total immersion language class. No English, no French, no Italian, only German, which forced one to think in German, key to learning any new language. "Guten morgen!" he would greet his fellow classmates as he arrived to take a seat at the rear of the room. The classroom was jam packed with young, zealous students, eager to gain their fair share of knowledge that might set them apart, if not above, their counterparts.

Three exceptions were himself and two other American undercover agents, each aware of the other, yet intentionally paying no heed to one another. From a distance, Paul recognized the lanky, boyish-looking man named Sean Hall slouched in his chair among the others, the picture of innocence. Nothing about him would suggest his true identity, that of a seasoned agent from the Nebraska ATF office. Housed in the no-frills dorm, his mission: to sleep, eat, and study like any other aspiring young scholar privileged enough to be part of this select international exchange program. Blond haired, freckled, with a gap between his two front teeth, he reminded Paul of Opie from the *Andy Griffin* show, except he was one of ATF's top snipers, known among his peers as Top Gun.

The third undercover agent was a female out of the New York office whose assignment was masquerading as a dorm mother, rotating floor to floor, with five other women who held similar positions. She was already comingling with her neighbors by the time Paul settled in, asking names, where they were from, and how many siblings they had back home. Some folks have the gift of making you feel you've known them for a lifetime. Against good reason, you find yourself confiding in them as if they were that childhood friend you regretted losing touch with decades ago. That was Cheryl Cookingham, which made her invaluable for what would be expected of her in the coming months.

"Lasst uns beginnen!" shouted the German professor, loud enough to be heard at the back of the hall. Everyone pulled out notebooks and pens, and faced to the front with an obedient hush, excited to delve into a new way of thinking and communicating for the next eight hours, and for the next fourteen days.

Der Staat University was not alone in its fear of terrorist infiltration, and rightly so. It's why Paul and his partners were here. College campuses around the world were feeding grounds for candidates worthy of malevolent indoctrination. Leaders of such groups ferreted out highly educated, socially adept young people, hunting their prey like the predators they were. When Paul was in law school, it was recruiters from high paying NYSE companies who scouted universities, competing for the brightest, most industrious students to join their celebrated firms. He was the first to admit times had changed. There was far more evil in the world on every level. "Damn shame!" he sputtered, conceding to his own rant.

His initial meeting with German authorities led him to believe they had already fingered Americans at the root of the university bedlam. Paul listened submissively, stifling alternative judgment until he could delve full force into the investigation himself. No disrespect, but he had his own theories, best kept to himself. But, this morning, squinting at the board from the back of the lecture hall, he turned his attention to the immediate order of the day: that of conjugating the verb 'to be' with Professor Steiglitz. Giving forth a rowdy, guttural wail, he heard himself bleat in chorus with the others: "ich bin...sie sind...wir sind."

It was a lame, white haired, elderly janitor on night duty who spotted a cache of wooden chests stored behind a heating unit in the basement of dorm B. At first glance, he took them to be a heap of trash covered by a loosely fitted tarp. Hobbling over for a closer look, he realized each chest had a padlock securely attached, except for one in the very back. Lifting the cobwebbed cover, he grabbed the wall, as he tottered, struggling for balance as he viewed its unsightly contents. A hoard of military-looking weapons and boxloads of ammunition stared up at him as if to say, *"What the hell you looking at old man?"* He lurched backward, allowing the lid to slam shut, and quickly staggered away. Mumbling his way up the stairs, dragging his lifeless left limb behind him, he headed straight for campus security.

German authorities engaged ATF upon discovering the caseloads of armor had originated in the U.S. Since the arrival of Paul Martin and his team, the stockpile of weapons had not been tampered with. It lay in waiting, surrounded by newly installed security cameras, soundless laser alarms, and an automatic advanced taser pulse system that would immobilize intruders. The highly trained agents, Hall, Martin, and Cookingham, had access to live coverage of the scene via iPhone with the push of a button anytime, night or day. *Someone clearly had a plan, but who?* Students, professors, office staff, department heads, visitors; all were suspect. As for Paul, he had a lifetime to outwait the culprits; one of the benefits of being a single guy with zero responsibilities. Worst-case scenario, he'd be speaking fluent German before returning to the states.

Paul and Sean had rifled through the armed contents uncountable times, opening each lock without detection. Diligently registering any and all markings over the span of weeks, in the dead of night, the two men appraised each metal chest as if it contained the original crown jewels. Ensconced in the stench of the mildewed basement, they sorted through the array of weaponry, selectively itemizing those to be shipped to labs in the states. Latest evidence traced the bulk of handguns to a troublesome, violent gang residing in upstate New York. Paul was convinced this international case could, on any given day, erupt into a fatal, explosive front-page storyline. "Christ, somebody make a move!" he pleaded to the moonlit sky.

Cheryl Cookingham's detailed reports provided home office key information, particularly as she zeroed in on three dorm residents with connections to Albany, New York. Privy to ongoing late-night conversations, as she laughed and joked amongst the scholars, she would return to search their vacant rooms the following day, dusting for fingerprints, and photographing anything unusual. Paperwork, journals, and personal correspondence lay about on unmade beds, in piles on cluttered floors, and strewn across study desks. With a modest amount of imagination, she had uncovered a mass of evidence, enough to keep the folks back home in the labs busy well past their eight-hour day.

Tuesday evening found her videotaping an unusual meeting at a local pub between these same three law students and four local men. Coming across a discarded, scribbled note in the dorm bathroom waste bin, she logged the time and place for what the three students, two males and one female, referred to as a 'meet-up.' In attendance was a criminal justice professor who Agent Paul Martin had called out in his reports as "deceitful and suspect." Huddled in a corner booth of the dark, dismal pub, Cheryl nursed a chilled nonalcoholic barley malt beer, shielding herself behind the pages of a *National Geographic* magazine, her NY Mets baseball cap pulled low.

She watched as diagrams, maps, and lists were passed surreptitiously around the table by a grim fellow attendee in a tattered skull cap. One never knows what one is viewing but it didn't appear to be the planning of a day at the beach. The professor appeared to be in charge as he leaned forward to speak in hushed, inaudible tones. Cheryl called on her long ago acquired lip reading skills only to find her German less than proficient to understand a single word. "Damn!" she heard herself sputter. Each of the American students around the table appeared to fully understand the dialogue, nodding agreement as they listened, posing questions in fluent German. The four local men seemed unusually comfortable with the others, as if this was not their first tryst.

Agent Cookingham trailed the group to the parking lot as the bartender was announcing his final round. She captured photos of the three separate license plates as each vehicle headed its separate way. With the time difference in the states, she realized she could still get off a full report to D.C. tonight. Within the hour, her superiors would be probing the detailed written account, surveying the tapes, and giving feedback on how to proceed.

"Good work, Cookingham!" flashed across the screen from D.C. as she toweled off from her nightly shower, and flung herself on the bed. She crunched into an apple left over from lunch. That was dinner. No wonder she was losing weight. She sent off two short texts to her partners that read: *Meet me at 0300 hours behind the library*. Fully exhausted, she slid beneath the coverlet, and shut down the light.

42

BOOK CLUB

Élise had no idea it was so late. The ladies would be arriving any minute and her hair was still damp and snarled. "Oh, well," she frowned at the frenzied image leering back at her from the armoire mirror. Her mother, Jacqueline Saint-Cyr, would have spent the morning having her hair touched up, and acrylic nails French-manicured before presenting *herself* at an afternoon book club. These days, there was hardly enough time for Élise to fret over appearances. A sleeked-back pony tail had become her hairdo of choice. Yet another reason for her mother to be horrified.

After Dru's death, Élise could barely keep up with the onslaught of what she categorized as *sympathy invites* as the community reached out to the newly-widowed young mother. Often, she would head to Luke's grocery store at odd hours simply to avoid running into well-wishers wanting to stop and chat at great length. Gone were the days of dashing in and out, grabbing needed items, and being on her way. Just last Wednesday, she found herself backing out of the dairy section when she spotted chatterbox Lilly Ryan hovering over a tub of low-fat cottage cheese. Though there was not a drop of milk at home, she'd have to come back later.

Admittedly, there were many people in town Élise would like to come to know better. One such person was the town librarian, Elizabeth Frost. It was over a cup of coffee with Elizabeth that the idea of a 'Shakespeare and Thee' group came to be. "Perhaps it's time I reacquaint myself with serious literature," she confided to her newest coffee companion, not entirely sure if the two were friends yet. This was New England after all. "There was a time I could recite passages from most every Shakespearean play, from *Romeo and Juliet* to *Henry V*. Heck, I named my second child after the Bard of Avon and my cat is named Othello!" The librarian laughed aloud as she reached for a second lump of sugar.

"You know," Elizabeth said, setting down her coffee cup, "I've often thought it would be wonderful to organize a Shakespearean book club here in Lexford. I'd be the first to sign up! Would you ever consider leading such a group?"

"Ummm…" Élise stuttered through the next few sentences, ending with, "I guess I could." Next thing she knew, she was offering to hold the first meeting in her newly furnished, glass-encased conservatory. When fifteen people signed up the very first week, she couldn't help but wonder, "What have I gotten myself into?" Assuming many might be more interested in scouting out the Sullivan House rather than what Shakespeare had to say, she predicted most would drop out after their first go-round.

As it turned out, Hazel Bloom, the notorious town gossip, hoped it was okay that her college-age niece came along. "She's going to be an English teacher," she boasted, while Marge Maitland, the waitress from Leo's Place, arrived with her newly purchased *Complete Works of Shakespeare* tucked in the crook of her arm. Two of Will's elementary school teachers drove together, and brought three friends. And, the doctor's wife was accompanied by two married daughters and a sister-in-law. It was crazy!

"I thought we would begin with a favorite, *The Merchant of Venice*," Élise announced with authority, while inviting everyone to take a seat. Some of the ladies were familiar with the Venetian play, and its characters and its plot, while others, admittedly, were pure novices. It didn't seem to matter. They all joined in, posing questions, comments, opinions, and views, making for a surprisingly stimulating hour and a half.

Elizabeth Frost took on the role of Shylock, the troubled moneylender, delivering his nefarious lines as if it were she herself demanding the pound of flesh owed! Will's teacher, Beth Flynn, took to the front of the room, delighting the group with a flawless read of the notorious lines of the wealthy, wise, and witty heroine, Portia. No stranger to literature, Miss Flynn proceeded to set up the pivotal trial scene in which Portia would shamelessly derail Shylock's evil plea. "Tarry a little; there is something else!" she cried out, pointing adamantly to the written law. "This bond doth give thee here no jot of blood."

"Bravo!" wailed the ladies in a rousing round of applause as Beth delivered the closing verdict in which Shylock is led away, humiliated, insolvent, and adrift.

"Oh, my goodness," remarked Marge Maitland to Laura Webber, her neighbor lady. "Who'd have thought we'd be studying Shakespeare?"

Élise was dumbfounded by the enthusiasm of the attendees as they gathered their belongings; extending smiles, hugs going round, thanking her a million times for playing host. "*King Lear* next month!" she announced, handing out an introductory synopsis as they filed their way to the front room exit.

"Who plays piano?" asked Mrs. Petricone, eyeing the magnificent Steinway in the middle of the grand room.

"My son Oliver and I have both started taking piano lessons," smiled Élise. "Chopin I'm not. It's just something I've always wanted to do. It was my grandfather's piano. He played beautifully," she added.

"How wonderful," the older woman glowed as she ran her fingers across the ebony keys. "I wish I had done that in my younger days. It's a little late for me now."

"It's never too late," Élise offered kindly. "I'll give you the name of our teacher if you're interested." Mrs. Petricone's face lit up as though she'd just won the door prize rather than been handed a simple word of encouragement; perhaps they were one and the same.

It was after three o'clock when Sarah Austin pulled in the drive with the three O'Neil boys. "What would I do without you?" gushed Élise to her devoted housekeeper. Sarah had become indispensable, especially since the former Wall Street broker had taken on teaching an economics class two evenings a week at the local campus; an extension of Boston College.

The kind-hearted Sarah couldn't have been more thrilled to find Élise had set up a room just for her off the hallway on the third floor. Often, she would stay the night rather than drive cross town after dark, and eventually took to adding personal items brought from home: a reading lamp, framed photos, and a favorite chair. The boys understood this room was off limits. "That's Sarah's private space," their mother would remind them.

"Do you ever have a bad day, Sarah?" asked Élise one afternoon as the two women worked side by side peeling apples for pies.

"Not really," was the woman's reply. "I'm so grateful for all I have."

The simple response caused Élise to set down her knife in the midst of coring an apple. She was well aware her housekeeper's life had been what many might describe as tragic. There had been an alcoholic, abusive husband in her past, and far too many miscarriages. Believing he would change, and desperate to have a child, she had tolerated the cruelty until the day two broken ribs and a concussion landed her in the emergency room. It was her married, sister, Ruth Cameron, who convinced Sarah to leave the miserable brute.

Ruth had shared the painful story with Élise one afternoon over tea when Sarah was off to the laundromat. "My husband and I were happy to take her in. She's been with us ever since," Ruth's face furrowed, as though it were she whose heart had been broken all those years ago.

Yet, looking at Sarah, this gentle soul now sitting across the table sifting flour, you would think she hadn't a care in the world. Never once had she uttered, "Why me?" Élise had much to learn from her dear friend. For anyone keeping score, Sarah was far in the lead when it came to overcoming misfortune, and putting past hurts aside.

Perched in his corner highchair, smug and content, Jean-Jacques squealed as he munched noisily on a plateful of apple peels. His days were spent waddling about, holding on to chairs and tables, falling down, bumping his head and getting back up, and throwing a tantrum when things didn't go quite his way. All to be expected in the life of a hearty, willful baby boy.

As the backdoor slammed shut, two rowdy rioters, Will and Oliver, came bustling through the kitchen, waving a handful of newly delivered mail: catalogs, advertisements, and a letter-sized envelope postmarked Paris, France, addressed to *Élise Saint-Cyr and family*.

"Let's see that!" Élise said, wiping her hands on her spattered apron.

"We know someone in Paris, France?" Oliver asked, as the two boys clamored for a prime spot on the kitchen bench, eyes glued to the envelope as if it were the deed to their inheritance.

"45 Rue Cherche Midi," their mother read the return address, equally curious. "I don't think we know anyone in Paris," she stammered, confused.

"Open it! Open it!" shouted the boys, twitching in their seats. Jean-Jacques was clapping and jabbering, adding to the family revelry. Even Argos crawled out from under the table, standing tall and alert, his head cocked to one side, licking his tongue as if the letter might contain good news for him. Slicing open the envelope with a bread knife, Élise immediately recognized the scrawled, hurried handwriting:

Hey guys!
Finished up our case at Der Staat University, Germany last week. Taking a week's break before returning to the states. A friend, one of the agents on the case, Cheryl Cookingham, offered an invite to show me around Paris which I couldn't refuse!

Hope all is well.
Love, Paul

43

COMING HOME

Chuck Connelly welcomed the three ATF agents, Paul Martin, Cheryl Cookingham, and Sean Hall into his office with such gusto one would have thought they had been marooned at sea these nearly six months. "It's a long time to be out on assignment, especially out of the country," he spouted, acknowledging the astonishing role each had played in unraveling and thwarting the plans of terror targeted upon Der Staat University just weeks ago.

"Hardly recognized you, Agent Martin, with that beard," joked the supervisor, giving his employee a hearty welcome home handshake, and escorting the three into his office. "Great job guys…and gal!" he added, with an apologetic wink to Cheryl Cookingham.

"No worries, sir," she laughed, while pulling up a chair next to Sean Hall. "I'm proud to be part of the brotherhood.

Comes from being raised in a family with four brothers." The supervisor could see the young woman was no prima donna as she sat herself down with conviction and assurance.

"And, how about you, Agent Hall?" Chuck asked, turning to the boyish-looking man who smiled back sheepishly. "I hear you're quite the marksman. Top Gun, isn't that what they call you?"

"Not sure about that, sir," he replied. "I did shoot my first rabbit by the age of five, I can tell you that." They all laughed, acknowledging that guns and rabbits were a way of life for many a young boy from Nebraska. "The difference is, now I aim for much larger prey," he added, settling back into his leather seat.

"And, far more dangerous," the supervisor replied. "Well, you all did a great job. Not everyone would be up to taking on such a lengthy and critical assignment away from family and friends. So, again, thank you."

"Well, we're all single," Paul added, trying to make light of it. "It's not like someone was sobbing in their pillow every night while we were gone." The two others agreed with a knowing nod.

"True that!" chirped Cheryl.

Homecoming niceties aside, Chuck Connelly rose to close the office door and the conversation turned serious. Step by step, the three agents depicted, first hand, the long-drawn-out events leading up to the arrest and conviction of the nefarious group who had infiltrated the campus of Der Staat University. Six students, two law professors, and four primary locals were all charged, and currently awaiting trial. It took months for the miscreants, working with larger, more practiced terror cells, to build a concealed arsenal of firearms in the dorm basement. Their plan was to *take out* an entire dorm of international law students in the blink of an eye as they slept in their beds in the dead of night.

The hardest part was the waiting, they all agreed. "We watched the stockpile sit, undisturbed, like a tsunami you knew was heading your way. It was simply a matter of time for the word to be given: Destroy, maim, kill!"

"Let me tell you about these two," Paul said, pointing to his partners. Agent Cookingham here, she hovered over the students like a troubled mother, surveying every action, questioning every word. Hell, she read their letters from home, and searched their sock drawers. Nothing was sacred under her watch. And, as for Sean, well, you've never seen a guy with more knowledge and skill of every make and model of firearm known to mankind. It's all in the reports. I'm sure you've read it all," he said, eyes directed at Chuck Connelly. "And, our lab guys here in the States, they were phenomenal, making themselves available day and night. Believe me, it was a team effort. In no way was it all about us."

Humble as they were, Connelly knew his people had performed their ultimate best. Even German authorities had given ATF a glowing send off as they led the guilty parties away into custody. "I hate to say this," said Paul, somewhat hesitantly, "but German authorities were none too helpful through this whole process, glowing report be damned!" Both Agent Cunningham and Agent Hall jumped in to agree.

"Once we arrived," stated Hall, "the Germans, for all their fawning, practically walked away. Tired of the waiting, they said they had more pressing concerns. It would have been one hell of a massacre if we hadn't hung tough. It was Paul who remained calm and cool, start to finish. I can't tell you how much I learned working this case with him."

The three agents were excited to finally make their way downstairs to the second floor to meet up with the D.C. lab staff. It was the technicians who ultimately matched the armed shells to a case in upstate New York that proved to be the beginning of the end for the crazed villains. Chuck watched as the men and women greeted each other as if it were one giant love-fest; everyone handing kudos to one another, none taking glory for themselves. The Resident Agent in Charge couldn't imagine being prouder of his agency, of his team, and of his people. For Chuck Connelly, it was a moment he'd remember for years to come.

Sean had an evening flight to catch after a whirlwind walkabout through downtown D.C., ending in a celebratory dinner at a high-end well-known restaurant. "Order like it's your last supper," Chuck said. "Dinner's on me!" The supervisor had reserved a window seat for his prized guests with a view of the White House.

"Would you look at that!" awed Agent Hall, as he flashed his Nebraska boyish grin. "What a sight!"

"Too bad you're heading home so soon, Sean," Cheryl elbowed him kiddingly. "Bad planning right there!" She was staying on a day or two in D.C. since Paul had offered up a room at his place.

The three had created a great working bond in their six months abroad. It wasn't as easy as it seemed to be returning home, Paul realized. Somehow, he was grateful to have Cheryl stick around to ease the stark reality he knew was coming. It had done him the world of good to be away. He worried about returning to everyday life, the muddled one he had left behind. "Who will I speak German with?" he gestured, bragging on his fluency as if he'd earned the Nobel Prize. "What good will it do me now? Chuck here, he doesn't speak a lick of German," he added, all in good fun.

"Afraid I can't help you there," admitted his boss, buttering a steamy, warm slice of herbal bread.

"Rufen Sie mich an," said Sean. "I'm always up for a chat in German."

Cheryl would have no part of it. "Don't call me!" she joked. "French will always be my second language." With that, she thrust her nose dramatically in the air.

Over rack of lamb, dover sole, and lobster salad, the party of four sat back, enjoying the live piano music softly playing in the background. The agents reminisced about their final week together, camped in Paris in a fourth-floor walkup apartment in the 6th arrondissement. "It was tight quarters, but we made do," said Cheryl, with a jovial smile. The five hundred square foot *pied-a-terre* on rue Cherche Midi, within walking distance to Jardin des Luxembourg and Le Bon Marché, belonged to her Parisian born mother…"who, fortunately for us, happened to be out of town," she added.

"How gracious of your mother!" Chuck added as he leisurely sipped his Courvoisier.

"My mother, Adeline, is one hundred eighty degrees opposite of me," the young woman admitted. "After four boys, she was over the moon to have a baby girl. But, as you can see, I'm no Barbie doll. I may just be her greatest disappointment."

Awkward!

Paul wiped his chin excessively with his white linen table napkin while Sean slurped his Mocha Coffee, and Chuck gingerly brushed bread crumbs to the side from beneath his dinner plate. None had a response. Each supposed it was the drink rather than their dinner companion talking. They let her continue without interruption.

"I might as well have been another boy but that's a long, drawn-out tale," she said as she finished off the remnants of her third glass of white wine. "We have nothing in common," she added. "She's into opera, ballet, and fashion week. I'm into football. When I enlisted in the army straight out of college, well, that was like the kiss of death for Adeline. C'est la vie!" she quipped, in an uncomfortable attempt to summarize her heartache.

Working through a mouthful of *Apple Tarte Tatin*, Paul nodded sympathetically to Cheryl's regrettable mother issues along with the others. His mind quickly flashed on the difficult relationship between Élise and her mother, Jacqueline Saint-Cyr. "You're not alone Cheryl. Mothers and daughters are not always like-minded. Sad, but true." He hoped he didn't sound too pompous. She's probably heard it all before from her four brothers, if not from her father, he supposed. Come to think of it, he had never heard mention of a father and Paul wasn't about to go there now.

As Chuck tallied up the check, and the server cleared the table, Paul's mind was lost on *when* and *how* he would contact Élise, if she's even still talking to me. He'd have to take things as they came. For tonight, he would see Sean off to the airport, then work on sobering up his overnight guest so they could 'do the town' as promised.

"Thank you, Mr. Connelly," Sean gushed, extending a hand of gratitude. "Great dinner! Pleasure meeting you, and feel free to call on me anytime if I can ever be of help."

"Same here, Top Gun!" replied Chuck. "And, we'll see you in the office next Monday, right Paul?" Chuck confirmed.

"Yes sir. I'll need a week off to get back on track," he said, glancing about the room in search of any familiar faces. It was strange to hear English being spoken as people dined and mingled. Washington D.C. was feeling more foreign to him than Heidelberg ever did.

"Ms. Cookingham, come back to see us anytime," Chuck offered graciously, walking side by side with her toward the exit door. "And, by the way," he added, "I'd be proud to have you for a daughter."

44

DOGGIE BITS

Hannah Connelly grabbed a hot cup of coffee and her phone, and dialed up Élise. It had been much too long since they had chatted. She hated having to begin a conversation with an apology but, "Oh my God, I am so sorry," she huffed. "Time just got away from me. You doing, okay?"

"Oh my gosh, Hannah, no need to apologize! It's forever crazy on this end, too. And, now with the boys on summer break, it's about to get even crazier," she laughed. "So, how are you?"

Hannah ran through the latest updates among their mutual women friends, and family news, and how desperately she wished Élise was nearby to help with her on-going redecorating projects.

"And Chuck, working hard as ever?" Élise asked, knowing full well the answer before it left her mouth. Chuck

Connelly's every waking hour revolved around his work, his agents, and his ongoing cases. Roosters would lay eggs before that would change.

"You know it!" replied her friend, with a sigh of submission. "Just yesterday, he welcomed Paul Martin home from his six-month assignment in Germany. Seems they finally wrapped up a monster case over there. Chuck has been strutting around puffed up, prouder than a first-time dad! Yet another feather in ATF's hat. He said Paul is looking rather debonair and dashing, sporting a well-manicured beard."

"Oh, nice," said Élise in the most casual voice she could muster. *So, Paul was back. Who gives a damn?*

Hannah glanced out the front window just in time to see three neighborhood children trampling through her newly planted azaleas. "Oh, no!" she cried.

"What?" shouted Élise, alarmed.

"Lord's sake, my flower beds just got stomped on by the little darlings who just moved in next door," Hannah groaned. It wasn't the first time they had tried her patience.

"Oh, boy," she sighed. "Anyway, where were we? Oh yea, Paul's beard."

Élise didn't care to hear about Paul, or his beard, but she listened politely as Hannah described Chuck's celebratory dinner from start to finish. "Actually, all three ATF agents who worked the case at Der Staat University were there. Along with Paul was a young agent from Nebraska, a sharpshooter of sorts, and a woman agent from the New York office. Chuck raved on-and-on *ad nauseam* about all three. I've never seen him more impressed."

Hannah paused, awaiting a reply that never came, which seemed odd considering her long-time friend was ordinarily full of inquiries.

"Sounds like a grand evening," replied Élise, envisioning the woman agent to be witty, poised, and probably beautiful to boot. This same woman agent Paul mentioned in his quickly drafted postcard. The one he stayed with in Paris; the one he said, *"he just couldn't refuse."*

Élise had heard enough!

"Hey Hannah, I'm really sorry but I'm going to have to cut out on you. I've got my own *little darlings* in the other room hooting and howling, having way too much fun, which is always suspect. But, listen, I'm glad you called," she ended with an ounce of good cheer. "Let's talk again soon."

"Debonair and dashing, my foot!" she stammered, quick to disconnect the line. Élise rarely had a moment to spare these days while Hannah's days were filled with nail appointments, charity luncheons, and hot river stone massages. Clearly, talk of play dates, tumble classes or lunch at Pizza Town were off the table. Élise, feeling a little more than envious, wondered if she and Hannah had *anything* in common anymore. Yesterday, the weary mother of three had carpooled six kids to the local bouncy house and, on Monday, attended a birthday party for four-year olds. Summer schedules didn't bring out the best in her, she supposed, as she hurdled a mound of toppled wooden blocks. Rounding the corner, she came to an abrupt stop long enough to belch an ungodly screech that echoed off the wooden beamed ceiling!

"What on earth! What is going on here?"

Argos stood motionless amongst an upturned bowl of doggie bits scattered from one side of the kitchen to the other. Oliver and Will were laughing hysterically, stomping each kernel into the stone floor with the heels of their cowboy boots.

"Boys, stop that!" the overwrought mother hollered, clenching her fists to catch a second breath. "I'm so-o-o angry right now!"

The boys stared back, big-eyed, like two frightened rabbits caught in a hunting trap. The plan for a leisurely family day at the town lake just went up in smoke. Instead, the enraged mother ordered her two hooligans, "Get the broom and dustpan, and clean up this mess!" Argos made his way to the corner, avoiding eye contact, shamelessly hoping to pass himself off as an innocent bystander. "And, you too!" Élise scolded, fingering his sniffling nose as he scurried from the room, head down, tail between his legs, in search of a safe space.

"What about our swim?" pleaded Will.

"Not happening!" said his mom.

After Dru's death, Élise knew she had been way too lenient with all three boys. Life was tough without a dad, undeniably, but it was time to set new rules! She sent the juvenile offenders off to their rooms, watching as they trudged solemnly up the stairs.

"Mom is mean," mumbled Oliver.

"What was that?" demanded his mother, sounding every bit a wicked shrew.

"Nothing," replied the eldest son, as though he'd been sentenced to death row.

Sarah Austin arrived shortly afterward with baby Jean-Jacques tethered to her hip, and a multitude of grocery sacks dangling dangerously from either arm. "Mama!" called out the young boy, running to throw his chubby arms around his mother's leg. Élise hugged the little guy, ruffling his dark crop of hair with her long fingertips.

"Mighty quiet in here," Sarah couldn't help notice. "Where is everyone?" she wondered aloud, having noted Argos uncharacteristically hunched in the corner of the mudroom next to Othello. That was strange in itself since the two were openly at odds with one another; one might say hostile. The cat grimaced, while Argos slumped apologetically, eyes down, chin resting on his extended paws as if he'd been told he had only days to live.

"The boys got into a bit of mischief while you were out," explained Élise, without looking up, as the pots and pans clattered loudly and the cabinet door slammed itself shut.

"You, okay?" asked the observant helper, sensing something awry.

"Of course. Why do you ask?" replied Élise.

Sarah had been around long enough to know when to leave things unsaid, and simply go about business as usual. "Would you like me to pack a small picnic for you and the boys to take to the lake for your afternoon outing?"

"We won't be going," was the curt response. *No explanation.* "But, if you could put the baby down for his nap, that would be a great help," she replied. "I'll go ahead and get these groceries put away," she continued, having already emptied half the bags of goods. "Thank you, Sarah," she offered, absent her usual warm smile.

"Of course," said her housekeeper, whisking Jean-Jacques into her arms with a gentle squeeze. "It's story time for me and my special boy!" she said with a toothy grin, hoisting the diaper bag over her shoulder, and hauling her small charge from the room.

Élise hated everything about herself at times like these. Exploding like that with the boys, and giving short shrift to Sarah, the most obliging woman in the world, and cutting Hannah off so brusquely? *Who is this horrible person I've become?* It wasn't like her sons had set fire to the house, or worse. It was a damn bowlful of doggie treats and two little boys being boys.

Dropping her full weight into the wooden rocker, heavy-hearted as a wrecking ball, eyes burning, she fought the crushing need to sob. From the corner of her eye, she caught sight of Argos edging his way toward the doorway. He halted as if out of respect, motionless as a palace guard, until he got the nod to approach, and lay his chin atop his master's foot. "Sorry, ole boy," she wept.

"Be glad you're a dog," she uttered, stroking the soft, furry head. "Life is so much simpler for you canines." He looked up, tail wagging, happy to be back in her good graces. A soft guttural growl emerged instinctively as he spotted Othello out the side window, strutting across the driveway like a pompous emissary. If only humans had doggie doors, thought Élise. They too could escape unseen. Argos leaned heavily against her thigh as if wishing himself a lap-sized kitten instead of a thirty-five-pound pup.

I guess Dru knew me better than I knew myself, she thought, realizing her husband had left behind such a loving gift; this perfect dog she had wanted no part of. For it was Argos who had pulled her through so many a sleepless night. Shadowing her down the stairs in the darkness, he would snuggle up to the hemline of her nightdress as, together, they would stare out the window at the moon, awaiting the rising sun. Corny as it sounds, it was true what they say about man's best friend. When family, husbands, or friends leave you, willingly or not, the dog remains ever loyal, ever true.

"So, Argos, you heard about our friend Paul taking up with another woman?" she spoke softly to the growing pup. "It's not as if we were a couple, you know? So, why do I feel cheated on?"

Argos looked up, wanting to understand. He knew today's outrage was never about spilled doggie bits. The hurt went far deeper than the antics of himself and his two accomplices. He sighed, feeling he wasn't being much help, but he would stay here as long as it took. He had nothing but time.

Suddenly, Élise unfurled herself, standing tall, looking down at his sweet face, and announced, "Come on boy. We've got work to do." Argos answered in silence as dogs so often do, following her closely up the winding stairwell to the second landing, to offer apologies to two little boys who were feeling awfully bad about themselves. She would still have Sarah and Hannah to make amends with…all in good time.

45

AIMI

Rose O'Neil shuffled her way to the front door to collect the noon hour mail, as she did every day, as if expecting good news to fall through the mail-slot amidst the arsenal of useless advertisements. With a beefy grunt, she retrieved the handful of leaflets and flyers, and fumbled her way to her corner chair to give each piece a shrug and a passing glance. "Heavens!" she said, lifting a tattered, oversized manila envelope from the pile. Its cover was smeared with a ghastly layer of grime. Tugging at her glasses, which hung from a pearl chain necklace, she fiddled with them till they sat firmly over the bridge of her nose. "What have we got here?" she muttered, swiping clean the face of the parcel with her handkerchief.

"Oh, Lord, have mercy! Patrick, Patrick!" her shrieks echoed through the three-story homestead, causing a neighbor to pause and glare as he passed by the open window.

Patrick came running from the downstairs basement where he'd been replacing the weathered felt cover on the aged family pool table. "Calm down, Rose. Calm down!" he hollered, hastening to catch his breath, and settle his wife down from yet another of her imagined life-threatening events. He sighed in relief to see her sitting in the living room with no signs of an intruder holding her at gun point or the ceiling ablaze. "What on earth is going on?"

Without a word she handed him the envelope, while fanning herself heatedly with a mangled supermarket flyer featuring a bonanza sale on chicken breasts. *Buy one, get one free.*

"This is what all the shouting is about?" Patrick posed the question, holding the harmless looking envelope up to the light. "God sakes, Rosie, I thought someone was being murdered," he said, squinting as he flipped the mailing back to front, front to back. "Let's see now..." The old man paused a second, clenching his stern chin solemnly as he took in the handwritten address emblazoned in bold, black marker. It read *ATTN: AGENT DRU O'NEIL*

"It's addressed to Dru." He offered his trembling wife his hand, and led the way in his usual commonsense manner to the dining room table. "Come on. We'll open it together." Rose hesitated before falling into step beside him. It had been seven months since losing their son. She could not speak of

Dru without shriveling, wilting like a neglected potted plant that had lost all purpose.

"It's postmarked Tokyo, Japan," Patrick announced, as if submitting hard core evidence. Dru had spent his four-year tour of duty as a U.S. Marine in Tokyo, assigned to the American Embassy. "Well, your guess is as good as mine, so let's get on with it," he said with a shrug.

Rose slumped into the padded dining room chair, kneading her arthritic hands, fighting the too-often tears that escaped silently, her cheeks wet with grief as though she had received the horrific news only hours ago. *Your son is dead.* No mother should ever face such loss. The long-time married couple grieved together, but also each on their own terms. As patriarch of the family, Patrick had pushed on. That's what soldiers do. Thankful for the many blessings life provided, life goes on. He owed that much to himself. To his family.

"Ah, here we go!" he muttered, as he bore into the triple layer of mailing tape. A smaller envelope dropped from the bubble wrap onto the table. Both husband and wife stared at it a moment before Patrick reached out to claim it. He unfolded the two-page handwritten letter, and began to read silently, his face growing ashen with the turn of each page.

"Well?" sputtered his wife, awaiting what she could only imagine to be dreadful news.

"Perhaps you should read it yourself," he offered, handing the first page over before she could refuse, allowing the grief-stricken mother no choice.

Dear Dru O'Neil,

It has been many years since your appointment to the U.S. Embassy here in Tokyo in your service as a United States Marine. Our daughter, Hana Shinsato, was contracted to the same embassy at that time as a translator. We remember when you both met and we welcomed you to our home. It was a happy time.

It is now with great sorrow that we find we must write to inform you of our daughter Hana's recent passing from complications resulting from heart surgery. In her final days she made us promise we would contact you if she should not survive. She told us she had corresponded with you after your return to the United States. She said you had gone on to become a federal agent. The last address she had for you was this one. She believed it was that of your parents.

With her passing we now find we must inform you that you have a daughter. Hana never wanted you to know, nor wanted you to think you had any responsibility to her or the child. But now, it is different, you see.

Enraged as she scanned each line, Rose threw the letter to the table. "Pure rubbish! Dru would not have gotten himself involved with…!" she hollered, her face flushed, wretched with disbelief, doubting truth to any such accusations. Struggling to stand, she grasped the tall high-backed chair for support, unwilling to pay heed to *this ridiculous nonsense*. "Will this nightmare never end!" she cried; her feeble plea more desperate than that of a non-survivor at the moment the ship's nose began to sink into the sea.

Patrick rose, grasping his wife's arm gently. "I won't let you walk away. You need to face this along with me. We're in this together, remember?" He settled her back into her seat, directly across from his and, after giving it a moment, he asked, "Ready?"

He waited for Rose's half-hearted nod and resumed to read the letter. This time aloud…

> *Hana's final words to us were to reach out to you, Agent Dru O'Neil, hoping you will embrace your daughter. The child, Aimi, is now fourteen years old. We are older folks, with little understanding of raising a young girl. Our wish is you will step forward and acknowledge this unexpected news from afar.*
>
> *We anxiously await your reply.*
> *God bless you.*
> *Mr. and Mrs. Niko Shinsato*
> *Tokyo, Japan*

Rose went silent in her predictable reaction to life's happenings. Stretching across the table, Patrick hesitated before handing his wife a school type photo of a beautiful young Asian girl with the name *Aimi Shinsato* written below.

Rising and staggering dumbfounded from the room, Rose looked back over her gloom-ridden shoulders and mumbled, "Call Katy. She'll know what to do."

46

SUMMONS

Élise O'Neil stuffed a little black dress into her overnight bag *just in case* before closing it shut. "There!" she stammered, towing the roller bag behind her down the long flight of stairs. This was going to be a quick turn-about trip to D.C.

"You sure you're up for this?" she asked, glancing at Sarah, who happily continued to flip French toast from the griddle onto a row of Mickey Mouse breakfast plates.

"Of course!" the much-appreciated live-in housekeeper answered, placing each dish on the table in front of the three newly awakened O'Neil boys. Yawning, and rubbing sleep from half-opened eyes, the three resembled a trio of ducklings whose feathers had been boorishly rustled. Sarah passed around warm morning hugs along with each silver fork. The scent of Vermont maple syrup and melted butter filled the kitchen with a sense of comfort in the way Élise imagined home ought to be.

"Mmmmm…smells delicious! What would we do without you, my lovely Sarah?" the grateful mother gushed as she leaned over to give her friend a warm morning embrace. Turning to her three pajama-clad off-spring, she quietly explained, "Mommy will be back late tomorrow night. I need you to promise you'll all help Sarah by being the very best you can be."

Wrapping her pinky finger around each of theirs, one by one, they nodded, "I promise."

"Bless her heart. Right on time!" said Sarah with a wave out the kitchen window as her sister pulled into the circular drive in her little red Honda.

Ruth Cameron had become as much a part of the family as her sister Sarah; the two always willing at a moment's notice to come to the rescue. An orthopedic pillow tucked beneath her arm, and duffle bag slung over her left shoulder, she burst through the door with a cheerful, "Good morning, everyone!"

"Looks like someone's ready for a slumber party," Sarah said laughingly as the giggling boys wiped their sticky chins on the length of pajama sleeves rather than the napkins at hand.

"And, look, I've brought popcorn for tonight!" Ruth said with an air of self-importance, holding up a giant-sized bag that brought Argos crawling out from beneath the wooden table with nose atwitter like a trained hound dog.

"Miss Sarah says we're going on a picnic, and then fishing at the lake," shouted Oliver, as much to put his mom at ease, as to assure his younger brothers he was okay with their mom's unexpected travel plans. Amazing how the oldest child instinctively steps up to the plate without an inkling as to why. His mother smiled, silently lamenting that her firstborn's innocence may too often be at stake. Yet another guilt trip to add to her list.

The taxi beeped its horn as Élise scurried about the table, passing out good-bye kisses and *be goods*. "Love you!" she hollered over her shoulder as the back door slammed shut and the sound of roller wheels echoed down the gravel drive. It was never easy leaving the boys, especially overnight, even if left in the best of hands. But, today, the wearied mother assured herself, she had no choice.

When Katy called last evening to say, "I can only tell you I really need your help. Is there *any way* you can come to D.C.?"

Élise had answered in her most comforting voice, "Let me see what I can do," while her brain was screaming, '*What the hell*?'

Her young sister-in-law would never ask for help unless something was outlandishly wrong. "It's not something I can discuss over the phone," Katy clarified apologetically.

Minds run wild, and completely skid off the rails at times like these when one only imagines the absolute worst. She's pregnant, thought Élise…or terminally ill? Or, has murdered someone, and needs an accomplice to help hide the body. *Okay, that's crazy!* Thanking the cabdriver, she signed off on the tab with a haphazard scrawl, and hurried into the terminal to catch the early bird flight, Boston to D.C.

Katy, likewise, had been baffled when her father called with a summons to *come home* in a tone she recognized clearly as an order rather than an invite. Within the hour, she packed a bag, and set off for Connecticut through the rain-swept evening, without a second thought. Her parents stood abreast, rigid, like two aged sentinels posted at the open storm-door, as Katy pulled up to the curb. Rose O'Neil, wrapped in an oversized, unflattering nightdress, waved a *'thank God you're here'* greeting as her daughter trudged up the walkway, and climbed the weatherworn steps leading to the dimly lamp-lit porch.

Homecomings are far less joyous now, sighed the weary traveler, dropping her bags in the familiar vestibule. Yet, with a cheerful smile, she reached out to her mom and dad with a hug and a matter of fact, "What's going on guys?"

Within the hour, the three sat hunched over what had since been referred to in the O'Neil household as *The Letter*. "This should explain," said Patrick remorsefully, as he handed over the opened envelope and its contents.

Katy read, then read once again, the ominous line…*we now find we must inform you that you have a daughter*. "Christ Almighty!" she declared, the words spilling out unfiltered.

In days gone by, Rose would have instinctively chastised the slightest curse word or God's name spoken in vain under her roof. But tonight, she simply slumped in the corner, browbeaten. Head down, she remained focused on unraveling the last row of knit one, pearl ones from the sleeve of an ongoing knitting project which Katy could only hope wasn't yet another cardigan meant for her. The older woman had decided she wanted nothing to do with what she deemed a sordid matter having nothing to do with her.

Patrick exchanged a knowing look with his daughter, as if to say, *'Let's just let the sleeping dog lie.'* Rising, he silently poured another round of steaming decaf. Katy wished it were something stronger, like whisky.

"You've talked to Dennis and David about this, right?"

"Yes, they've both read *The Letter*," her dad replied.

"And?" the young daughter eyed him with a probing glance.

"Neither care to be involved," the old man said softly, his shoulders sagging knee-deep into his flannel shirt.

Clearly, *the problem* was being laid at Katy's feet.

Holding the photo of the young Asian girl to the fluorescent light, she searched for a speck of likeness to her brother Dru but, instead, found almond-shaped eyes, honey-colored skin, and straight, black, shoulder-length hair. Not a freckle or a hint of auburn hair in sight. The face of a sweet girl; a child who likely had no say in the matter. A pawn caught innocently in a melodrama unfolding half-way around the globe in the O'Neil household.

The hour was late. Rose was struggling to stay awake, knitting needles resting idly in her lap, while Patrick muffled a polite yawn. Both had aged drastically in a mere seven months. Dru's death was written on their lined faces like a roadmap of unrelenting nightmares. Losing a brother was the most shattering experience the young college girl could imagine…but, burying your child; damn, she had no words.

From across the room, the youngest of the O'Neil children had come to terms with the fact that the tables had turned. In an instant, she was no longer the kid in the room. Like it or not, she would have to jump in feet first, grab the bull by the horns, and deal with her brother's mess-ups, if that's what it came to. It was blatantly apparent that her father, and most certainly her befuddled mother, were incapable of dealing with this uncertain turn of events. As frightening as it was, the matter at hand had become her problem.

"Mind if I take a look in the attic tomorrow?" she asked Patrick, taking note of his sluggish gait and visibly thinning hair. "Dru once mentioned he had left a battered, old trunk of memorabilia upstairs in the family attic. I'm wondering if there might be answers up there among the spider webs."

"It's worth a look, sweetheart," he replied. "No one's been up there in years."

Rose shuffled off to bed without a solitary parting word.

Okay, that was weird.

"Goodnight, mother," mouthed Katy, to no one there.

Patrick rose from his chair, and thanked her for making the long drive, while lightly planting a goodnight kiss on his daughter's forehead. "Anything you need before I shut down the lights?"

With a wide-spread stretch, she whispered, "I'm good, dad. Get some rest. I'll be right behind you."

Gathering *The Letter,* along with her belongings, she headed for the stairs, and her girlhood bedroom at the end of the hall. How strange it felt to be back here. The people in the house, including herself, had all changed drastically. But, the Disney wall coverings and her mother's hand-sewn laced curtains remained the same. Dog-tired from the day, and exhausted from thoughts of what might lie ahead, she flopped on the bed fully clothed, and fell into a restless night's sleep, dreaming of cobwebs, bats, and Japanese orphans.

47

THE ONE

The next morning, Katy clambered up the rickety old stairwell, plowing her way to the farthest corner of the attic loft. Intuitively, she knew exactly where Dru would store his *stuff*. There, in the faraway corner, rested an obscure metal trunk shrouded in dust, strapped shut with heavy leather bands. Sneezing through the musty, stifled air, she zigzagged over and through stacks of boxed up family relics; all of which would one day be tossed away, unwanted and unclaimed. Muscling her way to the deep end, beneath the alcove, her handheld flashlight paved the way to the murky, raftered crawl space.

Approaching the chest, she could see the metal clasps securing the lid had rusted enough to warrant a forceful hammering. "Dammit!" she muttered, wrestling with the heavy metal lid until it finally wedged itself loose.

"There we go!" she said, hunkering down awkwardly into a cross-legged position. Leaning deeply over the opened trunk, she felt extremely nauseated at the mere thought of what she could be about to uncover.

Dru's Marine uniforms stretched out across the entire top rack. Her hands were visibly shaking as they scanned the stiffened lapels and the brim of the hats he had worn so proudly. "Damn you, Dru, dying like that!" she heard herself snivel, wiping away the unexpected rush of tears with the hem of her oversized shirt.

"Christ, I hate this," she stammered, holding up a high school football shirt with number 22 emblazoned across its back. A tattered yearbook fell open to pictures of pony-tailed girls with names like Amy, Jenny, and Sue. Tarnished trophies and a stockpile of long forgotten baseball cards, all once treasured, now meaningless, filled the center bin. In the farthest corner, beneath a pile of yellowed news clippings lay a beat up, rubber-banded shoebox. Katy took extra care to maneuver it upright and intact.

A bundle of letters bound by pink ribbons spilled out into her lap. Attached was a silver framed photo of a beautiful young couple sitting on a bridge overlooking a river. The girl, in a flowery silk dress, laughed sheepishly while a very young-looking Dru held his arms full circle around her waist, as if to keep her from running away. Pasted to the backside of the small frame was a note. Katy immediately recognized Dru's handwriting. It read: *My darling, Hana, no matter where life takes us, you will forever be THE ONE.*

Looking closely at the girl in the framed photo, it became apparent that the beautiful almond eyes matched perfectly those of the little Asian girl who would have her believe she was Dru's daughter.

The ribboned letters, postmarked Tokyo, Japan, addressed in a delicate hand, were clearly those of Hana Shinsato. Katy drew in a deep breath, realizing this was what she'd been searching for. She would have to read each one, word for word. But, not here. Not now. She would take them home, along with the photos and *The Letter.* Closing down the chest, and walking away, she felt completely overwhelmed. How could she be expected to handle all of this alone? Her parents were far from senile, *but let's be real.* They were entirely too old and her brothers didn't care. With clenched fists, she headed back down the stairs with her breakthrough find in hand.

"If only Dru were here, he would tell me exactly what to do," she thought aloud. Instantly, as if from a voice within, she heard the answer. "Call Élise."

48

SECRETS

Élise would have preferred the solitude of a suite at a nearby Georgetown hotel but Belle made it perfectly clear, "I won't hear of such a thing!" If only her host knew how heavenly an overnight in a plush hotel sounded right about now. Nonetheless, as the restless traveler slipped into a nightshirt, and climbed up onto the downy sofa bed, she felt more than grateful for Belle's southern hospitality, and homespun patchwork quilt. Mildly speaking, it had been a long, exhausting, emotional day.

Thank goodness she had thrown the little black dress in her overnight bag. Otherwise, it would have been mom jeans for the unforeseen meet up with Paul at Maestro's. Katy had run into Paul Martin unexpectedly on the streets of Georgetown, and haphazardly mentioned that her 'favorite sister-in-law' was in town. "He said to say hello," Katy added with a casual smile, unmindful of the estrangement between the two.

"Oh, gosh, I wish you wouldn't have," grimaced Élise. The last person she needed to think about on a day like today was Paul. *What an abominable day!* thought Élise, reaching up to soothe her pulsating temples. It's not every day you discover your husband of seven years *might* be the father of a teenage Asian love child. Twisting her hair up off her neck into an unruly topknot, her mind flashed to Dr. Katz, and how he would analyze this utterly *shitty day*!

"This is not going to be easy," Katy had prefaced her remarks before handing over the packet containing *The Letter* and enclosed photo of the young girl. If an asteroid had come crashing through the ceiling, landing at her feet, Élise could not have been more horrified. She listened, half numb, not believing any of what was being said, as Katy briefed her on what could only be categorized as a painful situation. "The Shinsato family are claiming Dru is the biological father of their granddaughter," she said, pointing to the photo of the Japanese school girl.

"That's absolutely crazy!" cried Élise, as much in denial as in disbelief. Heart racing and fists knotted, the besieged ex-wife bit her lip to stop from trembling. Her eyes focused on the image, searching for anything resembling her husband, or any O'Neil for that matter. Her mind circled to the family. "Your father, mother, brothers…what have they to say?" This was, after all, a family matter of which, legally, she was no longer a member, as Rose O'Neil had made convincingly clear on more than one occasion.

"Collectively, they've laid the entire affair in my hands," Katy answered with a dismal shrug. "My brothers say it's hogwash; won't even discuss it. My mother, well, you can imagine." *Élise would rather not.* "And, my dad, between you and I, he tries, but he's far different since Dru's death. So, looks every bit like I own it."

Élise shook her head in defiance. "That's absurd!" she said, wrapping her arms around her young sister-in-law, who looked as if the world had unloaded the mysteries of the universe on her shoulders. Face to face, eye to eye, articulating each word slowly and clearly, as one does in the reciting of a vow, "Look," she said, taking a long, deep breath. "I'm glad you thought to call me. I can't deny I'm blindsided! I don't know if any of this is true *or not*, but I promise you this. If we put our heads together, you and I, we will get to the bottom of it." With that, the two raised hands in a mutual high-five, sealing the deal for whatever lay ahead.

How could the O'Neils do such a thing? thought Élise, shaking her head in wonder, yet quickly reminding herself that solutions were not to be found floundering about in the mud. "It's time to move on," she sighed, bolstering herself with a smattering of self-counseling as so often was called upon these days. It goes without saying she was no expert but even a novice would know there were ways to prove or disprove paternity claims; DNA, for one. It was time to gather her thoughts and get on with it.

"Where do we begin?" she asked, pulling up a chair, determined to bare the secrets left behind by the father of her three children. *The Letter* spoke for itself. Élise's stomach lurched, threatening to heave, as she digested every word. "Good God!" she groaned, eyes racing across the page. *"But now, it is different, you see..."* Élise concluded, as she grappled with the written words of the elderly couple as though they were lyrics to a sad, sad song.

"There's more," said Katy, flinching, feeling as if she were stoking a blazing fire. "I also found this bundle of letters in the family attic in a chest with Dru's belongings. Letters written by Hana Shinsato to Dru." Hesitating, she clutched them to her chest. "You might not want to read them..."

Élise already had her hand stretched out. "Of course, I *have* to read them," she uttered bravely. But it was the photo in the silver frame that stung as if it were a poisoned arrow. There he was! Brazen as a full moon on a clear, dark night. Dru, his arms entangled around a young Asian woman, sitting on a wooden bridge. "Damn!" was all she could say. Eyes burning, she turned to the attached note written in Dru's perfect handwriting:

My darling Hana. No matter where life takes us,
you will forever be THE ONE.
Love, Dru

Without a word she began to untie the ribbons.
Dear Dru ... the first letter began...
As I explained on our final night together, I could never marry you and leave my family or my beloved Japan. America could never be my home. I'm so sorry. I do love you, but you must go on without me. Love Hana

Wow! *That explains a lot*, thought Élise. clutching the stack of letters to her pounding chest. She was not naïve enough to believe Dru had never been involved with other women, but his having proposed marriage…and now to learn there was a love child. Well, that was a bitter pill to swallow. Not that her reputation in her college years was on par with that of the Virgin Mary, but damn, there were no offspring to account for. And now, to come across the fact that she was his *second choice,* didn't sit particularly well either.

Her mind flashed to an incident long ago when Grandfather Saint-Cyr had asked that she select a birthday gift for herself. "Pick something beautiful you will treasure forever," he had said with a beaming smile.

That afternoon, she and a friend visited a well-respected jewelry store, where a pair of marquis-shaped black onyx earrings nearly jumped out of the lighted glass-case. Élise had smiled into the mirror as she tried them on.

"They're exquisite!" she said, delighted to find the perfect gift.

"Maybe you should look around," said her college friend. "You might find something you like even better. We can always come back later."

After a day of shopping and lunch, the two headed back to collect the onyx earrings, only to be told the precious earrings had been sold; they were the last pair in the store and no longer available.

Élise, begrudgingly, settled on what had been her second choice; her birthstone surrounded by tiny diamonds. Now, whenever she wore them, no matter how many compliments she received, she always longed for the beautiful black onyx earrings. *Her first choice.* She couldn't help but wonder if that's how Dru felt when he thought about Hana.

With a deep solemn sigh, she returned to reading the letters that her husband had preserved, all intact, and so beautifully bound in their colorful ribbons.

Katy turned away, leaving Élise to have a moment to herself.

"Be right back," she mouthed over her shoulder, heading for the kitchen just as her cell phone rang.

"Oh, hi! Just a minute. Let me get her." Élise could hear Katy's voice trailing down the hallway as she walked back from the kitchen, holding out the phone. "It's for you!"

"For me?" a confused Élise lifted the phone to her ear.

"Hello?"

"Élise, it's me, Paul.

49

MAESTRO'S

They agreed to meet for an early dinner. "It could only help our cause if I meet with Paul," Élise said, compelled to rebuff any starry-eyed ideas that this evening might be construed as a date. Katy smiled to herself as she watched her sister-in-law dab bronze blush to her cheeks, and blow-dry her hair into loose, casual waves.

Katy offered to drive but Élise insisted on a cab. "No, you get some rest. This day hasn't been easy on you, either." Actually, Élise didn't expect to be gone but a few hours.

"Don't wait up!" she teased playfully as she wrestled with the front door.

Her sole reason to connect at all, she repeated to herself from the rear seat of the taxi, was simply to establish if Dru had ever confided in his trusted friend. Had he ever mentioned anything about a love affair he'd had during his military service in Japan? The answer should take no longer than a whisky sour and a Caesar salad. She thanked the driver as he pulled up to Maestro's, and quickly headed toward the revolving door.

Paul, already seated at a table when she arrived, waved from across the room as the maître d' led her through the dining room, and pulled out a chair. "Great to see you again. Looking lovely as ever!" Paul all but chanted as he rose to kiss her on each cheek, European style. She smiled a gracious *thank you* in return. The entrees had been ordered for two, he explained. "I took the liberty of selecting the plat du jour," he gestured, whipping a white hotel napkin across his lap and, waving for the sommelier. Drinks poured, dinner on its way! Obviously, he's anxious to get on with this, pay his dues, so to speak, and rush on back to his lady friend. *Just as well,* thought Élise laying her purse aside.

Over steamed crab legs and sautéed mushrooms, the conversation moved past how the boys were getting on, if New England was treating her kindly and, eventually, to his extensive stay in Germany. She hadn't planned on a four-course meal, though it wasn't going all that bad, comparing news and catching up as old friends do. As the perfectly grilled filet mignons were set before them, and the clinking of wine glasses subsided, Élise took a deep breath, and braved on to the subject at hand. "So, Paul," she began, her voice low and thoughtful. "I've wondered if Dru ever mentioned to you a love interest he had when stationed in Japan?" With eyes lowered, she continued to fuss with a pad of chilled butter, and a slice of steamy all-grain bread.

"Why do you ask?" he wondered, eyeing her curiously from across the table.

"Well," she replied, hearing herself speak in an unfamiliar uppity tone, "it seems the O'Neil family has come across correspondence hidden away in a locker in their upstairs attic. Letters, to be exact, addressed to Dru from a certain Japanese woman. It appears the two dated while he was on embassy duty in Tokyo. Would you know anything about that?"

Paul fidgeted a bit before answering, as though measuring how much or how little to divulge. "You know," he said, slicing into the tender filet, "he did say there was a girl but that it was long, long ago."

Élise proceeded to dip the crusty bread into the au jus. "Funny, he never once mentioned it to me. You suppose it was serious?"

"I don't know," he replied, shaking his head, and pausing to scatter fresh bacon bits atop a manly-sized Idaho potato. "He didn't elaborate. He simply said it didn't work out. Hell, people move on; they marry, have kids…" With that he gave a self-demeaning chuckle. "Well, not all of us marry or have kids, but life goes on. We both know that."

"But, let's say there were children involved," she said, eyes focused on the honey baked carrot dangling off the end of her fork. "Then, it would be different."

"Yeah, well, that's a whole other ball game right there," he said, lifting his goblet to take in a lingering sniff of cabernet. "So, what exactly are you saying?" he asked, leaning forward with an involuntary twitch of his impeccably, manicured beard.

The beard was distracting. This Paul, the one with the beard, was disturbingly distant, prim, proper, and rigid. Where was her old friend? The man who had laughed hysterically, scurrying about her living room setting up buckets to catch the rain in the middle of a drenching Nor'easter? The Paul in the apron who sang Acapella while taste-testing a pot of chili over her kitchen stove. The one who threw her boys over his shoulder, and strutted up and down the circular stairs to the tune of a Sousa march. Had he changed so in such a short time? *But, then, another woman in the loop can do that to a man,* Élise reasoned.

"Issues, actually rather complicated issues, have surfaced since Dru's passing," she continued, tiptoeing through the conversation in generalities. "It's a family matter," she explained with a devil-may-care shrug of her shoulders as she reached out to finger and sniff the fresh flowers in the vase between them. "Mmmm...lilacs. Lovely!"

Alphonse, the colorfully flamboyant server, came round to refresh their water glasses for the umpteenth time, hovering a bit too long over each pour to inquire if all was satisfactory. "Do *we* need a refill on the bread? More wine for madam?"

"No, we're good!" replied Paul abruptly, in a dismissive tone.

"Everything is perfect, Alphonse! Thank you," smiled Élise, wondering when Paul had become so short-tempered.

"Look, if I can help, you know I'm here for you," Paul said, attempting to pick up where they left off. There was more going on beneath this act of hers than she was letting on. He'd bet the ranch on that. He hadn't been an undercover agent this many years to be fooled by the obvious. He had zeroed in on her body language as soon as she sat down: the downcast eyes, the bogus voice intonation, the way she diverted the conversation. None of it was adding up.

As their waiter whisked away the last of the dessert plates, Paul turned to Élise, "Would you be up for a short walk? Maybe catch an after-dinner drink at my place on the way back? I've got a fifteen-year-old cognac I think you'd love. What do you say?"

"Ohhh...I don't know," pondered Élise, struggling for a comeback. "I have to ask. What would Cheri have to say about that idea?"

"Who is Cheri?" Paul asked, startled. "Help me out here because I'm totally flummoxed."

"Cheri, or is it Sherry? The woman agent you wined and dined all over Paris. The one, as I understand it, who stayed on with you here in D.C. when you returned from Heidelberg." The words spilled rapid-fire from her mouth. Élise knew full well her friend Hannah wouldn't make up such a story. "Don't get me wrong. I'm happy for you both. Really, I am."

"What the living hell are you talking about!" Paul raised his voice, catching the attention of the diners at the adjacent table who were now staring directly at them as though stage curtains had parted, and the first act was fully underway. "You can't mean Cheryl...Cheryl Cookingham?"

Élise could feel her spine arch upright like feathers of a riled peacock as she glared across the table. She hadn't planned on getting into this discussion. Not tonight, not ever.

It was just one more thing for her weary head and heart to deal with. "Not that you owe me or anyone an explanation, but if she's that woman, then I guess that would be Cheryl Cookingham."

The three women seated at the corner table glared, all ears, looking as if they had already taken sides. "You think your lady friend would approve of you inviting me to your apartment for drinks?" Élise countered, as the three women all but cheered her on.

Suddenly, it felt as if the entire left wing of the dining hall had fallen silent, waiting on what might follow.

It didn't take but a minute for a flustered Alphonse to sprint into action as Paul thrust his hand in the air to signal for the check and, without a word, scribbled his name to the bill with a series of unintelligible circles and dashes. "Obviously," Paul muttered to Élise, "you and I have lots to talk about. But, first, let's get out of here." As they rose, heading for the street exit, the balding man and his oversized wife across the way scowled as they passed. Paul forced a smile, wishing them each a good evening as he took Élise by the hand, and walked away.

Curbside, Élise fumbled clumsily with her wrap, avoiding eye contact. "You know, I think it best if we call it a day. It's been a very trying day."

He had no idea!

"I was hoping we could talk," Paul contended. He was certain something serious was going on. Whatever it was, she was keeping it to herself. This wasn't the first time he'd had to dance the dance to get her to talk. He'd been here at times like this with her before but, back then, he would have known what to do and what to say. It was all quite simple then. But clearly, anything he had to say tonight would only fall on deaf ears.

He wanted to tell her there was no other woman. It had always been Élise. The guilt of it preyed on him night and day. To have fallen in love with his best friend's wife. That sucks! Why did she think he stayed away for Christ's sake? He left the country for six months, hoping to change how he felt. It hadn't changed a damn thing. Watching her now fidgeting with her hair, tapping her heels on the cobblestone, and keeping her distance as if he had the goddamn plague. But, right now, he knew her well enough to know that it was in his best interest to back off.

"Okay," he said with a brisk kiss to the top of her head, "just remember, I'm here. I've always been here." With that, he called out a loud two-fingered whistle, the kind only men are masters of, and raised a hand to hail the oncoming taxi and, just like that, he watched as she sped away into the night.

50

AIRPORT

"Well, last night didn't go exactly as planned," Élise grumbled into her morning coffee cup as Belle placed a platter of Belgian waffles in the middle of the table. Katy and Belle looked at one another, daring each other to ask, "Why? What happened?" Neither uttered a word as they continued to rearrange the melted butter, hot maple syrup, and fruit plates as if preparing for a *Bon Appetit* photo shoot.

"It ended awkwardly, in fact. Very awkwardly," Élise carried on, as her two curious BFFs had high hopes she would. "I don't think Paul will be showing his face at Maestro's for a while." Without encouragement, she began a play-by-play of the scenario, from Alphonse all atwitter, the trio of cheering ladies at the corner table, and the bald man and his plump wife joining in the fray. "It's a lot more amusing this morning, I can tell you that," she admitted.

"Paul was blind-sided by our conversation. Honestly, he was at a loss for words and, by the time Alphonse served our lemon-blueberry cake, he was decidedly irate. Very unlike Paul," she added.

Katy had brought Belle up to speed on the claim that Dru might have an Asian teenage daughter living in Japan. "Mercy me!" Belle declared. "Guess we'll have to get to the bottom of that now, won't we?" The older woman was always ready for whatever she could do to help her girls. Katy coming to live with her was a godsend, especially since her ailing husband, Cliff Stevenson, was failing by the hour. Most days were spent by his side at the Lakewood Nursing Home, though he rarely recognized her anymore.

When the phone rang mid-afternoon, Élise suspected who it would be. "Don't hang up!" Paul said before she could say hello.

"He wants to take me to the airport tonight," she said, setting down her phone, and turning to Katy. "I guess I owe him that much."

"Maybe Paul could offer a man's perspective if he knew what's really going on here," Katy offered.

Élise would have to decide tonight on the drive to the airport whether *or not* to share the unabridged story with him. She was leaning toward the *or not*. The relationship with what's-her-name, Cheryl somebody, loomed jadedly between them. And, quite frankly, Paul hardly seemed the same man she remembered so fondly. Everything was different now. So, why would I consider dragging him into more of my messes?

she asked herself. *Perhaps it was simply time they went their separate ways.*

The two young women spent the better part of the remaining day compiling action plans as to how best to respond to the Shinsato family. Since the Greenwich, Connecticut O'Neil contingency had washed their hands of the possibility that young Aimi Shinsato could be family, the burden of proof lay at the feet of the young, aspiring PhD student, and the steadfast ex-wife of the deceased Agent Dru O'Neil. It was an unlikely state of affairs but that's where things stood.

At 9:00 p.m. on the dot, Paul called to say he was out front waiting. Élise hugged her sister-in-law and sweet friend Belle, inviting them both to visit anytime. "There will always be plenty of room at the inn for you two!" she shouted, heading out the door.

Paul doffed his hat to the two women waving at the door while he tossed Élise's travel bag into the backseat of his car. With a friendly tip of his baseball cap, and a smile, he greeted her with, "At your service, ma'am."

"Want to talk?" he asked as they pulled onto the freeway heading toward Reagan National Airport. Élise had already made her mind up. She would keep the conversation light, thanking him for the ride, and briefly apologize for her poor manners of last evening. "No worries," he said, as he played into her hand, shifting gears, moving on to other topics. "So, Katy's working on her PhD. That's huge!"

As they sped past terminal B, and turned into the parking garage, Élise spun around. "Where are you going? American Airlines is back there."

Paul knew the airport like the back of his hand. There was no confusion on his part as he winded up the ramp, and pulled into a third-floor parking spot. "Here, let me get that bag for you," he said, proceeding to run around to open the rear door.

"It won't be necessary to walk me in," she said, flustered by his assumption she might need help in finding her way through the terminal.

"No bother at all," he smiled whimsically, rolling her bag behind him as he led the way. "My momma taught me you *always* walk a lady to the door. A gentleman would never drop his lady friend off at the curb," he added, stepping into the elevator. They exchanged cordial goodbyes at the airline desk as she thanked him with a wide handwave and strode away toward the check in and passenger gate.

"Give my love to the boys!" he hollered.

By 11:00 p.m. she was on board her flight, exhaling a deep sigh of relief. It was good to be heading home. Not that the unsettling paternity developments were apt to disappear but she felt confidant she and Katy could work it out. Settling back into her seat, she buckled up for the one-hour and forty-minute flight to Boston. Passengers came streaming by, lifting bulging carry-ons high into the overhead bins while attendants walked the aisle, monitoring those in need. A fragile, elderly woman nodded hello as she crammed a large sack beneath the seat beside her. Élise nodded, quickly turning to face the window, praying her seat companion would not be a talker. She was in no mood for idle chit-chat at this late hour.

Just then, from the corner of her eye, she caught sight of the red baseball cap. Paul was boarding the flight! He winked at her as he passed by and took a seat in the rear of the plane. "What the hell?" Élise spouted, causing the woman beside her to sit up at attention, as though she'd seen a field mouse scurry by.

"What's happening?" the woman asked, holding her breath in alarm.

"Oh, sorry," an embarrassed Élise said. "It's nothing. Really, it's okay."

But now the elder woman was distressed. "I have a bottle of water here if that would help. I have anxiety issues, too, when flying, especially when I fly to the west coast to visit my daughter. She lives in San Francisco. I don't see her often as I like, as you can imagine, or my grandchildren for that matter. I have six. Three girls and three boys…"

Élise interrupted before the woman could divulge their ages, and which of them most favored herself. "Thank you. You're very kind," she said. "I just need to close my eyes and rest. It's been a long day." With that she tucked her legs beneath her, shutting her eyes, not daring to move an inch for fear her neighbor might attempt to re-engage.

Even on a good day Élise wasn't big on small talk, especially not with strangers. *Please, I don't know you. We've never met. We'll never, ever meet again. I'm sure you're a wonderful person, but please let it be.*

As the plane landed, and the passengers began gathering their belongings to deboard, Élise stole a quick look to the rear of the cabin, and clearly caught a glimpse of the offending red cap.

Her neighbor lady asked, "Feeling better, dear?"

"Yes, thank you," she replied hastily. Her mind was already at work on a game plan to grab her rolling bag, whisk her way through the terminal, and hail down the first available taxi. That would be the end of it. She'd be home within the hour. Just then, she turned to see Paul approaching from the rear with the airline attendant in the lead, escorting him up the aisle as if he were His Royal Highness.

"Excuse us, please. U.S. Marshal coming through. Thank you."

Élise watched open-mouthed as the two moved unhampered through the line, toward the cockpit, as folks moved aside to clear a path. As she exited into the terminal he stood, leaning against a pole, waiting.

"Don't worry, I've booked myself a hotel room," Paul said with a sheepish grin.

"What are you doing here?" she spurted, not sure whether to be angry, intimidated, insulted or glad. Damn him!

"We need to talk," he said, not backing down.

"What do we have to talk about?" she asked indignantly,

"You tell me," Paul answered as she began to walk toward the moving stairs. "You know as well as I, we are long overdue for a good heart-to-heart. I have a town car waiting for us downstairs.

"After you," he said, stepping aside to let her pass. "By the way, I hate your beard," she said, falling into line behind him, too exhausted to argue.

51

OPHELIA

The town car dropped the twosome off at 2:00 a.m. adjacent to the back-entry door. Paul followed Élise's lead as he wrestled with his backpack and her one overnight bag. He reminded her he had a reservation at a nearby hotel but Élise snapped, "Don't be ridiculous!" As she turned the key, and stepped into the mud room, Argos sprinted through the hallway, tail wagging, as if he'd been waiting up to greet her the entire two days and nights.

"Hey, boy," said Paul, scratching the dog's ears. "What's this?" he asked with a chuckle, pointing out the floral bandana tied about the dog's neck.

"Good lord!" spouted Élise, kneeling to throw her arms around her four-legged companion. "Look at you! They've managed to sissify you in a matter of two days."

"The troublesome part is, he doesn't seem to mind," Paul joked. The two weary travelers shared a laugh, as if their recent differences were a thing of the past.

"I'm afraid to think of what other surprises might be in store for me," she smiled light-heartedly for the first time in several days.

"If I remember correctly," said Paul, "there's an iron fold up cot out in the solarium. How about I'll set my bag out there, and hunker down for the night. Stay out of everyone's hair best I can, and let you catch up on your beauty sleep."

Nodding, she added, "I'd better leave a note for Sarah to alert her we have a houseguest." Pulling a pencil and piece of notepaper out from the kitchen draw she wrote:

Sarah,
If you see a tall, dark, handsome man walking about the house, don't panic! I brought home a friend.
Élise

"Glad she warned me," sighed Sarah, as she entered the kitchen with Argos at her heels, and spotted the handwritten note posted to the refrigerator door. It was barely 5:00 a.m. The house was quiet, just the way she liked to start each day, before the babies awakened. "A houseguest. Oh my, this could be interesting," she thought with a chuckle as she filled the doggie dish with crunchy morsels, and opened the shutters, before setting off to grind coffee beans for breakfast.

By the time Élise made her way down the stairs to the thrill of three little ones jumping for joy, as children do when a traveling parent returns home, there stood Paul. Looking up to greet her while flipping flapjacks alongside Sarah, he looked as if he'd landed a job at a Michelin five-star restaurant. "Sarah put me to work," he smiled.

"Uncle Paul is here!" shouted Oliver, as his brothers clapped with excitement.

Taking a second look, Élise's mouth nearly hit the floor. She couldn't believe what she was seeing. The beard was gone!

Sarah's sister, Ruth, cheerfully rushed to hug Élise, and pour her a mug of freshly brewed coffee. "Good to have you home, mama bear! And, what a wonderful helper you brought with you." Obviously, the ladies had already been charmed by the guest of honor and his winning ways.

"What the devil?" Élise squealed, nearly jumping out of her chair, as a fluffy ball of grey-and-white fur rubbed against her ankles before strutting across the kitchen floor like a Dior model. "Good God!" she gasped, swiping her forehead, half-believing she was hallucinating. *She'd read stress could do that to a person.*

Ruth and Sarah exchanged apologetic looks while Will hollered, "Please, please, can we keep her?" Jean-Jacques wiggled his nose, bouncing up on his tip toes, wanting to chase after the cat who strolled away as if it had not a care in the world. "We thought you'd like her if we named her Ophelia," posed Will, pleading his case on behalf of the newly adopted feline.

"Oh, my heavens," she sighed. "We'll talk about this after I've had caffeine," the drowsy mother replied, with a defeated whimper, knowing full well how this would play out.

By late morning, Élise had treated herself to a much-needed luxurious herbal bath. As she unraveled her long hair from its plush turban towel, shaking it loose like a lion's mane, she glanced out the upstairs bedroom window only to see Paul bent over, head thrust beneath the hood of Ruth's car. The boys were collectively handing him a wrench, and then a screwdriver while Sarah offered a dampened towel to wipe his brow. Ruth held a rubber hammer as Argos looked on, as if enjoying an appointed supervisory role.

How do you compete with the likes of Paul? Traitors all of them!

Élise turned abruptly to notice her newly acquired resident, Miss Ophelia, perched atop an adjacent window sill, soaking in the morning sun. "I know we've hardly met," the mistress of the house spoke kindly, moving across the room to run her fingers through the coat of soft, fluffy fur. "But, from where I sit, it's looking like you may be the only loyal one here." The cat assumed an unspoken, haughty posture as Élise continued. "I *suppose* you can stay. But you need to understand, I *barely* like cats." The newest addition to the household chose to disregard the underlying insult by lowering her head, closing her eyes, and exhaling a long-winded, self-indulgent purr.

52

BORN TO BE WILD

Paul placed the black and white photo in front of Élise without as much as a word. It was late at night and the house lights in the study room were dim. The O'Neil boys were long asleep and Sarah had escaped with Ruth for a few well-earned days of R&R. "Who's this?" she asked focusing on the man in the photograph or…*was it a woman*? On second glance she wasn't sure. With the military boots, oversized camouflage pants, leather jacket, and shorn hair, it could be either. "Am I supposed to know this person?" she asked, searching Paul's face for a clue.

"That's a buddy of mine from the Heidelberg trip," Paul explained, as he placed a second photo face up on the marble top coffee table. "Now, this shot here," he said, pointing to a cheerful looking group. "That was taken our final day in Germany. We just got word we were finally heading home!"

he added jubilantly. "And this fellow," he said indicating a boyish-looking man with freckles standing center front, "that's Sean Hall, a sharpshooter out of Nebraska ATF office. Hell of a guy!"

"Okay," nodded Élise, confused as to where this conversation was heading.

"To Sean's left is Professor Lindsay and Professor Young. On the right is me, alongside my friend and colleague, a dynamite ATF agent out of New York." Élise eyed the *dynamite agent out of New York.* It was in fact the same person with the shorn hair, beat up boots, and leather jacket. "My friend there," Paul continued as he rolled up his sleeve to demonstrate, "has a truly wicked tattoo. Damn thing stretches from the shoulder all the way down to the wrist. Never seen anything like it!"

Élise attempted a polite smile. She would never understand people who imagined you might have the slightest interest in shuffling through photos of people you hardly knew or, in this case, would never know. Her mind flashed back to the dreaded holidays when Rose O'Neil would drag stacks of photo albums from the hall closet, and begin the never-ending history of every family member beginning with her dearly departed grandmother.

"There's a huge skull up here on the shoulder," Paul continued with his fixation on his friend's tattoo. "In bold black letters, the words *BORN TO BE WILD* run down the entire arm."

The best Élise could muster was a compliant, "Well, that's sure to set your friend apart."

"Wish you could see it, but the jacket has it covered…"

"Okay, you're scaring me now," she said, noting the dozen or more pictures in his hand she might be expected to suffer through. "Been a long day," she said covering a yawn as she stood up, massaging the kinks that had settled in the crook of her neck. *She hated to be rude but, on the other hand…*

But Paul hadn't finished. "So, this agent, the one with the tattoo, is a genuine ballbuster. Someone you can count on to have your back when the crap hits the fan." Now he was talking louder, as if to drive home a point.

"I suppose this person has a name?" Élise added, hoping to move this showcase along, and be done with it.

"Who, that one?" he asked laying his thumb on the person of questionable gender. "Why, that's Cheryl Friggin' Cookingham!" With that, he dropped into the corner chair, arms stretched over his head like a man who had just crossed the finish line at the Boston Marathon.

"THAT is not Cheryl Cookingham!" Élise wasn't sure if she had screamed the name aloud or to herself as she sat back down to take a closer look. "You're kidding, right?" This was the woman she had worried herself about! *Well not really worried*; *more like been curious.*

"Now, why would I kid about a thing like that?" He was toying with her now, like a Maine Coon with a ball of catnip.

"No way!" she replied, nose nearly touching the photo, scouring the face as if she might be called upon at a later date to identify said person in a criminal lineup.

"What's the matter?" Paul bit his lip to keep from gloating as he watched her eyes flash back and forth between photos, trying to assimilate what she now knew to be true. Clearly, Cheryl Cookingham was never, ever Paul's type!

"I'm just a little surprised is all." Élise attempted to backtrack, though the lines gathering above her brow betrayed her every word.

"Surprised? Why would you be surprised?" He was quite enjoying this.

"Well, you roomed with her in Paris and then she traveled home with you to D.C. It seems rational to assume…"

"Assume what exactly?" he asked playfully. "You assumed we were what? Lovers? Am I right?"

"Yeah, I suppose so. But, why would I care?" she lied, stammering over her words, her face flushed crimson red.

"So, that wouldn't have bothered you? Me and her being lovers?"

"Of course not," she replied, quick to discard any such notion. Crossing the room in long, quirky strides, she hovered over the antique settee, readjusting the row of perfectly aligned needlepoint pillows.

"Here, let me help," Paul said as he began to clumsily fluff a pillow or two. "If I told you that could never happen, me hooking up romantically with another woman, that is, would you care to know why?"

Élise pretended she couldn't imagine why.

"Let me tell you why," he began as he felt his legs go limp. He had waited way too long for this moment to arrive.

It wasn't that he had ever been a wallflower when it came to women. But he'd never before ached for a woman, until now. Death-defying terrorist assignments in foreign lands, no problem! But this crazy relationship with Élise, if you could call it that, had taken him to the woodshed over and over and over, again and again. "You need to hear me out while I have the courage to say what I need to say." With that he took a deep breath, and muscled on, his heart pounding. "Because, honest to God, I've been carrying this around for far too long."

Élise felt her chest tighten as she flopped back down, tucking her bare feet beneath her on the sofa, calming herself by focusing on the painted landscape over the fireplace. He could wait as long as it took for her to look up at him.

"I don't know where you're at right now in your head, or in your heart," he began after a long, heavy pause, "but I do know exactly where I'm at." He watched her every move to detect a read. *Nothing! Not even a twitch.* He had no choice but to brave on. "I'm ready to be whatever you want me to be," he said, his hands flashing every which way. "Your call! Your best friend, your lover, your husband, or just good ole Uncle Paul. You tell me because, unless you tell me otherwise, I'm not going anywhere." He watched as her head dropped deep into her hands and she began to sob.

"I'm sorry," she muttered through a flood of tears.

Sorry! Good grief, what the hell does that mean? He hadn't a clue what he was expected to do or say but was not about to back down now. "Yes, I said 'your husband.' I've never said that to anyone," he added, eyes lowered, as though he couldn't quite believe his own words. This might be his death march but he was going in for the kill. "Please don't cry," he said, taking a seat beside her, and gently pulling her to him. So many times over the years he had been her shoulder to cry on but this was different. He had to remind himself to breathe.

Élise was visibly shaking like a child awakened in the night, believing there were gremlins beneath the bed; her mind a jumble of senseless thoughts. Her maze of hair tangled itself around his wrists as he held her, and pressed his lips to her forehead for what seemed hours; neither daring to move or speak.

"I've loved you for a very long time, right or wrong, Élise," he whispered, brushing her long locks aside. "If you don't feel the same, I'll understand. Whatever you tell me, know we'll be okay, you and me." Reaching in his pocket, he pulled out a white linen handkerchief, and began to dry her tears. They rocked back and forth in a wordless embrace for what seemed a very long time.

How many sleepless nights had she dreamed Paul would return, and profess on bended knee his love for her, never believing it would actually happen. The reality of it left her blubbering like a schoolchild, unable to think or string two words together coherently. It was as if floodgates, harboring years of hurt, grief, longing, hope, and fear had lifted, spilling out, running down her face in an ugly, uncontrollable deluge of tears the size of hailstones.

"You, okay?" Paul asked.

"No," she answered, shaking her head.

"It had to be said," he ventured. She shook her head in agreement even as he reached for her hand, both of them caught up in their own crazy emotions; each in need of answers.

After a series of tongue-tied exchanges, Élise half-audibly whispered into the night, "I don't know what's wrong with me. It's been a fretful couple of days. I feel I need to pull myself together, maybe get a decent night's sleep. I'm so confused."

"It's okay," he answered as he watched her climb the stairs one solemn step at a time, and tiptoe silently through the hall. He listened until he heard the soft click to her bedroom door which, from where he stood, sounded like a virtual kiss of death. Running his hand through his hair, he shook his head, "Damn, I screwed that up!"

The night felt strangely surreal as he headed to the rusty cot in the drafty solarium, reminding himself that, when a woman is quiet, it's never a good sign. He stopped to gaze at the full moon out the wide span of windows. Whatever the outcome, he was relieved this day had come. He repacked his belongings into his travel bag, setting it by the exit door. It was the first time he'd ever put himself at the mercy of a woman; but this was not just any woman. This was Élise Saint-Cyr O'Neil.

Around the corner came Argos. "Hey, boy. How did you know a brother was hurting?" he said as the honorable pup settled beneath the cot, laying his head between his paws. "Ever been in love, Argos?" he asked, staring up at the stars through the skylight. Argos answered with a snort.

"Guess not," assumed the weary guest as he fumbled with the bed sheets for what undoubtedly would be a miserably fitful night.

Upstairs Élise, never a huge fan of Virginia Woolf, reached for the volume of *Mrs. Dalloway* from the top of her corner bookshelf before falling into bed. Her mind was a jumble of irrational thoughts, rushing in a million directions, much like Woolf's strange stream of conscious writings. In the darkness of the room, she clutched the slim book to her chest, surrounded by a barricade of downy pillows. It wasn't that she planned to read, but rather felt an affinity to the only other woman she knew to be wholly more disorderly confused than herself.

A part of her wanted to run downstairs barefooted to the solarium, and curl up next to Paul for the night on the rickety old cot. But, of course, that was hardly an option in her messed-up state of mind. She closed down the lights, and stared into the darkness, wiping tears from her eyes. Ophelia's purring in the nearby antique rocker was the only sound in the dead of night.

Paul and I. Simple. Noncommittal. Friends. Dru, arms around a beautiful girl. No, he's dead. My fault. Aimi Shinsato. Not my problem. I love my single life. Me and my boys. Argos. New England. Dr. Katz. Book club. Online classes. Sullivan house. Mother Jaqueline failing. Rose O'Neil hates me. Paul. Remarriage. I just can't. The boys love him. Why do I hurt people? Call Hannah. Belle. DNA test. Paul. Tokyo. Piano lessons. Return Símone's call. Paul downstairs, hurting. I do love him.

53

THE YELLOW BOX

Dr. Katz was halfway to his office when the call came in. It was nearly 7:00 a.m. Only a handful of patients had access to his private number; Élise O'Neil was one. The last time they spoke was just after the death of her agent husband at which time she appeared to be adjusting reasonably well. As a neuropsychologist, Dr. Katz's days were primarily spent attending to depressed, anxious, heartbroken, and often neurotic individuals who sobbed and raged through each session, declaring life unfair. His patient, Élise O'Neil, was the exception. She would arrive with a well thought out plan, seeking counsel primarily as a supportive or negating measure. From where he stood, their exchanges were concise, measured, well-reasoned, and one might say enjoyable. As he swung his Mercedes into the parking garage, he found himself pleasantly eager to make her his first call.

"Thank God you've called!" she gasped, as his name flashed boldly across her screen. "My life is in total chaos, Dr. Katz," Élise began, without so much as a hint of her customary gracious manner.

"How so?" he replied, rather startled by her needy tone. Sitting back in his high-backed chair, he listened without interruption as Élise's tearful plea spilled over the speaker phone, filling the entire room. He gave an occasional, "I see," jotting notes along the way, while withholding comments, questions or remarks. Her *crisis*, he quickly determined, was twofold. First came the discovery that her late husband likely fathered a foreign-born child; a situation she says has fallen almost entirely in her lap, begging immediate action.

"This recently orphaned child may well be half-sister to my three sons," Élise cried out. "It's not something I can just wish away."

The doctor muttered, "Yes, of course," as the second half of her state of affairs came to light, smiling to himself, anticipating what was coming.

"There is a man in my life," she confided as though confessing a mortal sin. *Which nine cases out of ten was cause for a woman's hysteria.* He'd seen it a million times. He let her talk it out at great length before jumping into the fray.

"I believe I've got the picture," he professed guardedly. "And, when you're ready, I have some thoughts to offer."

"Please do," replied Élise, clutching the phone as if it were a lifeline.

He had to agree that a college-aged, unmarried sister-in-law, no matter how mature, was not a likely candidate to take on the rearing of a teenage niece. That said, should a heretofore unknown child of a *deceased ex-husband* give cause to throw one's own life in disarray? One must carefully consider the ramifications of introducing such an additional dynamic into an existing household. Taking on another's child is hardly something one decides upon overnight.

Élise found herself nodding to the phone. "Right."

"Secondly," Dr. Katz moved on, "regarding this man of yours…" It sounded outlandish to hear Paul referred to as *this man of hers*. She thought of correcting him but decided to let it be. "You say he's a longtime friend, which tells me he is most probably honest, loyal, trusting, and kind." He paused, waiting for assurance. "Again," the doctor continued, as if in a private conversation with himself, "the crux of the matter, as I understand it, is that he is downstairs, awaiting an answer to a marriage proposal, or a commitment of some degree, yes?"

"Yes, he wants to know where we are and where we're going in terms of a relationship," she responded.

"That's only fair, wouldn't you say?" the counselor advocated.

"He's always been there, not only for me but for my boys as well. They adore him!" she explained, sounding triumphant by her own admission.

"That's a real plus and, may I say, rarely the case," Dr. Katz opined, acknowledging that, in most second unions, half the hurdle was the children's unacceptance of a new partner.

That said, by no means would he suggest considering marriage solely for the sake of children but he did see it a windfall that her sons already loved this man. This was a positive scenario no matter the outcome, he rationalized. She had created a healthy, happy, family environment of which he congratulated her, but questioned if, given time, single life would remain enough. "You're a young, beautiful woman and children do grow up and leave home, you know?" He said this as though he had suffered a personal experience.

"Did I mention he's a black man?" Élise added, as if to throw in a curve ball.

"Is that a concern?" he asked, slightly caught off-guard.

"Not at all." It was never anything she gave thought to. The doctor smiled as she began to elaborate. "He's everything a woman would want in a man," she gushed. "Except, he's a federal agent." These last few words were spoken as if she had declared him a serial killer.

"I see," noted Dr. Katz. "Regrettably, your prior experience, as wife to a federal agent, turned out to be *unsuitable* at best but perhaps it was more about being married to the wrong man, and less to do with his being an agent. Just a thought!" he quickly added. "You know, as a rule, first loves are hopelessly euphoric. It's a lovely time, never to be forgotten."

"Yes, 'L*ove is merely a madness,*' William Shakespeare, *As You Like It*, Act 3, Scene 2," quoted Élise, which brought a chuckle from Dr. Katz.

"I'd forgotten I'm dealing with an authority on the Bard of Avon," he recalled with laughter, before reviving his thoughts.

"Yet, in the second go-round," he continued, "love might look and feel calmer; as though it were something *less than* the real thing. No fireworks igniting when he walks through the door, for instance but, also, less fuss, less drama, and less of a spectacle; which doesn't make it any less real. Moreover, we perhaps were expecting a person or an event to appear on our timeline in a yellow box and, instead, it presents itself now, in a silver box with orange tassels."

"Exactly!" Élise sighed as she slipped her foot into her bedside floppy slippers.

"Sometimes opportunity arrives at an inopportune time; or so we think at the time," said the good doctor, whose advise sounded more like that of a family friend than a paid professional. "Think hard on what feels right, Élise. Only you know what that is."

"So, it's all about timing, isn't it?" she quipped.

"Yes, indeed," he agreed, but added, "sometimes we're more ready for the next step than we realize."

With that, his smart-phone vibrated, alerting him his next patient was waiting. "What I'd like you to take away from today's session is that both your concerns, that of the orphaned child and the unforeseen marriage proposal, while lifechanging, neither are life threatening. Some might say quite the opposite. Life has many surprises awaiting us. Our job is to decide wisely."

With that, he scripted his final notes to the file with a flair. "Promise me you'll call next week, same time?" he concluded as he tamped his pipe with his preferred tobacco, a gift from his wife of twenty-six years, and smiled at the way his day had begun.

54

LIFE CHANGES

Chuck Connelly wasn't all that surprised to receive a call from David Mills, ATF's Boston regional office RAC. After all, they'd been friends from way back. What he was surprised at was to hear Dave had met with Agent Paul Martin over the weekend to discuss the possibility of a transfer out of D.C. to New England. "I'm always open to bringing on seasoned agents as I know you are, Chuck," David said cautiously. "I just wouldn't want to step on anyone's toes, especially yours."

Chuck wasn't blind. He was well aware Paul was struggling to settle back into the D.C. office upon his return from six months in Heidelberg. The horrendous death of Agent Dru O'Neil had taken its toll on the entire team, but maybe more so on Paul Martin than anyone. As supervisor, it was always a difficult call to know how far to intrude into someone's private world. Chuck was giving it time. He knew Paul to be an upright, extremely bright young man from a well-heeled family, graduating top of his class with a pedigree law degree from University of Virginia. He had good reason to believe a smart guy like him would sort things out on his own.

"I wish he had come to me first," Chuck confessed, sounding a bit bewildered. "Must be losing my touch."

"I doubt that," his friend assured him. "Life takes unexpected twists. You and I know that better than anyone." Over the years, the two men had walked each other through a never-ending series of transfers, all in the name of furthering their careers, even if it meant upending the entire family. Dave himself had worked his way up the chain, with posts in Wyoming, Georgia, New Mexico, and Indiana before being awarded his coveted spot in Boston. No doubt it came at a price. Like Chuck Connelly, his first wife decided she'd had enough. Somewhere between New Mexico and Indiana, she announced she was taking their four kids, and heading home. It was a tale told too often among aspiring federal agents.

"I'd go easy on the guy," offered David. "Paul Martin had only praise for you and the D.C. team. Nothing to do with you, I assure you."

In retrospect, Chuck felt he should have read between the lines when Paul's late-night text came through saying he had business to attend to in New England. "The guy's loaded with holiday leave, vacation and sick time, too. I never gave it a second thought. You know how that works, use it or lose it," he chuckled.

Truth was, Paul was set on making a change no matter what. If not Boston, then somewhere. He couldn't bear to stay in D.C. Every time he walked through that office door, it felt like a dreaded homecoming to the house your mother died in. You see and feel the loss at every turn. Nearly every case he worked in D.C. involved Dru. If the *ghosts* would not go away, he would.

A clean cut from ATF would mean abandoning his early retirement plan for the future. As it stands, he could sail into the sunset with a federal pension before turning fifty. He'd have to think long and hard about that one. One thing was certain, he wouldn't be joining his father's law firm; not that that option was still on the table. He and his father hardly spoke, other than the obligatory Father's Day and Christmas Eve calls. Nothing much to talk about after the loss of his beloved mom. His father, Paul Martin Sr., had all but disowned his only son when Paul signed on with the ATF more than twelve years ago.

"Picture me sitting behind a cherry mahogany desk pushing papers?" Paul would quip, when asked why he hadn't carried on the family tradition established by his esteemed grandfather. The father and son couldn't be more opposite. Paul was warm, charming, and quietly savvy while Paul Sr. was a shrewd, brash, calculating individual. Perfect for his line of work.

Approaching nearly his fourth decade, Paul found himself with no family to speak of and, not only open to, but yearning for a family of his own. The feelings for Élise O'Neil and her boys had come out of left field. Nothing about it was planned or underhanded. It just happened. In the early years, he found himself taken aback by his friend Dru's seemingly uncaring manner regarding his beautiful, brilliant wife and young family. How many times he felt himself drawn to Élise by what he could only read as an unspoken sadness; a pining for life to be *other than* the one she woke up to each day.

A concerned bystander was how Paul would describe himself back then as he watched his partner increasingly obsess over each new case as some agents are apt to do. Work, it seemed, took precedence over all he said, thought, and did. Paul had known agents willing to steamroll their mother's grave to gain the next big breaking case. Whether it be ego, or the habitual need for adrenalin, he couldn't say. As for himself, he loved what he did, but not at the cost of being a decent human being.

As far as careers, both he and Dru had each turned down any number of offers to head up departments. To them, ATF would always mean working the streets. Gun raids, undercover assignments, and surveillance operations was what kept them eager to clasp on a holster, take up a badge, and risk their lives each day. The D.C. *talking heads* could keep their titles and lofty corner offices in high-rise city buildings, staring at computer screens, and punching keyboards. Dru and Paul had no argument when it came to that.

Over time, it became shamefully obvious to Paul that Élise had something up her sleeve. There was a newly adopted bounce to her step as she delved out donuts and coffee to Dru's agent friends as they met around her kitchen table to review the previous night's explosion in a high school boys locker room. It was 4:00 a.m. They'd been up all night, as their grisly beards and sweaty bodies could attest to. Each nodded a weary thank you while she, wrapped in a terrycloth bath robe, hair askew, smiled her winning smile; her familiar sullenness replaced by the intensity of a woman in the midst of deriving a genius plan. The only one who didn't seem to notice was Dru. Was he blind with overconfidence or did he just not care?

Paul admitted on a number of occasions he had weighed the consequences of cornering his longtime friend for a serious *come-to-Jesus* intervention. Maybe after a few cold beers he'd ask point blank, "What the hell are you doing, man?"

Or, do you keep your nose out of it and your thoughts to yourself?

Anyway, what the hell did he know? A single guy, monkey-barring his way through one groundless relationship to the next. He knew, as well as anyone, some lines aren't meant to be crossed, even between the best of friends. In retrospect, he wished he had. Consequences be damned!

"Hey, Dave, thanks for the heads up," Chuck replied as he bit off the ragged tip of a thumbnail, a nervous habit lately acquired. "I certainly hate to lose a straight-up guy like Paul Martin. If it comes to that, it's definitely your gain and my loss." He shook his head, not sure exactly what his next move should be. He stood up, taking in a limbering stretch before crossing the room to open the blinds. Suddenly, he had an off-handed thought as he picked up the phone to call home.

His wife, Hannah, reached for the phone as she sprinted from the shower, dripping wet, to wrap herself in an oversized bath sheet. "What's up, babe? Something wrong?" she asked with concern. It was unusual for him to call from the office on a busy Monday morning after a long weekend.

"Quick question," Chuck countered. "Have you talked to Élise O'Neil lately?"

55

WHAT WILL PEOPLE SAY

"I think I just got engaged to Paul Martin!" said Élise, nearly causing her brother, Símone, to drop the dozen eggs he was unloading from his grocery bag.

"What the hell does that mean?" spouted Símone, who hadn't heard from his sister in months. He laid aside the six-pack of Sierra Nevada, and leaned into the phone. Ironic that she found herself ringing up her bachelor brother for relationship advice but, then, she had few friends, at least the kind you share your heart with. There was Hannah, but then Chuck Connelly was Paul's boss…so, no. And, her dad, Henri, had his hands plenty full dealing with his wife, Jacqueline Saint-Cyr. So, that left Símone.

Paul had run off to the city that afternoon after the two had gone head-to-head for three intense days of discussions about their future. "We're working things out," she confided.

"It's not been easy." Her biggest concern was *'what would people say?'*

"Who cares what people say?" Símone replied, tossing the butter tub into the fridge. "I got over that kind of shit long ago. You deserve your happiness." He remembered first meeting Paul at Dru's funeral. "Seems an upright guy, respectful, bright, all of that. I'm just honestly surprised. I thought you were all into the independent single life, no?"

Talking aloud to herself, as much as uncharacteristically unburdening on her brother, she explained there was no need certainly to rush to the altar but, sometimes, decisions must be made here and now. "This feels right is all I know," she conceded. "The boys love Paul, too. To them, he's already family."

Símone rinsed the red peppers and head of cabbage while they continued the unusual conversation. His younger sister was the rational thinker in the family so he had to wonder who this person was he was listening to.

It seems Paul was almost assured a transfer to the Boston ATF office. It boiled down to a simple nod from the higher-ups. He was open to compromises far beyond what Élise ever dared ask. They agreed he would look into taking a flat in the city where he'd stay throughout the week, joining the family on weekends. He wouldn't subject her and the boys to the crazy life of gun raids, mug shots, and the rest of a federal agent's daily life she so detested. That would all stay in the city, at least for now.

"Can you believe I would even consider becoming an agent's wife *again*? Absurd, right!" She shared bits and pieces of the session with her longtime therapist who understood her, and opened her mind to think differently. "I'm content in my single life but I do wonder if, in time, as the boys grow up, it would be enough. Sometimes, when the right person shows up on your doorstep, you may have to act on it. No one's going to wait around forever while you second guess your options. Chances are, they'll move on, leaving you drowning in a sea of regret, or at the very least wondering...*what if?*"

Símone didn't know about such things since Miss Right had yet to knock on his door. "The question is, you love the guy, right?" he probed, feeling like a pervert prying through a peephole, asking things he had no right to.

"I do. I didn't know it until there was another woman involved."

Hearing the groan on the other end of the line, Élise was quick to explain. "I *thought* there was another woman. There wasn't, of that I'm certain! When I believed there was, I was miserable. I didn't admit it, but I was crushed. I thought Paul would always be there...until he wasn't."

She realized she was babbling.

The tomatoes were far from ripe, green actually, Símone realized as he turned them over, placing them upside down in the strainer. "So, it sounds like you're taking things for a test run?"

Gosh, she hadn't thought of it that way. It helped that Paul had witnessed first-hand how she'd been treated in her marriage to Dru. Hence, his extra caution to *not be* that kind of partner. It was his idea to take a flat in Boston, and ease into a life together as man and wife. It would give themselves and others, like the children and her family, time to get used to the idea.

"Could you imagine the response if we jumped the gun, and ran off to get married?" she asked, with alarm at the very thought. "The rumors would be insane!" she added. They would be accused of having had an affair behind Dru's back *and worse*. Neither wanted that.

Paul had gone as far as considering leaving ATF if that's what it took. He could teach college law. However, she wouldn't ask that of him. He assured her he was willing and able to do whatever it took to make things right. Because of that, she, too, found herself open to undue compromises, even if it meant bending her own rules.

"The solarium is serving as his private domain at the moment." A man needs his own space after all, she explained.

"Of course, you do know eventually the iron cot is going to have to go?" Símone added laughingly. Paul was already planning to bring in a desk, *if that was okay*, the one he had battered, scarred, and loved since college days. 'Pretty much an eyesore,' he had admitted unapologetically. That was an understatement.

"And, the blessed event will take place when?" her brother dared ask.

"Not until next year is what we're thinking," she answered, glancing down at the heirloom ring on her left-hand finger. "Give people a chance to see us together, and adjust to the idea of me marrying Dru's best friend," she said, cringing with undying guilt.

"Hey, what are friends for?" Símone quipped, hoping his sister would see the humor. He shook the bottle of orange juice noting the pulp rise to the top while quickly whisking the melting ice cream into the freezer with an, "Oh damn!"

"And, then there will be the matter of Jacqueline to contend with," she said with a pause, taking a sip of tepid coffee. Uppermost in her mind was how her mother would take the news. Henri would be pleased as punch, but her mother... Well, one could only imagine the drama. And then, of course, Rose O'Neil. Good Lord, the roof would surely cave in at 49 Aspen Road when she heard the ghastly news. But, Símone was right, she and Paul deserved happiness, so it was full steam ahead.

Élise kept the best for last. "And, to top it all off," she continued, after pausing so he could brace himself for this one. "It's come to light that Dru *likely* fathered a newly orphaned Japanese daughter..."

"Okay, now you're playing with me!" Símone hollered into the phone as the bag of apples toppled across the floor.

She admitted, quite honestly, that she believed the news of Aimi Shinsato would be the deal breaker for Paul since 'bringing the girl to America seemed the only decent thing to do,' she'd explained. But, Paul had only to glance at Aimi's school picture to be one hundred percent on board. "How can I help?" was his only question, and immediately began contacting the embassy to check out the endless red tape facing them. "You think there's room in the Sullivan house for a daughter *and* a new husband?" he joked in his usual cheerful manner.

Símone found himself reaching for a cold beer, and plunking down at his kitchen table. "Any more surprises, sis?"

"Not today. I pretty much emptied my holster," she laughed. "You, okay?"

"I'm not sure," he added, raking his hands through his long, dark thick hair, thinking how much he relished his simple life. At the end of the day there was just himself and his old dog, Augustus Too Short III.

56

THE APARTMENT

Paul had no problem finding an apartment in downtown Boston in a historic brownstone district within walking distance from his new office. It was strange to find himself reporting to David Mills, ATF's Boston RAC, after years of working with Chuck Connelly. The transition had gone without a hitch, but change, even good change, can be harrowing when you're the new guy on the block. Adopting new work habits and adjusting to the quirks of new teammates could be tricky. It would be hard to find a better crew than the one he left behind in D.C. but it was all part of moving on.

He still had to pinch himself to believe that he and Élise were engaged to be married. Everyone in the D.C. office was taken by surprise, yet ecstatic, when Paul delivered the good news. "That's wonderful!" Chuck Connelly had shouted his congratulation over the phone. He couldn't have been happier if it had been his own son getting married.

While Élise was busying herself, booking the church, shopping wedding dresses, and scouting photographers, his tasks, as the groom-to-be, were comparatively minor.

"Who will you choose as your best man?" she had asked.

He had no idea; he had no brothers or close relatives to choose from. Crazy to think about, but it would have been Dru, if he were still alive. But then, I'd be marrying his ex-wife, so… hell, that would never fly.

Paul knew he would have to call his father, the esteemed Paul Martin Sr., to announce his upcoming nuptials. "So, you're marrying a white girl?" the older man replied in a voice that resonated disapproval.

Somethings never change, thought Paul as he closed down his phone. He was sorry he had bothered to make the call. Best his father not be invited to the wedding.

The apartment was shaping up as his short-shrift, second-hand bachelor furnishings from the D.C. flat finally arrived. Paul confessed he had never bought a stick of furniture over the years. They were all donations from his newly-married buddies whose brides banned each *'perfectly good piece'* from ever entering their new homes.

"Would you have need of a sofa, table and lamps?" Sam had asked, only weeks before walking down the aisle.

As for the used beds and kitchen table, they were offerings from his pal, Jeffrey Campton, when he decided to put-a-ring-on-it. "Hey buddy," Jeff had said, sounding slightly ticked off. "My fiancée wants to know if you can use a set of twin beds and a wooden kitchen table?"

"Sure," said Paul. He was glad, at the time, to discard the orange crates he'd been eating off for years, and it would be nice to have a bed to sleep on instead of a foldout couch. *What was wrong with these women?* Paul wondered, as he stood admiring his roomful of furniture.

Élise had come to the apartment one weekend to see how things were coming along. "You have only the one pan?" she asked politely, as she explored the kitchen cabinets.

"One pan, one mug, two dinner plates, and some silverware," he replied. "It's not like I plan to do a lot of entertaining," he gestured.

"Where's the T.V.?" she wondered aloud.

"Why would I need a TV. I've got internet and a laptop," he laughed.

"Spoken like a true minimalist," Élise chuckled.

"I'm hardly ever here," Paul said. "This apartment is a place for me to shower, get a good night's sleep, and have a place to store my stuff."

"I see," she said, while thinking of a million ways she could make this place more livable.

They had a wonderful weekend together taking in the sights at the Boston Common, hanging out at her favorite café in Harvard Square, and dining on fresh lobster down by the wharf. This was all very new to them, having time alone. Usually, they were surrounded by children, and taking care of the many chores around the Lexford manor home. She planned to be back soon for another weekend when they could get tickets to the Boston Pops Symphony.

Paul was already working out the logistics of *how*, and *if*, they could bring young Aimi Shinsato to America. If he could help make the young girl's world happier and more secure, he felt it was a way to honor Dru. He was waiting on word from the embassy in Tokyo on how to proceed. Meanwhile, Élise was immersed in reaching out to the girl's family with the kindness of a loving mother, as if the child was her own. He wondered how many women would open their heart and home, to an ex-husband's foreign daughter, to be loved and cared for in such a way.

His new neighbors greeted him with a smile and a wave when he passed them on the street. As far as they knew he was an insurance salesman. His only hope was they never ask him any technical questions. Chances of that were slim, since he never dallied long enough to harvest a conversation, always acting as if he were running late for an appointment. But then, that was common amongst city dwellers, just as it was in D.C., where people paid little mind to each other's comings and goings at unordinary hours of the day and night. In his line of work that proved extremely helpful.

With a host of ongoing work cases, and weekends in Lexford whenever time allowed, he truly did lead a double life. Élise referred to him as 'Double O 7.' She was grateful that he kept his gear locked away, sight unseen, in a closet in the Boston flat. A household devoid of guns, ammunition, and surveillance paraphernalia suited her fine. His idea of keeping a separate apartment was the perfect solution to keeping life simple, at least for now.

She had to admit, she was growing fond of his one-bedroom apartment, dropping by every now-and-again to bring new linens for the beds, place mats for the table, and a new juicer for the kitchen counter. Slowly, the place was taking on the makings of a weekend hide-a-way. Fortunately, Sarah and Ruth, her supportive household friends, were always up for staying at the big house with the boys whenever they were needed. Could that be any more perfect!

Paul felt privileged when his boss, David Mills, called him into the office to ask if he would be interested in having his name submitted for ATF's National Response Team training. The elite team of agents selected would be trained to investigate interagency criminal cases, reconstruct fire origins, and identify their causes. They would also provide expert witness testimonies and prepare search warrants and grand jury subpoenas.

"Your law degree would give you a huge advantage to be considered for the team," Mills reasoned. "That is if you're interested," he added.

Paul was all ears. So far it sounded like something he could dig his teeth into. "Tell me more," he said.

"Well, the NRT members work with cutting-edge technology including state of the art robots," Mills added, as if to seal the deal.

"Sounds amazing!" Paul replied. "So, what's the downside?" he asked.

"Well, your travel would definitely accelerate," Mills clarified. "Since NRTs are required to travel anywhere in the nation within 24 hours, you'd have to be ready to turn around on a dime."

Paul had to admit he would welcome the idea of branching out into something other than the usual cases he'd been working on for years. "Of course, I'll need to talk it over with Élise," he added, "but as far as I'm concerned, count me in!"

"Sleep on it and let me know by Monday," Mills said with a nod of approval.

"You sure you're okay with this?" he asked Élise. "It's not just my decision that counts anymore," he added. Paul would never agree to do anything detrimental to their upcoming union.

"Go for it!" she said without hesitation. She wouldn't stand in the way of such a great opportunity. "Your apartment will be in good hands in your absence," she laughed. It wasn't as if she were a twenty-something ingenue anymore. She could stand on her own two feet and care for the home and retreat to the Boston flat *when*, and *if*, things became overwhelming.

When Paul's acceptance to the NRT training program was announced, it was indeed an occasion for a grand celebration! His recognition was a testimony to his outstanding achievements and an all-encompassing formal welcome to the Boston ATF office. David Mills organized a congratulatory *Happy Hour* for him at a local bar, where his new team-mates happily cheered him on.

Élise couldn't wait to reserve a cozy table by the window at their favorite Italian restaurant in the North End for a romantic Saturday evening dinner for two. "Well done, my darling!" she said, applauding her husband-to-be with a raised goblet of aged Chianti Classico wine.

57

TALK OF THE TOWN

At Leo's Place, downtown, the well-known waitress, Marge Maitland, poured another round of coffee for her friends, Hazel Bloom and Lilly Ryan. "As flies to wanton boys are we to the gods," she quoted, with a smile and, a knowing wink.

"*King Lear*, Act 4, Scene 1," spouted Hazel, with the pride of one who had had just won the ten-thousand-dollar question.

"Excellent!" said Marge, moving briskly, as she hustled her way to the adjacent booth. How unexpected it was, to the women of Lexford who gathered each month at the Sullivan House, to find themselves becoming fast friends. Élise Saint-Cyr's book club, *Shakespeare and Thee*, had managed to bring them together, in a way, quite unimagined. School teachers, housewives, widows, doctor's wives, young mothers, college students, all side by side, meeting to celebrate a newborn common interest. Who knew that was possible?

"Have you heard the news?" Barbara Nelson asked, as Marge flitted by, her hands chockfull with platters of biscuits and gravy.

"What news is that?" asked Marge.

"It seems, our neighbor, Élise Saint-Cyr, got engaged," Barbara announced.

Of course, Marge knew. You couldn't work at Leo's Place and not be privy to everyone's personal business being hung out to dry.

Oscar Brown, the organist at St. Michael's Chapel, had spilled the beans, on the very day, Élise had inquired into reserving the church for a summer wedding. "The wedding's not until next August," Oscar pointed out, seemingly pleased with himself to have scored the latest inside scoop.

"Who's she marrying this time?" asked Ned Joslin, with a sarcastic chuckle.

"Has it even been a year since her first husband died?" snapped Bill Levin.

"Strange goings-on up there on the hill at the Sullivan House. Remember that fiasco when she secretly harbored that young boy?" asked Ned. "I can still see the convoy of television crews that descended on our little peaceful town."

"She's trouble, alright," replied Fred Flanders, biting into a crusty cranberry scone.

"Well, I heard, she's marrying that black fellow. The one she was, *supposedly*, just friends with," said Al Gersten, with a sour grimace.

"Yea, that's the fellow," Bob Kelly assured the group, as though he got his news straight from the horse's mouth. "He's an agent...an Internal Revenue Agent, I think they said."

"Oh Christ! Just what we need, the IRS breathing down our neck," croaked Jeff Kramer, as if he had just uncovered a dead fly afloat in his coffee mug.

Biting her tongue, Marge, made her way around the table of cantankerous silver-haired men who gathered every Saturday morning at Leo's Place. *Who gave them the right to publicly bash her friend?* she thought, as she sloshed a tad of coffee on Al Gersten's table napkin.

"Is it Élise Saint-Cyr? Or does she still go by Élise O'Neil?" chirped a woman's voice from across the room. "Anyway, she came by the high school last week to inquire about registering her *soon-to-be* stepdaughter for fall classes. She told us the girl is Japanese, but speaks perfect English."

"Sounds to me like she's running a boarding house up there on Longwood Lane," added Dan Lipton.

Elizabeth Frost, the town librarian, and friend of Élise, had been sitting quietly in her usual corner, listening to the onslaught of distorted information being unfurled. She'd heard just about enough of their chin-wagging. Standing tall, she laid a generous tip on the table, and smiled at Marge, before making her way to the cashier's counter.

"Lovely day," she said to Leo, as he passed through the dining room on his way to the kitchen.

Turning to face the tableful of testy older men, she greeted them each with her warmest forced smile. "Have a good day, gentlemen! I'm off to join our neighbor, my good friend, Élise Saint-Cyr. You all know her, right? We're meeting with her caterers this afternoon. Shall I give her all your best regards?"

She watched the men squirm in their seats, side-eyeing one another, as if wondering who they could lay the blame on for their wayward remarks. One by one, they wiped their chins, and prepared to disassemble to go about their business of facing another day.

"See you all at church tomorrow, fellows!" waved Oscar Brown.

"Amen, brother," she heard them chime in unison.

For sure, they could all use a prayer or two, thought Elizabeth, leaving a trail of bells jingling behind her, as she headed out the café door, and jauntily hurried to her parked car. She loved small town life, even the crotchety old men at Leo's Place, who had nothing better to do but gossip. Oh well, she thought, they weren't really hurting anyone. They were just being sassy old men!

58

THIS IS IT! ... *One year later*

Out of town guests began arriving late afternoon, many staying at local inns on the outskirts of town. Liz Summer and her son, Devon, Hannah and Chuck Connelly, Katy and Belle; mainly those attending the posh rehearsal dinner held at the yacht club on Lake Wikiup.

Élise couldn't believe a year could fly by with the snap of a finger. Tomorrow, Sunday, August sixth, was to be their wedding day. Doctor Katz was right all along. This second time around was proving entirely different than the first. This day would belong to her and Paul, unlike the staged event she and Dru endured years ago to please parents, and a host of guests they hardly knew. This, however, was to be a celebration of their nearest and dearest family and friends.

Katy simply glowed in her slinky black jumpsuit as she leaned on the railing of the rented yacht. With a shrug, she shared, "My mum is no longer speaking to me." Rose O'Neil was appalled that her only daughter would agree to stand in as maid-of-honor at Élise's wedding to *that man*. The mere thought inexcusable to the vengeful ex-mother-in-law. "Nothing new, same-o same-o," said Katy, slowly sipping champagne. On the other hand, Patrick O'Neil had slipped a handwritten note in Katy's hand, asking her to give Paul and Élise his blessings on their special day. The rest of the O'Neil clan remained silent as mice. None among them willing to offer good cheer at the expense of facing the wrath of mama.

Símone awakened in the king-sized guest room of the Sullivan House, whose cathedral ceilings and wooden beams were befitting a best man. "I always thought the groom just showed up," Símone laughed, as he greeted his sister over a freshly brewed latte. "That is, until your husband-to-be strong-armed me into trying on my tux *one more time* so he could tweak whatever needed tweaking. Apparently, I've been tying bow ties incorrectly all these years," he added with a wink.

One additional member of the family was busy meeting and greeting folks, in some cases for the first time. Fifteen-year-old Aimi Shinsato had joined the household nearly five months ago. Paul had worked tirelessly to make that happen without a snag. After months of documentation, and endless conference calls, he flew to Japan to accompany the young girl to the U.S. to meet her new family. Élise and Katy rushed to the gate in San Francisco, ecstatic to greet the flight as it landed on American soil. For Aimi and her new step-mom, it was love at first sight as the excited teen dug deep in her satchel, handing Élise a giftwrapped silk kimono. "For you," she said in perfect English with a shy smile.

Anxious to adopt the American ways, her English was amazingly good. Her mother had taught her early on the importance of bilingual skills. The new arrival burst into tears at the sight of a framed photo of her mom, Hana, and her American dad, Dru O'Neil, placed on the bedside table of the room that was to be hers.

But, today, the teen was occupied with the handsome young boy, introduced to her as Devon Ost, who boasted, "I, too, once lived at the Sullivan house. Just up there at the top of the stairs," he gestured.

The two ventured through the old house, retelling tales of their short, yet exceptionally venturesome lives. His, growing up in Arizona, the wild-wild west, was as intriguing to the young girl as living in Japan seemed to Devon. She imagined him in rawhide boots and a Stetson hat, riding bucking broncos, while he conjured images of her meandering the streets of Tokyo in the family rickshaw. *Both indoctrinated by Hollywood misconception.*

The two sisters, Sarah Austin and Ruth Cameron, likewise, had taken to experimenting with miso soup and tempura for Aimi's arrival, only to discover she much preferred pizza and chicken wings. But today, keeping the three O'Neil boys engaged was the primary focus on what was to be a momentous day. The fresh-faced youngsters trailed Paul up the driveway as he flagged the in-coming floral truck to an opening beneath the big oak tree.

"Can we help?" Paul offered as the driver began unloading festive floral arrangements from the coolers.

Will was none too pleased to hear he was expected to wear a boutonniere to the wedding service. "That's for girls!" he moaned, while Oliver smiled with a devil-may-care shrug. With all the excitement, Jean-Jacques dashed about the courtyard, half-believing the circus had come to town. He was dancing, clapping his little hands, and glancing down the driveway, as if expecting dancing bears and circus clowns to arrive any minute.

A large white tent stood in the area behind the grand old house, beckoning the start of the day's festivities. The musical quartet was set to arrive late afternoon, following the wedding ceremony at St. Michael's Chapel. Caterers scurried about, preparing for the evening banquet, while a bar was being set up near the edge of the tree-lined drive.

Henri Saint-Cyr rang from his hotel suite to say, "Good morning, luv!" As for Jacqueline, one could only guess how she might conduct herself at her daughter's nuptials. Most probably, she would aggrandize her role of mother-of-the-bride while professing the union to be a wonderful blessing. This, after a year of ongoing rage and condemnation of the unwelcome engagement news.

"Let's not let anyone steal our joy!" Paul had said to his future bride as he wiped away her tears. Though fully expected, Jacqueline's harsh reaction to their startling news was yet another never-ending lunge to the heart.

"Wouldn't you think I'd be used to it by now?" she said with remorse.

As for Paul, he hadn't stopped smiling since the moment Élise uttered '*yes*' to his emotional proposal. These days, he could be heard spouting quotes from Shakespeare: "*Never was monarch better feared and loved than is your majesty,*" he would declare, genuflecting, as he backed out of the room to empty the kitchen trash.

Élise would respond in kind: "*King Henry V*, Act II, Scene II, Earl of Cambridge." He had yet to trip her up; not yet anyway. It had become one of their many playful challenges from the start.

"Can you teach me to shoot?" Élise asked with trepidation one evening as they curled up fireside, sipping sherry.

"Of course, I can!" Paul replied, utterly flabbergasted by the unforeseen interest in firearms. In no time at all, she could clean, assemble, disassemble, load, unload, find her stance, aim, and fire his Glock 19, 9mm pistol. "You're amazing!" he would say, as she adjusted electronic earmuffs, and lowered metal eye shields to protect her eyes. Saturday mornings at the shooting range had become *a thing* for the duo. Something neither would have ever expected in a million years.

No doubt about it, they had become a solid team over the past year; over-the-moon in love, and anxiously looking forward to their long-awaited wedding day!

Paul's agent friends had arrived; some from the Boston office and a half dozen or more who flew in from D.C. "Wouldn't miss this for the world!" they cheered. Amidst back-slaps and mindless jokes, they headed to his downtown city flat, each clamoring to claim a spot to hunker down for the night. Some flopped on the sofa bed, and others on the twin beds, while the unlucky ones settled for floor mattresses and bedrolls.

"Just like old-time fraternity days," Agent Rob Taylor said half-awake as he staggered to the john.

"Beats those flea-bitten hotels the ATF puts us up in," coughed Mike Finn as a pitcher of beer made the rounds.

"Hey, how 'bout letting a guy get some sleep over here?" hollered Paul, from where he sprawled uncomfortably on a lumpy divan. "Big day tomorrow!" he growled, his head submerged in a mound of pillows. His request generating a roar of guffaws and deafening boos.

On the magical wedding day, the photographer and his assistant chased about, lugging satchels, cameras and tripods, and snapping photos and videos throughout the day. But, the ultimate favorite photo Paul and Élise would choose to hang above the mantle was the one with everyone squeezed in neck-and-neck in front of the huge white tent. The one that included everyone in attendance, including Argos, Ophelia, Othello, and the not to be forgotten, Augustus Too Short III.

Élise was elegant in an exquisite, ivory tea-length Vera Wang gown, hair cascading loosely down her back, beaming head to toe, arm and arm with Paul, and mingled amongst the joyous guests. "Wonderful to see my girl smiling again," said Belle, wiping happy tears from her eyes.

Jacqueline Saint-Cyr looked enchanted as she waltzed on the arm of her son Símone. As luck would have it, Élise was pleasantly surprised to see her mother actually enjoying herself. *You see, you never can predict these things.*

Meanwhile, Henri, the predictable parent, greeted each guest, exuding his usual charm. "So, how is it you know the bride and groom?" he would ask with his gracious smile.

The O'Neil boys got to stay up way past midnight, which was an unheard-of treat. They danced among the guests to the music, feasted on sweets, being made much of as they celebrated their new family. The three had unquestionably adopted Aimi into the fold as their big sister. Oliver, especially grateful to no longer bear the burden of being the eldest sibling, appeared relieved to simply be a lighthearted boy again. Will was bothered that Aimi's last name was Shinsato, not O'Neil.

He asked, "But why?"

Paul, whenever possible, set aside a weekend for fishing, camping, hiking, baseball, soccer practice, or a concert with the children; always decided by unanimous decision. Together, they might head to the lake to burn hot dogs by the fire while he retold stories that included him and their dad; always making Dru out to be the hero, and himself the fumbling sidekick. They all, including Aimi, loved to hear the much-exaggerated antics of the two federal agents as they chased down bad guys and hauled them off to jail.

"Your dad, he loved red hot chili peppers on his hot dogs," Paul would explain, as he toasted the hot dog buns over the fire. "The hotter the better! He'd take a big bite, and then rush to guzzle down an entire bottle of water, all the while gasping for breath!"

They would giggle and shout, "More, tell us more!"

It hadn't been easy getting to this place, thought Élise. But, becoming Paul's wife meant waking up each day eager to see what life had in store. That's not to say that she didn't expect challenges along the way. *That would be naïve now, wouldn't it?* But this was one journey she couldn't wait to begin. The stage was set. The players all in place.

"Bring it on!" she chanted, lifting her glass to a round of cheers. Wrapping her arms around Paul, the two twirled about the dance floor to the music and applause, for their first dance as man and wife. Such a beautiful sight!

59

COMING FULL CIRCLE... *11 months later*

Dr. Katz, his work done for another week, loosened his silk tie, and eyed the hoard of unread reports and correspondence piled high on the corner of his desk. No rest for the wicked, he thought, as he began to transfer the stack neatly into his leather satchel.

"Darn!" he grunted as a solitary envelope escaped his grasp and drifted to the floor. "Well, well, well!" he said with a grin, while glancing upon the return address. There was only one person he knew who lived in Lexford, Massachusetts. He hadn't heard from her in quite a long while. Leaning forward to grasp the pearl-handled letter opener, a gift from a cantankerous patient long ago, he smiled at the thought of Élise O'Neil. Adjusting his glasses, he unfolded the enclosed letter.

Dear Dr. Katz,

How can I ever thank you for your patience and wise counsel? At a time when my world made little sense, you were there to redirect, encourage, and listen without judgment. I am forever grateful.

My husband, Paul, travels often on assignment, but knowing I am always in his heart and mind makes all the difference. Our three boys are growing too fast for our liking and our adopted teenage daughter has a boyfriend…so there's that!

Our big news, however, is we are weeks away from welcoming a new baby girl to our family! We are ecstatic!

Thank you for your kind and professional skill through the years. Be well always,

Yours truly,
Élise Saint-Cyr-Martin

He thought back to the very first day when he had welcomed her into his office as a new patient. As she sat before him, distraught and angry, it was clear, even then, that she had a plan in place. She didn't know how it would all play out, only that, she was ready to begin that day.

Closing the shutters, and shutting down the lights, he reflected on the fact that not all his patients had the luxury of a grandfather's trust fund to afford them a ten-room manor house in New England. But people don't need such things to move on. Nonetheless, he was overjoyed to think he had played a very small part in the making of a new life.

As he tucked Élise's letter into his satchel, he couldn't help but think that sometimes you see a patient make it to first base, second base, or even third. But sometimes you see them hit the ball out of the park with bases loaded!

Bloody well done, Élise Saint-Cyr Martin!

With that joyful thought to end his long week, he jauntily swung his heavy case over his shoulder and headed home.

Milton Keynes UK
Ingram Content Group UK Ltd.
UKHW041100290923
429627UK00004B/353